An Act Of Murder

John Holt

Phoenix Publishing – Essex – UK

Conditions Of Sale

British Library Cataloguing in Publication Data.

A CIP catalogue record for this book is available from the British Library

Printing History

First published in January 2020

Preface

The story that follows is totally fictitious. All places and persons included in the story are totally imaginary, and any similarity to actual persons alive or dead, is totally co-incidentally, and un-intentional.

All towns, and places within those towns are imagined. They have been merely created for my own purposes, i.e. to serve the needs of this story.

I am grateful to Lauren Ridley, Cherryloco Jewellery for allowing me to base the Phoenix logo on her design

My sincere thanks go to Robin and Marian Lennox and the directors of Woodbury Village Hall, for permission to use their photograph as the basis for the book cover.

John Holt

Murder At Larkhall Manor
– A murder mystery in Three Acts

James Donovan	-	The Colonel
Catherine Barr	-	His wife Isabel
John Berry	-	The Butler
Timothy Saunders	-	The Police Officer
Rose Fuller	-	The House Keeper
Steve Ashton	-	A Stranded Motorist
Ian Jackson	-	A Weekend Guest
Clive Masters	-	The Doctor
Janet Cooper	-	The Director
Peter Gammons	-	Lighting
Guy Palmer	-	Scenery
Susan Turner	-	Props

Prologue
Five Years Ago

On the 20th February 2014, during a routine audit at the offices of Woodhouse Insurance, a substantial sum of money was discovered to be missing. It seemed that the money had been taken in small amounts over a period of twelve months. Although actual evidence was scant, suspicion fell on to an employee who had joined the company within the previous year.

For almost eight months Angela Hull had been living under a cloud of suspicion, accusation, and uncertainty. She had been arrested, and charged with stealing a sum of money from her employer. As a consequence she had lost her job, and many of her friends. For eight months she had been subjected to interrogation after interrogation, culminating in an appearance in court, charged with the theft, and facing a possible prison sentence of ten years minimum.

* * *

"Friday 4th October 2014 – West Sussex Gazette – Today in the Crown Court the trial of The Crown Versus Angela Hull came to a dramatic, and abrupt end when the case was dismissed by Mr. Justice David Lawrence, due to a lack of evidence. Miss. Hull had been charged with stealing £100,000 from Woodhouse Insurance, the company that she had worked for. Judge Lawrence was highly critical of both the Police and the Crown Prosecution Service, and in a scathing rebuke he stated that the case should never have been brought to trial. Miss. Hull, who has spent six months in custody, has been awarded an undisclosed amount in damages, and awarded costs. The Crown

Prosecution Service has accepted the criticism and accepted the Court's decision. Speaking afterwards a spokesperson for Miss. Hull said that although the settlement would never make up for what she had suffered, she was delighted with the outcome. The last eight months had been a nightmare that she would not wish on anyone. She thanked her Barrister, and her legal team. She added that she now wished to put the whole episode behind her."

* * *

Angela Hull tossed the newspaper to one side. Sure she was delighted with the outcome, who wouldn't be? Certainly she was glad that it was all over, and all behind her. The case had been dismissed, thrown out, damages awarded. *Compensation of a kind,* she thought. But there was still a problem. Guilty or not, case proven or thrown out, the whole episode was still on record. The case should never have been brought to trial, that's what the Judge had said. But it had been brought to trial, and that would stay with her for evermore. The details would remain in the public domain for years to come, and available for all to see.

So, the nightmare was finally over, and she could now try to rebuild her life, and go forward.

Or could she .....

* * *

Chapter One
'Murder At Larkhall Manor'

Janet Cooper was feeling quite nervous as she stood in the theatre wings watching the action on the stage. Though she would be the first to admit that the actual term theatre was, perhaps, overstating the facts of the matter, and was a slight exaggeration. In reality the wings of this particular theatre were located in a small village hall, which was, for the next five days, due to be home to the Wokingham Players, and their presentation of "Murder At Larkhall Manor", a murder mystery in three acts. Today was the opening performance.

It should, however, be said that Miss. Cooper always felt nervous on a first night, or indeed any other night for that matter. In any production there were a hundred and one things to think of, and she knew that each and every one of them could easily go wrong, and quite often did. And with any live performance, each one could prove disastrous to the production. Any such mishap could soon change what was meant to be high drama into a comedy. Scenery had a habit of falling down; lighting often failed; curtains would not open; doors would stick; props would not be where they were required to be; and actors were notorious for forgetting their lines, and/or their cue. To add to her problems, she was all too well aware that should anything go wrong, no matter what it was, no matter how slight, as the Director, it would be laid at her door. There would be no one else to blame, it would all be her fault.

This evening was to be no different. Indeed, if it were possible, she was actually feeling more nervous, being in charge of an amateur production like this one. She perhaps had just cause in this particular case. After all, it was a very poor script that had actually been written by one of the cast. Furthermore, it was an extremely poor plot that would never hold up under close scrutiny. The only true mystery about this particular play was why would anyone want to see it anyway? In truth, ticket sales had been poor, and the hall was only just over half full. There was nothing she could do about that, which only made the situation even worse. She hated being in a position over which she had no control. But it was all too late now. This was opening night, and in the best tradition of the theatre, the show must go on, come what may.

In Janet Cooper's opinion the poor plot was matched only by the poor title that had been given to the production. *'Murder at Larkhall Manor',* she murmured. It sounded like the title of a third rate B movie from the nineteen fifties. Admittedly, it was factual and straight to the point, but it was hardly imaginative was it? Hardly earth shattering, hardly worthy of a Purlitzer prize, or be in the running for the Bruntwood Prize presented to an outstanding playwright.

But that wasn't the only problem she had, was it? In fact, maybe the title wasn't that bad after all, all things being considered. There were many other, far worse, problems to be contended with. Top of the list was the acting. That was another issue altogether. Even allowing for the fact that it was an Amateur dramatic society producing the play, it was becoming increasingly clear that acting was not something readily understood by anyone in the cast. Although, she had to admit that although they did not exactly instill confidence in the director, the rehearsals had not been a complete disaster thus far.

Miss. Cooper had to admit that London's West End, or New York's Broadway, certainly had nothing to fear. Sadly there would be no Hollywood Producers come knocking on doors, wishing to bring the production to the silver screen. There would be no impresario willing to place it on the West End stage. Furthermore, there was very little chance of any Olivier Awards, or a Tony, coming their way anytime soon.

She looked out towards the audience. A wry smile crossed her face as she wondered how many drama critics were out there, siting in the audience, waiting in eager anticipation. Pens at the ready, words of wisdom already forming in their minds. She was gratified to know that the answer was probably none.

But for all her misgivings, Miss. Cooper had to admit that Act One had actually gone down without a major mishap, and had been reasonably well received by a very generous, and an extremely forbearing audience. Although the strong likelihood that most of the one hundred and twenty three members of the audience, were probably related to at least one member in the cast, or at least knew them fairly well, might have had some influence on their response.

So far Act Two had survived for twenty five minutes or so, despite a couple of mishaps that no one had apparently noticed, or perhaps they had seen, but had kindly not mentioned. She, on the other hand, had seen everything, but as the Director that was her job wasn't it. And she, unlike the audience, had no intention of ignoring any mishap, or of keeping quiet. She had made a note of the errors, and added them to her list of issues to be taken up with the cast directly after the performance.

She looked at her watch. Just another few short minutes to get through, and Act Two would be safely over. It was looking promising, and she began to relax a little. Then there would be just one more Act to go. Just another thirty-five minutes, and it would all be done, all over. *Perhaps it wouldn't be the unmitigated disaster that she had envisaged after all.* Despite all of the odds, it seemed that it was going to be alright.

Janet looked over at the stage. Catherine Barr, who played Isabel, the Colonel's wife, had just left the scene, exiting stage left. She was looking pleased with herself, and had clearly enjoyed the scene. James Donovan, or Colonel Mycroft as his character was called, lay asleep in the armchair by the fireside. Janet smiled. She knew that he wasn't actually acting, he was really asleep. A scotch or two too many in the Queens Head, were clearly starting to have an effect. *Just hope he doesn't start snoring,* she thought.

The stage was in semi darkness, and there was complete silence, except for the ticking of a clock. Janet looked over to the far side of the stage. Young Timothy Saunders was waiting for his cue. He saw Janet looking at him, and he gave a nervous wave. She waved back. 'You'll be fine,' she mouthed to him.

The clock on the mantle shelf started to chime the hour. There was the sound of a window opening. A wind began to blow, rustling the curtains at the window. Right on cue, the barrel of a gun could be seen poking through those curtains. The curtains slowly opened, and Tim walked on to the stage. He glanced around, and slowly made his way until he reached the centre of the stage. He stopped, and glanced around once more. Then he looked down at the figure lying asleep. He raised the gun, and pointed it directly at the Colonel, and gently, slowly, squeezed the trigger. There was a loud thud, followed by a gasp from the audience. The stage curtains came down indicating the end of Act Two. Janet heaved a sigh of relief. Despite all expectations, it had gone reasonably well after all. *Thank goodness,* she murmured. Clearly the audience were still enjoying the production, judging by the applause. Perhaps she had been worrying all of this time for no good reason.

Janet hated the noise of that gun. Even though she knew that the bang was coming, it always took her by surprise, and startled her. Tonight though it somehow seemed louder than normal, not like at rehearsal, but she knew that wasn't likely. It was just her imagination playing tricks, nothing more. She dismissed it from her mind. But then there was that smell of cordite hanging in the air. It was so realistic. She had never noticed it before, but tonight it was so strong. She guessed that it was probably something to do with the air conditioning, or the ventilation system. Or maybe it was because this was the first live performance, and someone had decided that they needed to add a bit more realism to the proceedings. *Not a bad touch*, she thought. *In fact, it was a good idea. It really did add something.* The audience seemed to like it anyway. She decided to speak to Susan Turner, who was in charge of the props, and gave it no more thought.

"Okay James, that was great. You can get up now," she said as she reached the centre of the stage. James never moved. "Come on James," she coaxed, smiling. There was no reaction. "James, we haven't long before Act Three, you know," she continued, as she tapped him on the shoulder. Clearly the whiskey had done its worst.

"Come on, now." He still never moved. "Enough, now, James," she said beginning to get angry. She didn't need this. She had more than enough problems to deal with, without his playing around. "The curtains have closed, the act is over. There's no more to be done. No one is watching you, not now," she pointed out. "I've no time for your silly games. I've a lot to do." She shook him. There was still no reaction. "James get up .... Now!" Still there was no reaction. Her anger was now beginning to change into concern. "James!!!" she called once again.

Others began to crowd around her. "What's going on?" asked John Berry. He looked down at Donovan. "As usual he is looking for the attention of his adoring fans." He did a mock bow. "We salute you, oh mighty one."

"What's the problem?" Rose Fuller asked, looking down at Donovan. "Drunk again I suppose."

"Dead drunk if you ask me," added Ian Jackson, as he joined the group.

"You and me both," added Berry. "So what else is new?"

"Why don't we just wheel the chair off the stage, his lordship and all?" suggested John Berry.

"James!!!" Janet called for a third time, as she shook his shoulder. Then she noticed the blood staining to his chest. It looked so real. *More realism,* she thought. She shook him once again. And then she let out a loud scream. "He's dead," she cried. "He's been shot."

She looked over to her right hand side. Tim was still there. He hadn't moved, and was still holding the gun. His face was ashen. He was breathing hard, and shaking violently.

* * *

The applause gradually lessened, and eventually stopped completely. The house lights remained switched off. Minutes passed by. Five minutes, ten, and then fifteen. The hall remained in darkness, with the exception of the Fire Exit signs that were still glowing. People started to become impatient, fidgety. *What was going on?* A buzz started to resound in the audience. First it was no more than a whisper, then gradually it got louder and louder. Questions were being asked. *Why the delay?* Someone wondered. *Has something happened?* Asked another. *Somebody has been taken ill,* suggested someone else. *Ah, you know what these amateur groups are like,* someone offered their opinion. *We've been forgotten,* someone muttered. *There's probably a fuse blown somewhere,* someone else said, followed by laughter. Then somebody started to slow clap. Slowly others joined in. Before very long the whole audience was clapping. Then the chanting began. *Why are we waiting? Oh why are we waiting?*

Suddenly the lights came back on, and the clapping stopped immediately. *They've found the light switch,* somebody in the back row called out. *More like they found some money for the meter,* came a retort, which was followed by more laughter.

Janet appeared from behind the curtains. She looked pale, and was shaking. The laughter ceased. "Ladies and gentlemen," she stammered nervously. She paused, and took a deep breath. "Ladies, and gentlemen, it is with deep regret that I have an announcement to make." She paused once again, and took another deep breath. "For reasons beyond our control, I am sorry to tell you that we are unable to continue with tonight's performance."

There was a loud gasp from the audience, followed by the shuffling of seats.

"If you would please leave your name, address, and seat number, with my assistant at the door, as you leave, arrangements will be made to provide you with a full refund," she continued. "Please leave as quickly as you can." She quickly turned around, and hurriedly returned behind the curtains. Tears were rolling down her face.

"Has anyone called for the police, and an ambulance?" she asked, as she looked at the lifeless body still lying in the armchair.

"All done, Janet. You don't have to worry," replied Guy Palmer, the person in charge of the scenery. He walked over and placed his arm around her shoulders. "They're on their way."

* * *

Chapter Two
Police Constable Harry Cutler

The village Police Station was located at number twenty-eight Mill Lane. To all intents and purposes it appeared to be a fairly ordinary semi-detached house. Ordinary that is except for the two year old Ford Fiesta that was parked in the driveway. Gleaming white, with a yellow and blue stripe running along the side. Emblazoned along each side was the single word in dark blue lettering, POLICE. Then there was the old fashion blue lantern hanging by the entrance door. And finally there was the notice board positioned by the front gate. In letters four inches high it announced *'Wokingham Police, telephone number 01907 522477. Officer in charge Police Constable Harry Cutler.'*

* * *

Police Constable Harry Cutler closed the file he had been reading. He placed it on to the side table. It had been a busy day, and he was looking forward to a nice quiet evening relaxing. Taking a well-earned break. Just himself, the family dog Lucy, who was already curled up asleep on the armchair, a couple of ice cold lagers, and the telly. Betty, his eighteen year old daughter was out with her latest boyfriend, and Mary, his wife, was at her evening class in the Church hall.

Computing for Beginners, P.C. Cutler murmured. *More like computing for the terrified. Whatever next,* he thought. *She'll be on that internet all day long, with that Facebook thingy, and emailing everyone and anyone.* He sighed, all of this technology was way beyond him. Oh yes, he had a mobile phone, but all it did was to make and receive telephone calls. It didn't have any of those app thingies, whatever they were. It didn't make the tea, or do the housework. It just made calls.

Still as long as she enjoyed it, he thought, *that was all that mattered.* He had to admit that the *Word Processing* course the year before last had certainly proved useful anyway, especially with the endless reports that were necessary.

He reached for the remote control, and switched on the television. A few minutes later, having searched through what seemed like thousands of channels, he settled on one of those police series, '*Midsomer Murders*'. *A bit of old nonsense really,* he thought, and so far removed from real life. But there again, who needed real life after a hard day's work, anyway? Besides, he had to admit that it was mildly entertaining, with no hidden messages, and none of that bad language that he couldn't stand. Though he did wonder, with so many murders going on in that village, who in their right mind would want to live there anyway. He certainly wouldn't. He was quite happy where he was. He also wondered, in view of the detection success rate, who on earth would even contemplate committing a crime in the village of Midsomer. They had no chance of getting away with it. *The question though was whether or not he could solve the crime before the end of the programme?* In truth he never could, mainly because he was usually asleep long before the end of the programme.

Unlike the village of Midsomer, nothing bad ever happened in Wokingham. It was just a nice quiet village that was all. Perhaps it would be considered boring to some, dull and even predictable perhaps, but it suited him perfectly. Not for him the hustle and bustle of the city. He liked the peace and quiet. He liked the predictability.

He poured himself a lager, and settled down. He took a long drink, and sat back in his chair. He fully expected to be joining the dog asleep in the not too distant future.

The programme started at nine o'clock. Twenty minutes later Police Constable Cutler was already fast asleep. That's when the call came through. At first he was sceptical. *It was nothing more than a hoax, a prank,* he thought. It had to be. Somebody was winding him up. Probably some of the youths from the village playing a joke on him. They had done it before. Several times in fact. It was annoying, but nothing more. No harm done. Cutler had spoken to their parents, and their teachers at the local school, and that was an end to it. *If this was another of their silly jokes there would be trouble this time, big trouble,* he vowed. After all wasting police time was a crime. They had been warned.

He decided to ignore it. Just hang up and forget all about it, and get back to the television. Then the nagging doubts started. *But what if it was genuine?* He couldn't risk it, could he? Better to go and find out that it was a prank, than not go and then find out that it was genuine. Besides, it was hardly likely that they'd joke about something like that would they, something that was clearly so serious.

Something like a murder.

* * *

Police Constable Harry Cutler arrived at the village hall five minutes after receiving the call. Just a few moments later the ambulance arrived. He soon realised that this wasn't a joke. It wasn't a hoax call. It wasn't just a group of kids playing around. This was no laughing matter, it was anything but. This was serious, deadly serious.

He had been a policeman serving the local community for more than twenty-five years. Everyone knew him, many of them actually on first name terms. He wasn't just a representative of the law. He was a friend to many, always willing to lend a helping hand. Someone who would do all he could for the community. And in all of that quarter of a century, he had seen nothing like the scene that now confronted him. A murder had taken place, right here in his back yard, right here in Wokingham.

* * *

Normally, Wokingham was such a nice, quiet, peaceful village, and nothing exciting ever happened there. He certainly had never been required to deal with a murder before. In fact, the only violence he had ever witnessed previously was a couple of young boys caught fighting a year or two ago, behind the church. They got a good talking too, and a call was made on their parents. Constable Cutler had considered that was sufficient punishment. Just good old fashioned discipline was all that was needed. You couldn't beat it. There was no more fighting.

The only other piece of excitement in recent times was when Billy Cartwright had got drunk, and drove his car into Mrs. Bennett's bakery shop window. Fortunately no one got hurt, a few loaves of bread were flattened, but that was all. Billy had his license suspended for twelve months, and was ordered to pay for the damage, and to work in the bakery for two weeks without pay.

* * *

P.C. Cutler walked over to the stage, and straight to the slumped body of James Donovan. He announced that the police doctor was on his way. "In the meantime don't touch anything," he advised.

He then went over to Timothy, who was still holding the gun, but shaking uncontrollably. Cutler had known Tim's family ever since they had arrived in Wokingham. Tim had been no more than three or four years old at the time.

He placed a hand on the boy's shoulder. "Give me the gun, Tim," he said gently, holding out a cloth in order to collect the weapon. Tim, still shocked and dazed, remained motionless. His knuckles were white as he gripped the gun even tighter. The police officer asked for the gun once again. "Come on Tim, you know me. I'm not going to hurt you."

Tim simply stared at the policeman, gripping the gun as though his life depended upon it. Janet Cooper walked over and spoke to Cutler. She took the cloth, wrapped it around the gun, and gently took the gun from the young man, and handed it to the constable.

Constable Cutler gave an audible sigh of relief, and took a deep breath. "Timothy Saunders," the police officer announced, as he walked back to the young man, his voice cracking. He was about to do something that he had never imagined in his wildest nightmares that he would ever do. He was about to arrest someone in connection with a murder, someone that he had known for many years.

He placed his hand on the young man's shoulder. "Timothy Edward Saunders, I'm arresting you on suspicion of murder." He paused trying to think of the correct words. "You aren't obliged to say anything, but anything you do say will be taken down, and may be used against you." He paused once again. He hoped that the words were correct, or at the very least, that they were close enough. He opened his notebook. "Have you anything to say?" he continued satisfied with his choice of words.

"I didn't do it," Tim blurted out, as he started to cry. He looked at Janet Cooper. "I didn't do it, you must believe me."

With a dead body in front of him, and a young man still holding the murder weapon, it seemed to Police Constable Cutler that any protests of innocence were of little, if any, value. *This showed all the signs of being an open and shut case,* he thought. He had a murder weapon, the person who pulled the trigger, and a dead body. What else did he need?

Nonetheless he knew that there was a procedure to be followed, and that he needed to go through the right motions. He also knew that there was still a lot of investigations to take place. He also knew that there was no way Timothy Saunders would kill anyone, and yet everything pointed to him being guilty of murder. He wrote the statement down, word for word. Then, satisfied that he had done everything necessary he called the police station in Weathersfield.

* * *

A short while later officers had been brought in from town. The area had been established as a crime scene. Officers were busily taking photographs, and measurements. The gun was then removed and sent to be checked for fingerprints, and to confirm that it was, in fact, the murder weapon. Timothy Saunders had been taken into custody, and driven to Weathersfield Police Station. The police doctor had arrived, and the body had been taken away. A post mortem would take place the following day, and a report would be issued later that same afternoon.

Satisfied with the arrangements, the police constable locked the hall, and placed the key in his pocket. He then returned to his office. It was almost ten thirty, but he still had a lot to do. He had some reports to write up. He also had some more phone calls to make. And he needed to go and speak with Tim's parents.

* * *

The following day the news was the talk all over the village, and beyond. A murderer in their midst was the theme. That's when the real questions began. Did Tim really commit murder? Certainly he had the gun, and certainly he had pulled the trigger. But why commit such a crime in front of so many witnesses? Did Tim really intend to kill Donovan? What was the motive? It soon became apparent to police constable Cutler that it wasn't going to be that easy to solve this case. It wasn't the open and shut case as it had first appeared. There were so many questions. Cutler eventually admitted that he needed help. Experienced assistance was required. A call was put through to Scotland Yard.

* * *

Chapter Three
Chief Inspector William Whittaker

Eighty five miles to the north of Wokingham, Detective Chief Inspector William George Whittaker was in the corridor just outside of his office, Room 4/24 on the fourth floor of New Scotland Yard. Coming up to his twenty-sixth year, Whittaker was an old fashion copper. A no nonsense copper. A copper who had seen it all before. Meticulous, and methodical were his watch words. Sift through the evidence, he would say, and don't take anything on face value. Check it out, and then check it again. And when you've finished checking, check it again just to make sure.

He was carefully balancing a bundle of files, as he reached for the door handle. *Why he had agreed to take them with him, and not allowed the constable to bring them, he would never know.* He eventually managed to turn the handle, open the door, and enter his office, without dropping any of the files. He kicked the door shut behind him. As he reached his desk Whittaker thankfully allowed the files to fall onto the desk, and he gratefully sat down. He stifled a yawn, removed his glasses, and started to rub his eyes. *Getting old,* he thought. *That, or more likely too many late nights stuck at the office dealing with seemingly endless paperwork.* He closed his eyes. *Just for a few minutes. Where's the harm,* he thought. *Five minutes that's all I ask, just five little ....*

His peace was short lived, broken by the ringing of the telephone. Startled, Whittaker opened his eyes. He stared at the telephone, hoping that the ringing would stop or, better still, the telephone would just disappear.

"That phone never stops," he mumbled as he reached for the handset. "Whittaker here," he said. It was the Commissioner. "Yes ma'am. Yes. I'll get right on it. Leave it with me, ma'am. Certainly ma'am."

He put the phone down. "Of course ma'am. You only need ask ma'am. Yes ma'am, yes ma'am, three bags full, ma'am. You'd think I was the only one here," he said to no one in particular. "Of course I'll do it, ma'am. Right away, ma'am. No, it's not a problem ma'am. Pleased to do it. As if I haven't got enough to do." He glanced at the pile of files on his desk. "Head cook and bottle washer, that's me. Give me a brush and I'll sweep the floor for you." He looked at the telephone. "Perhaps you'd like me to do a bit of cleaning as well, during my spare time. A bit of washing and ironing, maybe."

His ranting was interrupted by a knock on his door. *Here we go again,* he murmured. "Come in," he called out. It was Detective Sergeant Derek Chambers, Whittaker's assistant. "Yes Derek, and what can I do for you?"

"We've just had a call, sir. There's been a shooting in a village, somewhere in Sussex. A place by the name of Wokingham, about eighty miles away, as the crow flies. Happened last evening at about twenty past nine. It's a small place, about a thousand people, you know the sort of place I mean. The village shop, and the parish church, and a pub at both ends of the High Street, and that's about it."

"What no charity shop?" said Whittaker. "Or what about a betting shop?"

Chambers shrugged. "Probably got a couple of both, I'd say, sir."

"Go on, I'm listening," said Whittaker, trying to sound interested, but failing spectacularly.

"Well it seems that one of the local dignitaries, a ...." Chambers looked at his note pad. "James Donovan, has been killed. A single shot from a 9 mm pistol. The local bobby, a P.C. Harry Cutler is on site. He's a twenty five year man. It's a bit out of his league though I'm afraid, but he seems to have done the right thing. He has cordoned off the crime scene and taken somebody into custody, arrested on suspicion of murder."

"He has somebody already, that's pretty good going," said Whittaker suitably impressed. "So what about the call?"

"By all accounts, sir, it seems a pretty open and shut case," Chambers continued. "The whole thing was seen by eye witnesses. The Commissioner would like us to go down and just make sure everything is being done by the book. Should be easy enough."

Whittaker was puzzled. It was very unusual for a murder to be witnessed. "It was seen did you say? How come?" he asked. "Who were these eye witnesses?"

Chambers explained about the amateur theatrical group, and their production of a murder mystery. "Murder at Larkhall Manor, it's called, sir. One of those murder mysteries, totally unrealistic I know, but fairly popular for some reason. Anyway, about a hundred odd people saw the whole thing, right there on the stage."

"On the stage, you say?" said Whittaker.

"The opening night I understand," explained Chambers. "Quite a performance by all accounts."

"And the Commissioner wants me down there?" said Whittaker. "You're sure of that?"

"That's right, sir," said Chambers. "Just to cast your eye over proceedings, that sort of thing. Nothing too onerous."

Whittaker looked at the telephone. "Well, she's just been on, and she never said a word about it."

"I think maybe the call must have come in a little bit later sir," suggested Chambers. "I mean after she had spoken to you."

"Maybe so, but more likely she didn't want to tell me herself. Direct like, because she knew I'd have an objection," said Whittaker. "Guess she thinks I'm the only one here, and that I've nothing else to do anyway. I'm just sitting here twiddling me thumbs, waiting for that phone to ring, and when it does I'm supposed to jump." He glanced around at the mountain of files on his desk. He could complain and rant all he liked, but he knew that at the end of the day he really had no choice.

"Suppose they can all wait," he continued. "Well they'll have to won't they? Besides, obviously they're not that important are they? After all what do we have anyway? A couple of robberies, a murder or three, one or two assaults with a deadly weapon, a couple of missing persons, and a handful of drug dealers. Hardly anything at all." He shrugged. "Oh, and I forgot the one she did ring about."

"What was that one, sir?" asked Chambers.

"Oh, nothing important," said Whittaker. "Just that a body has been fished out of the Thames."

Chambers smiled. "Perhaps she thought it would be a nice day out in the country for you, sir," he suggested. "A nice change. You know away from the smoke and grime of the city."

"Very thoughtful of her I'm sure. Maybe I'll get in a spot of fishing, or improve on my tan," said Whittaker.

"Perhaps a round of golf," Chambers suggested.

"Maybe. You know I've never played golf, might be nice to give it a go," Whittaker replied. "How can I ever repay her? I hope she is as good to me when it comes to the time for my pension, and my gold watch."

"Oh, I wouldn't worry about that just yet. You've got years to go, sir," said Chambers. "No, she just thinks you deserve a bit of peace and quiet, you know. Some fresh air and some sunshine does you good, sir."

"Nice of her to consider my well-being," said Whittaker. "Very good of her. I must remember to thank her some time. Perhaps I'll send her a post card from, where's that place you said?"

"Oh, you mean Wokingham," replied Chambers. "In Sussex."

"Right, that's it then," said Whittaker. "I'll send her a post card from Wokingham. Now what shall I say?" He thought for a few moments. "I know. Wish you were here, instead of me. Having a well-earned rest. Thank you for your consideration." He sat back satisfied. "Oh, and please don't let anyone touch my files, I'll get right on to it upon my return. Yours ever W. That should do it."

"I think the Commissioner thinks it'll all be wrapped up in a day or two," Chambers said. "So I've taken the liberty to have your car ready for ten o'clock."

Whittaker grunted, and looked at the clock. "Nine fifteen," he announced. "Right, we've just got time for a nice cup of tea then and some of that nice Dundee Cake that Mrs. Chambers made. What do you think?"

"Good idea, sir. In fact, I'd already thought of that and taken the necessary action," replied Chambers.

There was a knock on the door. "In fact, I expect that'll be the Sergeant with it right now, if I'm not very much mistaken." Chambers continued

The door opened, and the Sergeant came in carrying a small silver tray. He looked at Detective Chambers. "The tea and cake you requested, sir," he said. He then turned to face the Inspector. "By the way that robbery last evening, sir. Well they found the car. In Deptford it were, down by the river."

Whittaker looked up. "That's something then. Probably linked to that body they found. Keep me posted. Just leave instructions about the car. Check it for prints, the usual. Find out where it's been. You know what to do."

"Will do, sir," said the Sergeant.

"And I'll want a full report on my desk when I return," Whittaker added. "And photographs, lots of photographs."

"It'll be there sir, never fear," said the Sergeant as he left the room.

Whittaker looked at Chambers. "That's something. At least they've just found the getaway car," he explained "Now where was I?" He reached for his cup and picked it up. He took a sip of his tea, and a bite of cake. He started to chew slowly. "Now that really is a piece of cake," he said, brushing the crumbs from the front of his shirt. He took another drink of tea. "Right, Derek. What do you have for me?"

Chambers took a drink of tea, and took out his notepad. "Well sir, as I said the victim is a James Donovan, aged fifty-two. Used to be a local magistrate. Served for twenty years. Widower. Retired due to poor health a few years ago. The suspect is Timothy Saunders, aged twenty six, lives in Wokingham, and works in a shipping office in Brighton."

"Any form?" asked Whittaker.

"Nothing sir," replied Chambers. "Not even a parking ticket."

"Anything else?" asked Whittaker. "Motive, for example?"

"Not at present sir," Chambers replied. "But when we arrive we'll go and see the police constable first, then we'll go on to the scene of the crime. We should find out a bit more by then."

"Fair enough," Whittaker replied. "Let Cutler know won't you?" He looked at his watch. "It's almost ten o'clock now. We should arrive in Wokingham, what did you say, eighty miles? We should be there at about quarter to twelve, if all goes well." He looked around at the office, and over at the files on his desk. "I expect they'll still be there when we get back."

Chambers smiled. "I don't doubt it, sir. And I wouldn't be at all surprised if there were a few more cases added to the pile."

"You can bet your Christmas bonus on it," Whittaker said as he walked wearily towards the door. "Okay, let's get going then shall we?"

As they reached the street Whittaker looked up at the sky. It was dull, and overcast. "Looks like rain," he said. "So much for enjoying the fresh air and sunshine. She's done this deliberately."

"The Commissioner you mean, sir?" asked Chambers. "She wouldn't do that."

"Wouldn't she indeed?" said Whittaker. He grunted. "Maybe, maybe not. If I catch pneumonia, she'll know all about it."

"Oh come on, sir, it can't rain forever." He opened the car door. "After you, sir."

Whittaker got into the car. "I bet you anything you like, the rain will never stop. They'll be no sunbathing, and no round of golf. I'll be spending the whole time indoors. You see if I'm right or not."

He turned to face the driver. "All right, what are you waiting for, I haven't got all day. Let's get going."

* * *

Chapter Four
Wokingham Police Station

It was almost twelve thirty by the time Whittaker and Chambers arrived in Wokingham, and made their way to twenty-eight Mill Lane, the home of the Wokingham Police. P.C. Cutler was waiting at the kerbside as they arrived.

"Found it alright then, sir," he said, as he opened the car door to allow Whittaker to get out.

"We got lost a few times," said Chambers. "That's why we're late."

"Modern technology for you," grunted Whittaker. "That Satnav thingy kept getting it wrong. And this wretched rain." He sneezed, and looked at Derek. "Told you, didn't I? Pneumonia. Is it ever going to stop raining?"

Derek merely smiled and looked at the Inspector. It had rained non-stop since leaving London, and the Inspector had complained the whole journey. *He'll probably mention it in his post card to the Commissioner,* he thought jokingly. *Having a good rest, weather appalling, wish you were here, instead of me.* He then turned to speak to the driver. "You go and get some lunch, and we'll see you back here." He looked at his watch. "At two o'clock, okay. If we need you sooner I'll ring."

The driver nodded, switched on the ignition, and drove away.

"Anyway, we're here now, sir," said Chambers. "And I'm sure this rain can't last forever."

"Yes, we are here alright," said Whittaker. "Though what we've done to deserve it, I'll never know." He looked at the Constable. "As the good Detective Chambers said, we're here now."

"And most welcome you are, sir," said Cutler. "Come in please, out of the rain." He showed them into the front room.

"Make yourself at home. The bathroom is up the stairs second on the right," he continued. "I'm sure you wouldn't say no to a nice cup of tea would you? I'll get the kettle on." He hurried from the room.

Whittaker glanced around the room. *Pleasant enough,* he murmured. "Quite nice really," he said to no one in particular. "As police stations go, that is."

"Sorry, sir, did you say something?" Chambers asked.

"Nothing important," Whittaker replied. He stood up and started to walk around. He stopped by a large sideboard. On the top were a number of figurines, and several photographs. In pride of place was a silver frame enclosing one showing a family scene on a beach.

"That's me and the wife, my Mary, and our daughter, Betty, sir. Brighton it was, about ten years ago," announced Cutler as he returned a few minutes later with the tea and some sandwiches. "Thought you might be hungry as well." He placed the plate on to the coffee table. "Help yourselves."

Whittaker returned to his seat. A bite to eat sounded good. A steak and kidney pie would have been more to his liking, but he had to admit that a plateful of ham and chicken sandwiches, wasn't too bad as a second choice.

He picked up a ham and lettuce, and took a bite. "So tell me about last night," he said, dusting a few crumbs off of his jacket lapel, and getting straight down to business. "Were you there?" he asked. "You know, when it happened?"

Cutler took a drink of tea. "At the hall you mean?" he replied. "Oh no, I was here, at home. I'd planned a nice quiet evening, relaxing. You see I'd been working late, writing reports, filing, you know general admin stuff. Nothing exciting. I didn't finish until near eight-thirty. I was hoping for a bit of peace and quiet. Wife and daughter were out you see. I thought a couple of lagers and the telly would be just the ticket. Wasn't to be though."

Whittaker smiled, he knew the feeling. *Head cook and bottle washer,* he murmured. *No rest for the wicked that's what they say.*

"Did you say something, Inspector?" asked Cutler.

"Oh no, nothing, really," replied Whittaker, taking another bite.

"So you don't know exactly what happened?" asked Chambers.

"You best speak to Janet about that," Cutler replied. "Janet Cooper, she's in charge up at the hall. But as I understand it, the shooting happened right there on the stage, in front of everyone."

"Not the sort of thing you would expect, when you go to the theatre," suggested Chambers.

"No I guess not," replied Cutler. "Although I doubt very much that they realised what had happened."

"Why do you say that?" asked Chambers. "I mean a shooting is pretty obvious I would say."

"Oh certainly it is, normally," replied Cutler. "But you see it was a play, acting you know. There's a shooting takes place in the play."

"You're saying that the scene actually included a shooting?" said Chambers.

"Correct," agreed the Constable. "Murder at Larkhall Manor you see, and the old Colonel gets shot. The audience might have just thought it was part of the play."

"Maybe so," agreed Whittaker. "I understand that you already have someone in custody. Timothy Saunders, is that right?"

"Yes sir, that's right. He wasn't hard to get either," Cutler replied. "Tim pulled the trigger right enough, and Mr. Donovan died right there on the stage. Shot at close range." He stopped, and looked at Whittaker. "No further than I am to you, sir." He took a drink of tea. "No question about it. Tim did it alright.

Simple as that. Open and shut case, or so it seemed at the time."

Whittaker had seen it all before. There was no such thing as an open and shut case. Never was, and never would be. Oh sure it might look obvious who pulled the trigger, or used the knife. But that wasn't everything was it. There were still a mass of unanswered questions. *Was it murder? Or was it an accident, or maybe self-defense?* Then there were the questions as to why. What was the motive? Was anyone else involved?

"Something tells me you don't actually believe that," Whittaker said, picking up another sandwich. "About it being an open and shut case I mean."

Cutler smiled. "Tim actually denies murdering Mr. Donovan," he said.

"Well he would wouldn't he? So no big surprises there," said Whittaker. "I've never yet met a murderer who admitted to his crime. In all my twenty-six years I've never got a confession out of anyone. Never heard an admission of guilt. In fact it was always the opposite. They would always deny all knowledge of the crime. I never did it. Must have been someone else. It was always two other fellows." He took a drink of tea. "Not me governor, I was nowhere near the place. Always the same story. Never fails. You know if I'd had a pound for every time I heard something like that, I could have retired years ago. Sometimes, I think they take this innocent until proven guilty malarkey a bit too far. Sure they're entitled to a fair trial and all, but sometimes, with a good barrister, they literally do get away with murder."

"Inspector, I've known the lad, Tim, for most of his life," Cutler started to explain. "Know his family. Why his dad and me we play darts on a Friday down at the Arms." He paused for a moment, and took a drink of tea. "Tim's gentle you know. Never been in any kind of trouble. Good at school you know." He paused for a moment. "Tell a lie, sir. There was just one time. He was about seven or eight I think. I actually caught him climbing the wall around old man Carter's orchard. He had been picking apples you see." Cutler started to smile. "Trouble is they were cooking apples, you know, big, green things. Granny Smiths. Well, he had about three in his hands, he was eating them. Well I can tell you he ended up with a real bad stomach ache."

"So what happened?" asked Chambers.

"He got a good talking to from me. Then his dad had a go at him. Finally Ted Carter had his turn, Young Tim had to work in the orchard for a week, picking apples," continued Cutler. "He never did it again I can tell you."

Whittaker grunted. "Perhaps it was his first steps on the road to crime," he suggested. "A road that eventually lead to murder."

"No sir, he's a good lad, is our Tim," insisted Cutler. "He'd do anything for anyone. He wouldn't hurt a fly. No he may have pulled that trigger but he never murdered Mr. Donovan."

Whittaker wasn't convinced. "People can change, it has been known," he suggested. "Maybe he had a grudge against Donovan. He didn't like him maybe."

"He didn't do it, sir," Cutler insisted. "Believe me."

"But he was seen," Whittaker responded. "Seen by a hundred and something people. He had the gun, and he pulled the trigger. There's no doubt of it."

"It was play acting, sir. The Wokingham Players, and their Murder at Larkhall Manor," said Cutler. "In the play Tim's character really does murder Mr. Donovan, or I should say he murders the Colonel. It should have been a prop gun, a fake, but somebody switched it."

"Play acting indeed," said Whittaker. "The trouble is we have us a real murder, with a real dead body." He paused for a moment. "What did Saunders think of Donovan anyway? I mean were there any problems between them?"

"I don't think the lad liked Donovan, if that's what you mean. I think he was nervous of him. Intimidated is maybe a better word," Cutler replied. "But if you are looking for a motive, sorry sir, but you are way off line."

"We'll see," said Whittaker, as he looked at his watch. "You've been holding Saunders for what, a little over sixteen hours. Another twenty hours, or thereabouts, and he will have to be charged, or released."

"I don't think we have enough to charge him, sir," said Cutler.

"Agreed," said Whittaker. "Not near enough."

"So what part did Saunders have in the play?" asked Chambers.

"Oh, he was the policeman," replied Cutler. "Except he wasn't really a police officer."

"So what was he?" asked Whittaker.

"I'm very sorry, sir," said Cutler. "I cannot tell you that, I'm sworn to secrecy."

"A lot of nonsense," Whittaker said. "Play acting indeed. We've a real life murder to investigate, not some airy-fairy pretend one. What about the gun? The murder weapon I mean, not the prop."

"A 9 mm pistol, could be ex-army," said Cutler. "It's at Weathersfield Police Station, at present. There's no prints, and no identification marks, I'm afraid."

Whittaker looked at Derek. "Well, we better get forensics to take a look, they might come up with something, who knows?" he said. "We'll get it back to the Yard, and see what they make of it. Not that I expect too much." He looked back at Cutler. "What about the fake gun, was it similar?"

"That's a good question, Inspector," Cutler replied. "As I understand it the prop gun was quite different. Different shape, and a lot lighter to hold."

"So why didn't Saunders notice the difference?" asked Chambers.

"I don't know," said Cutler. "But maybe he did notice, but just thought it was more realistic for the play. As I said it was meant to be play acting."

"So where's the gun now, the fake one?" asked Chambers.

"We've no idea, sir, it's missing," replied Cutler. "Whoever did the switch, has hidden the gun, or destroyed it I guess."

Pity, but not a surprise, thought Whittaker. "It might have told us something, who knows," he said. "Oh well can't be helped I suppose, that's how the cookie crumbles. No use crying over spilt milk."

"Never a truer word spoke in jest," Chambers said adding to the words of wisdom.

Whittaker glared at him. "Maybe," he said quite simply.

Cutler stood up. "Well, we're still looking for it," he said trying to sound hopeful. "We might find it, you never know. We live in hope …."

"And die in despair," said Chambers completing the phrase.

"Umm," replied Cutler, heaving a sigh. "More tea?" He left the room without waiting for a reply.

* * *

Cutler returned a few minutes later with a fresh pot of tea. "You know anyone could have switched that gun," he said as he sat down. "Anyone of them in that theatre group."

"Presents quite a few suspects, then," said Chambers.

"So what can you tell me about the group, this, what's their name, the Wokingham Players?" asked Whittaker.

"I don't know that much I'm afraid," Cutler replied. "They've been going a few years I think. Janet, Janet Cooper, she's the Director. She's the one to talk to if you want information."

"Are they any good?" wondered Chambers.

Cutler smiled. "What can I say? I saw their last production." He paused for a moment. "What was it called? Mystery at somewhere or other, something like that anyway. Once seen easily forgotten. A bit grim I'm afraid, pretty poor. Not my type of thing at all."

"I suppose you get what you pay for," suggested Chambers.

"Right enough, sir," agreed Cutler. "But I suppose I expected too much."

"And I guess that the audience got a bit more than they expected, last night," said Whittaker.

"You could be right, sir," said Cutler. "But they never realised what was happening, not then. But they certainly know now, the talks all over the village. We'll have the press here soon, and the local television station. Not looking forward to that I can tell you."

"You can't stop it, I'm afraid," said Chambers. "They will certainly want to speak with you, and us. Just be careful what you tell them."

"One more thing," Whittaker continued. "Apart from Tim Saunders, did you know anyone else in the group?"

"Oh, only Donovan," replied Cutler. "For many years he was a magistrate over in Weathersfield. He dealt with a few of the cases that I got involved with. Nothing too serious to be honest. Speeding, drunk and disorderly, things like that."

Whittaker looked at Chambers. "Right, I think we're done here, for the time being," he said and drained his cup. "You have been very helpful I must say."

"No problem, sir," said Cutler. "Is there anything else I can do for you?"

"Yes there is," Whittaker replied. "Can you arrange for us to see Saunders, tomorrow, say ten o'clock?"

"I'll get right on it," Cutler replied. "As soon as we've finished."

Whittaker paused for a moment, and then turned to face Chambers. "You know Derek, I think we will be here a lot longer than a day or two don't you?" he said. "Could you ring the office and tell them our thinking. And then we better find a hotel somewhere."

"Begging your pardon, sir," said Cutler. "I thought you'd be here a little while, so I've already made arrangements for you and Detective Chambers to stay at the Queens Head. It's at the end of the village. It's not fancy like your Ritz or Savoy, but it's quiet, clean and comfortable. Anyway there's two rooms waiting for you. Oh, and dinner is served from seven onwards."

Whittaker looked at his watch. It was five minutes to two. "We've time for a word with that Miss. Cooper then. Right Derek."

"Right you are, sir," Chambers agreed. "Our driver will be back in a few minutes, sir."

"Good," Whittaker replied, as he turned towards Cutler. "Thank you once again for your help Constable. We've got our work cut out methinks. So where can I find the young lady?"

"Well, she could be at the Queens Head, she's staying there as well," suggested Cutler. "Or you'll probably find her at the hall. With the play cancelled, there's a lot of tidying up to do, and I know that she wants to go through Donovan's things. You know he was a widower. His wife died several years ago. Cancer I think. There were no children, and as far as everyone knows there's no other relatives."

"Did he leave a will?" asked Chambers.

"Not that I know of," replied Cutler. "But Beavis are looking into it. Solicitors in Weathersfield. They've helped me out a few times."

"Keep me informed will you?" said Chambers. There was a knock on the door. "That'll be George, Our driver. Time to go."

"Right we'll be off then," said Whittaker, as he stood up. "I'll be in touch. In the meantime if you can arrange for that visit tomorrow, that would be good."

* * *

Chapter Five
Miss. Janet Cooper

The rain had finally stopped, and held up long enough for Whittaker and Chambers to drive to the Village Hall. Chambers, who was first out of the car walked to the door. He was surprised to find that it was open.

He peered into the hall. It reminded him of the hall at his old primary school. Herringbone parquet flooring, heavily stained through years of use. Thick heavy curtains up at the windows. Cast iron radiators. It even smelled like his old school. He looked over at the stage, his mind drifting back to when Miss. Painter, the headmistress would be standing there, saying morning prayers, or maybe giving out the school prizes at the end of term.

Whittaker followed a few moments later. "Any sign of her?" he called out.

Whittaker's voice shook Chambers out of his reminising. "Oh, yes I think so, sir. There's someone inside," he said as he saw Janet Cooper standing by the stage, her way blocked by the crime scene tape strewn across the stage. "I'm guessing that's her."

"Don't cross that line, Miss," Whittaker called out as he entered the hall, and walked over to where she was standing.

Startled she turned around to face the voice.

"Good afternoon, Miss. Cooper," Whittaker continued. "It is Miss. Cooper isn't it?"

"I'm Janet Cooper, yes," she replied, puzzled. "And you are?"

"I'm Chief Inspector Whittaker, from Scotland Yard, and this is Detective Sergeant Chambers. We've been sent down to investigate this tragic death."

"Constable Cutler said that you might be at the Queens Head, or here," Chambers explained. "We called the Queens Head, and obviously you weren't there."

"Constable Cutler did actually warn me that you would be coming," Cooper replied

"You really shouldn't be in here, you know," said Whittaker.

"Oh I know, I'm sorry, but I was just hoping that the tape would have been taken down by now," she replied. "There's a lot of sorting out to be done, and I need to go through James' things. And I was actually hoping that I could get some of my own things you see."

Whittaker looked puzzled.

She pointed "Over there, backstage," she explained, behind this tape. "With all that was happening I never gave them any thought before."

"I can understand that," said Whittaker. "It must have been quite a shock."

"It was," Janet agreed. "But now, with the play cancelled, I need to get everything packed away." She paused and brushed a tear from her face. "The worst thing is I can't do anything, and no one is telling me anything." She looked at Whittaker. "Could you help me? I could just pop over there, and then come back. Five minutes, that's all I need."

Whittaker smiled and shook his head. "I'm sorry. I just can't allow it," he replied. "I'm afraid that there's very little that I can do." He looked around. "It's still a crime scene you see, and you really should not be in here."

"I know, but how long will it be?" she asked.

Whittaker didn't know the answer to that. "As long as it takes I'm afraid," he replied. "How long is a piece of string?"

She looked disappointed. "There's some private things I would like to get in my handbag," she continued. "Things I need. My purse, my keys, credit card, money, things like that."

Whittaker was certainly sympathetic, but his hands were tied. "There's nothing to be done I'm afraid," he said. "A murder has been committed right here, up on that stage." He looked up at the platform.

"Yes I know, I still can't believe it though," Janet replied. "It's all very distressing."

"It is still being investigated, you understand," Whittaker continued. "And I'm sorry but that tape has to remain in place until that investigation has been completed." He turned to look at Chambers. "Derek you better speak to Cutler, this place needs to be better secured."

"Will do," said Chambers.

Whittaker turned back to face Miss. Cooper. "I actually wanted a word with you if you can spare me a few minutes."

"Well, I'll help if I can, certainly," she replied. "But I've already told the local police all that I know."

"Thank you, much appreciated," replied Whittaker. "Now, I understand that you saw the whole thing. Is that right?"

"That's right," she replied. "Along with about a hundred and twenty others sitting in the audience, watching the play."

"Murder At Larkhall Manor," said Chambers.

"That's right," said Janet. "But it was meant to be play acting."

"It was meant to be play acting," said Whittaker. "But when someone is shot dead, on the stage in front of an audience, then it becomes an act of murder."

"I never expected a real murder," Miss. Cooper continued. "Nobody did."

"No, I'm sure that they didn't," said Whittaker. "So tell me, what actually happened?"

"What happened was Tim shot James, as simple as that. Right there on the stage," she replied as she pointed indicating the murder scene "He just came from behind that curtain, walked up to James, took aim and shot him. Just as he was supposed to do according to the script." She started to cry. "You know, if I hadn't actually seen it myself, and someone had just told me that Tim had shot someone, dead, in front of everyone, I would never have believed it. There's just no way. It was horrible. It was meant to be acting, nothing more. Just a stupid piece of fantasy. There wasn't meant to be a real gun," she continued. "For the past week we've been rehearsing with a prop, a fake gun. Then comes the opening night, and it's suddenly a real one. I can't understand it. Where did it come from?"

"That's a good question," said Chambers. "And one that we must find an answer to."

Whittaker agreed. "If Saunders shot Donovan without realizing he had a real gun, then it looks like somebody switched the gun deliberately," he said. "Tell me, who would be in a position to do that I wonder?"

Janet thought for a moment. "Well, certainly any member of the cast could have done it," she replied. "And any of the backstage staff."

"Who is in charge of the props?" asked Chambers.

"Oh that'll be Susan Turner," Janet replied. "It's her responsibility to make sure that everything needed for a particular scene is there, in place, ready for use."

"So the fake gun would have been placed in position as required," said Chambers.

"That's correct," agreed Janet.

"So when would she have done that?" asked Chambers.

"Susan would have made sure that everything needed for Act Two was provided probably during Act One."

"So let me get this straight in my mind," said Whittaker. "What time did Act one start?"

"That was just a few minutes to eight o'clock," Janet replied.

"Right, and it finished at what time?"

"Just after eight thirty," Janet replied. "I reckon that Susan would have dealt with the props for Act Two, at about quarter past eight, something like that."

"Are you absolutely sure of that?" Whittaker asked. "Eight fifteen?"

Janet said nothing for a few moments. "Well, no I'm not one hundred percent certain," she replied. "But Susan did mention that's the time she had in mind." She paused once again. "So I imagine that's when she put the gun in position."

Whittaker looked at Chambers. "Make a note of that, Derek, and we'll check with Miss. Turner." He looked back at Janet Cooper. "And when did Mr. Saunders take up his position?"

Janet thought for a few moments. "Well I saw Tim waiting in the wings," she started to explain. "I never noticed the time, but I'm guessing it would have been about five minutes before he walked on to the stage. I would say, probably about ten past nine."

"So about fifty-five minutes in which anyone could have switched the gun," said Whittaker.

"Probably right, sir," said Chambers. "But I think whoever made the switch would have waited until the very last possible moment. They wouldn't run the risk of the switch being noticed and maybe their plan being stopped, would they?"

"Makes sense," said Whittaker. "Miss. Cooper, I shall want a full list of the cast, and the backstage people. That would give us a list of suspects, or at least a good start. All we need do then is find not just the people who could have done it, but the person who wanted to do it. Simple. Well at least that's the hope."

"I'll get a list written up for you Inspector," said Janet.

"That will be very helpful I'm sure," said Whittaker, more the optimist, than the realist. "Could I also have a copy of the script?" he asked.

"Why would you want that?" Janet replied.

"We think that the gun was switched between eight fifteen, and ten past nine, give or take a few minutes," said Whittaker. "With a bit of rough calculations regarding timing, a study of the script could give us some idea of where the cast were at certain times."

"Well, certainly you can have a copy if you think it would help," replied Janet. She smiled, and then laughed nervously. "It could prove to be quite historic. I mean, after all it's the play that closed after just an hour and twenty minutes on opening night, and never to be seen again."

"Why do you say that, Miss Cooper?" asked Chambers.

"I could never do it again," she replied, brushing a tear from her eye. "It would be too upsetting. I mean James wasn't the friendliest person I've ever known, but to see him murdered like that. No, it will never be seen again. I doubt that anyone would want to see it anyway."

"Maybe you're right," Whittaker replied. "But perhaps, with all of the publicity it will certainly receive because of the murder, it might take on a whole new life."

Janet thought for a moment. Certainly there was some truth it what the Inspector had said. What was it they said? *There's no such thing as bad publicity.* "You might well be right, Inspector, but if it does it will do it without my involvement."

"Oh, why is that Miss. Cooper?" asked Chambers.

Janet sighed. "I love the theatre. I love being part of it, even if it is a second rate tin pot amateur production like this one," she started to explain. "But I really would not want to be part of a production where a murder had actually taken place, and I saw the whole thing."

"I can certainly understand that, Miss. Cooper, but it still seems a shame," said Whittaker.

Janet took a deep breath. "Will there be anything else?" she asked.

"Addresses," replied Whittaker. "Can you also let me have a list of addresses for the cast members?"

"Addresses?" repeated Janet.

"Yes," Whittaker replied. "I'll probably need to get in touch over the next few days, so I need to know where they will be. I imagine most of them won't be hanging around the village."

"Oh, of course," said Janet. "Actually some of them do live here, in Wokingham, or maybe in Weathersfield. And some are staying either at the Queens Head, or the Wokingham Arms. It's a small Bed and Breakfast place, not really a proper hotel, like the Queens. A bit down market if you know what I mean."

"If you could just let me have the addresses, it would be appreciated," said Whittaker. "I imagine that now the production has been cancelled the cast members will be making tracks for their homes."

Janet nodded. It hadn't occurred to her, but certainly the Inspector was correct. There would be no reason to stay.

"You'll be going home as well, I expect," said Whittaker.

She smiled, and looked past the crime scene tape. "Well now you mention it, yes I will, when I can get my things."

Whittaker looked over at the tape. Amazing how such a narrow strip of tape, no more than fifty millimetres thick, could become such an impenetrable barrier. "Oh I see, yes that could be awkward," he agreed. "Which is your handbag?" he asked.

"Oh, you can't miss it, it's a large dark brown bag," she explained. "With a small teddy bear chained to the handle."

Whittaker started to laugh. "Well we can't leave poor old teddy chained up, can we?" he exclaimed. "I'll have a word, but I can't promise anything. In the meantime, where is home for you?"

"Oh, London," she replied. "Bayswater Road, it's a small one bedroom flat, nothing special, but it's convenient you know. Five minutes on the tube and you're in the heart of the West End and ...."

"The theatres," Whittaker added. "I know what you mean. I'm in Fulham myself. Handy for the old football you see."

"Oh, are you a supporter of Fulham then?" Janet asked.

"No, not on your life," said Whittaker feigning offense. "Chelsea is my team." He paused for a moment and looked at Derek. "Derek's a West Ham man, for his sins."

Chambers started to laugh. "Best team in the league," he announced.

"In your dreams," said Whittaker. He then turned back to face Janet. "So how come you are involved with a local amateur group?" he asked. "I mean living in London like you do."

"Oh, that's an easy one. I used to live in the next village, Hatfield," she started to explain. "I had always wanted to work in the theatre. Not acting though. I wasn't any good at that, but directing, stage managing something like that. I'd applied for so many jobs but no joy. I thought I might do better by moving to London, but to date, there's been nothing. Not a hint, but I keep trying."

"So tell me about this group," Whittaker continued. "How long as it been going?"

"Oh, this is the sixth year," she replied. "Quite a spectacular way to celebrate wouldn't you say."

"Quite so, perhaps a bit too dramatic though," said Whittaker. "But as I said the publicity might do you some good. You never know."

"Not for me, Inspector," said Janet, suddenly becoming weepy once again. "As I told you, this will be my last year with the group."

"That's a pity Miss. Cooper," said Whittaker sympathetically. "Nonetheless, I wish you well in whatever comes your way."

"Oh, I expect I'll find something," Janet replied. "Probably another amateur group somewhere. Maybe even one in London, who knows?"

Chapter Six
A Lot Of Questions

"I hope you find something suitable Miss. Cooper," said Whittaker. He paused for a moment. Then he took a deep breath. "In the meantime, however, I'm sorry, but I do need to ...."

Janet Cooper nodded. "Of course," she said. "You must have a lot of questions. Please carry on."

"Thank you. I'm intrigued about the play you were performing," Whittaker began. "Murder at Larkhall Manor. Where did it come from?"

"Oh it was actually written by one of the cast," Janet explained. "Steve, Steve Ashton. He plays the stranded motorist. Well he wrote it." She smiled. "He's no Shakespeare I can tell you. And Agatha Christie has absolutely nothing to worry about."

"Maybe, but at least I've never heard of a real murder take place on stage before. That's got to be a first," said Whittaker. "This, er Mr. Ashton, how long has he been a member of the group?"

"Just over four years," replied Janet.

"And has he written many plays?" asked Chambers. "I mean during that four years."

Janet Cooper tried not to laugh. "He has dabbled I think, but not actually produced a complete play before. Certainly he hasn't with us," she replied. "I really don't know if he did anything before coming to us. But judging by Larkhall Manor, I sincerely hope not."

"Oh, that bad, eh," suggested Chambers.

She started to smile. "Not really bad I admit, but it's far from good," she replied. "Let's just say that it lacked quite a lot."

Whittaker was puzzled. "If it wasn't that good, why did you continue with it?" he asked. "Why not just scrap it, and do something else?"

"Necessity," she replied. "Simple as that. To put on another play we would need permission from the author, or their estate, and probably have to pay a hefty royalty, which, quite frankly we couldn't afford. Steve said that he would write something for us. There was only six or seven months before we were due to perform here in Wokingham. You have to book these halls a long time ahead you understand. I really had no choice. I needed something. Besides I never expected it to be so …. So dramatic. Well, least said, soonest mended."

"What about Donovan?" asked Chambers. "How long had he been in the group?"

"Oh, he was fairly new," replied Janet. "Just this season in fact. He came about nine or ten months ago, something like that. Sorry to say he wasn't the greatest of actors, and certainly he was very hard to work with, but I have to admit that he was perfect for the part of the Colonel. He just looked the part, you know, definitely in command." She paused for a moment. "In fact it was actually Steve's idea. He said that Donovan would be ideal as the Colonel. Made for the part, I think Steve said. I have to say that he was absolutely right."

"I wonder why Ashton felt that way," said Whittaker. "I mean did he know Donovan before?"

"Sorry, I've no idea," Janet replied. "All I can say is that neither of them actually said that they knew each other."

"Umm," replied Whittaker, still puzzled. It just didn't seem likely that you would recommend a complete stranger, someone with unknown acting ability, for a major role in a play that you had written. "Had he any experience?" he asked.

"Before he joined us you mean? A little I think, but I don't have any details," she replied. "Though I have to say I probably wouldn't have taken him on, but he was determined to join, and well it suited my purposes, I guess."

"I wonder why he was so determined," said Chambers. "I mean with all due respects, from what I hear, and from what you have just said, Murder At Larkhall Manor wasn't that special was it?"

"You are absolutely right, Detective. It wasn't anything special at all," Janet replied. "In fact, I'm sorry to say this but it really wasn't that good. Do you know we only sold one hundred and twenty three tickets? We barely paid for our expenses. And even that money has to be refunded after what happened. Hopefully no one claims travelling expenses. You can't win."

Whittaker looked around the hall. "I would have thought you would have had a lot more than just a hundred people," he said.

"Hardly a sellout I grant you?" Janet agreed. "We could have handled at least another sixty or seventy people, maybe more. The hall could easily accommodate two hundred people."

"So not wildly successful, then," said Whittaker. "So, why was it so important to Donovan I wonder? Did he think it was actually good?"

"I really don't know," Janet replied. "But I got the impression that he knew someone in the group, or at least he thought he did."

"Did you know who it was?" asked Chambers.

"No, I didn't, and he never said, and I didn't press the point," she replied. "As I say I just had an impression, I could have been wrong."

"But if you were wrong, we're back to square one," said Chambers. "Why was he so determined to be in the group? It doesn't make much sense, especially if he actually lacked acting experience."

"Maybe he was looking to take up a hobby, or something," Janet suggested. "Or maybe he wanted company. You know he was a widower, and perhaps he was feeling lonely."

"Did he say that?" asked Chambers.

"No he never said anything," she replied. "Sorry, but I really have no idea why he wanted to join our little band. And sadly James is now dead, so we may never know."

Whittaker had to agree, but he was convinced that whatever the reason Donovan wanted to be in the play was, it had eventually lead to his death. "Getting back to the play," he said. "Were all of the cast required for the second act?"

Janet thought for a few moments. "Oh no, just a handful would have been required. There's Catherine Barr, she was in the Act. She plays the Colonel's wife, Isabel. And then there was John Berry, the butler. He brings the Colonel his nightcap." She paused for a moment. "The scene starts with Isabel and the Colonel sitting by the fire. It's getting late. Then the butler brings in the Colonel's drink, and then he goes. That just leaves the Colonel and his wife on the stage. They have an argument, a real ding dong I can tell you. Best part of the play in my opinion. Catherine was clearly having a great time with it. Then almost at the end of the Act she leaves the room. She storms off. The Colonel drinks his nightcap, and very soon falls asleep, and I think you know the rest."

"Yes, I think we do," Whittaker had to agree. "So apart from those two, Catherine Barr and John Berry, and of course Donovan and Saunders, there was no one else in Act Two."

"That's correct," said Miss. Cooper.

"So where were they?" asked Whittaker. "The others who were not required."

"Oh, I'm not really sure," she replied shaking her head. "Rose was hanging around back stage, helping out as usual. There's always a lot to do, and she likes to help out if she can." She paused for a moment. "Ian Jackson made a quick getaway, probably went down to the Arms, for a quick half, as he put it. Clive had disappeared for a gin and tonic, probably at the Queens Head. Oh, and John, John Berry, went for a smoke after he had finished his couple of lines. We keep telling him to quit, but, well, what can you do? I'm not sure about the others. Not very helpful I'm afraid."

"Well you never know," said Whittaker. "Somewhere in there, might be that one vital piece of information that solves the whole thing. We just have to keep looking, and hope we find it."

"Well I hope you do find it, Inspector," replied Janet.

"Tell me, purely out of idle curiosity, in your play who is the murderer?" asked Whittaker. "The Butler I suppose. It's always the butler isn't it?"

Janet was surprised at the change in questioning. "Well we do actually have a butler, as you know. John Berry." she admitted. "But no, not this time, he is completely innocent."

"So who did it then?" Whittaker asked. "I mean this young man, Tim Saunders, what part does he play?"

She wondered where this was leading, but decided to go along with it for the time being. "He actually plays the young police officer," she replied. "But he isn't really a police man."

"Of course not," replied Whittaker. "What is he then?"

"Ah, that would be telling wouldn't it? Give the whole game away," Janet replied. "If you want to know, then I'm afraid you need to watch the play. Now sadly, an impossibility."

"So the policeman isn't really a policemen," said Whittaker.

"Correct," agreed Janet.

"And I'm guessing that the Colonel wasn't really a Colonel," Whittaker continued. "He was actually, er, oh I don't know, perhaps he was the young man's long lost father."

"Wrong," said Janet, trying not to laugh. "He was definitely a Colonel."

"Ok, we'll leave that to one side shall we," Whittaker replied smiling. "But what about the motive? There's always a reason, so in your play why was the Colonel killed?"

"Sorry, but I can't tell you that either," Janet replied. "I'm sworn to secrecy, and so are the members of the audience. We won't let them in unless they swear not to divulge the culprit, or the motive."

"And they all agree," said Chambers. "Do you get them to sign a legal document?"

Janet started to laugh. "Oh no, nothing like that," she replied. "But I have to say they all go along with it. It's never a problem."

"Well that's fantasy for you. In real life you can't do that," the Inspector continued. "Withholding evidence is a crime. You could go to prison for a long time. In real life you must tell, you can't have secrets relating to a crime."

"Fortunately for me then that it's not real life," replied Janet. "But merely a play, a bit of fantasy."

"Oh yes, its fantasy, agreed, but even then all is not what it seems is it?" said Whittaker. "It's a pretend police officer who is actually the murderer in your play. In some ways fantasy and real life become merged don't you think?"

"In what way, Inspector?" Janet asked.

"Think about it, for a moment," Whittaker said. "By all accounts Tim Saunders shot and killed James Donovan. Murdered him right there on that stage, in front of a hundred odd people. Or so it seemed. But he didn't do it, did he?" He paused once again. "Or did he? That's the real mystery."

Janet looked horrified, and shook her head. "No, he didn't do it, Inspector."

"So you say," replied Whittaker. "And I'm not actually saying that he did, but you must admit that he had as much chance to switch the gun, as anyone else did. Maybe more so, because he was right there, in the right place, at the right time. Right where the fake gun should have been."

"He didn't do it," repeated Janet.

"Maybe you're right, maybe he didn't do it. That remains to be seen," Whittaker said. "But one thing is certain."

"And that is?" asked Janet.

"Unlike your play, we have a real body, and a real murderer to catch," replied Whittaker. "At present they are the only two facts we do have."

"I know, Inspector," Janet replied. "But why would anyone want to kill James anyway? It doesn't make sense."

Whittaker heaved a sigh. "Well, you know, Miss. it's a wicked world we live in, and some really nasty people that live in it," he started to explain. "People kill for all kinds of reasons. Money, that's a great reason for committing murder. Then there's revenge, or jealousy. And another old favourite is to kill someone to stop them from talking, from divulging secrets you might prefer to keep hidden."

"Blackmail you mean," suggested Janet.

"Blackmail," agreed Whittaker.

"But why James?" she asked.

"We don't know that right now," said Whittaker. "But we aim to find out don't you worry about that." He paused for a moment, then sighed. "Well we have a murderer to catch, so best be getting on, or we won't catch him …."

"Or her," added Janet.

"Indeed. Or her, as you so rightly state," agreed Whittaker. "Right, I'm afraid you'll have to leave now." He pointed to the door.

"She looked over at the door. "Right, well I'll say goodbye then."

"Goodbye Miss. for the time being at least," said Whittaker. "I expect I'll need to speak with you again."

She started to walk away. She suddenly stopped and turned. She raised her hand and waved. Chambers suddenly noticed something. "What have you done to your hand," he called out.

Janet looked puzzled.

"You've cut it," Chambers continued "You should put a plaster on that."

She looked at her hand. "I never noticed," she said. "I don't remember doing that."

"Well, I'd get a plaster if I were you," Chambers repeated.

She smiled. "Will do, thank you. Bye." She waved once again, and headed to the door.

* * *

Chapter Seven
Too Many Suspects

A small office area had been put to the convenience of the Chief Inspector. It had been set up as a base for the investigation. To one side of the room The Inspector had erected a pin board displaying a plan of the hall especially the stage area. A few notes had been pinned on specific areas indicating specific information, together with a time. One such note was pinned to the position of a small table, and indicated an estimated time when the prop gun had been placed there. Another note, placed at the centre of the stage indicated the time of Donovan's killing. Next to it was another pin board containing scant details of the cast members. At the bottom of the board were a number of pins of various colours.

Whittaker looked at the boards, and heaved a sign. "Just look at those pins, Derek. They represent the members of the cast of Murder at Larkhall Manor," he explained. "You know, for my money the murderer is one of them, no one else. And that includes Timothy Saunders and Miss. Janet Cooper, which means we have for too many suspects."

"Did you say Saunders, sir?" asked a puzzled Chambers.

"Yes I did," Whittaker replied. "You know he can protest his innocence all he likes, but he still could be the guilty party. He certainly had the opportunity didn't he? No, for the time being, and until I know different, he is still a possible murderer."

"Well he certainly didn't like Donovan, according to Constable Cutler," replied Chambers. "And he did have the gun, so."

"Harry actually said something about Saunders being intimidated by Donovan," said Whittaker. "I think he could have been frightened of Donovan."

"Hardly a reason for killing someone though is it, sir?" said Chambers. "In fact if he was that frightened, he'd be more likely to keep his distance wouldn't he?"

"You're probably right," said Whittaker. "Either way, we've got to get the number of suspects down. And we also need to find a motive." He turned away from the boards, and sat down.

For some minutes neither Whittaker, nor Chambers said anything. Whittaker sat back in his chair, his feet up on the desk. His eyes were shut. Detective Chambers was idly doodling.

He suddenly stopped scribbling. "I wonder why Miss. Cooper was so anxious to get her bag," he murmured.

Whittaker opened his eyes, and removed his feet from the desk. "What, what did you say?" he asked.

Chambers looked at the Inspector. "Nothing really, sir," he replied. "I was just wondering why Miss. Cooper was so desperate to get her bag. I mean she must have known that she shouldn't have been there."

"Alright Derek, what's on your mind?" asked Whittaker. "Let's have it."

"Oh, I was just thinking aloud, sir," replied Chambers. "My usual suspicious mind working overtime maybe. Probably nonsense."

"Go on," Whittaker coaxed. "If you've something to say, just say it. If it's nonsense I'll be the first to tell you."

"Well, she just seemed a bit too anxious, you know," replied Chambers. "A bit too impatient. I mean it hadn't exactly been a long time had it? It was only the day after the murder."

"Well perhaps she really did need her purse, and whatever else it was," suggested Whittaker.

"Perhaps she did," agreed Chambers. "But possibly it was something else, something she was hiding."

"The fake gun you mean?" suggested Whittaker. "The prop."

"Well it's a possibility isn't it?" said Derek, hopefully.

Whittaker had to admit that it certainly was a possibility. "I'm way ahead of you Derek," he said. "I had the same thought. I've already asked Constable Cutler to take a look."

Chambers smiled, and went back to his scribbling. Whittaker returned his feet to the desk, and closed his eyes once again. Chambers looked down at the sheet of paper. *Motive,* he wrote. It was heavily underlined, and a series of question marks had been added. He stared at the paper for a short time, then he picked it up, scrunched it into a ball, and then dropped it into the waste paper basket.

* * *

There was a knock on the door. "I expect that'll be Harry now," said Whittaker, once again removing his feet from the desk.

"I thought you were asleep, sir," said Chambers, as he stood up.

"Nonsense, me asleep, how dare you," said Whittaker. "I was merely thinking."

There was a second knock, then the door opened, and Police Constable Cutler entered the room.

"Hello, Harry, come in," said Whittaker. "Okay, take your seats gentlemen, I think we need to go over a few things, and decide on a course of action, shall we?"

"Well, sir, firstly I've made arrangements for you to see Saunders," Cutler replied as he sat down. "You're expected at ten tomorrow."

"Good. You better let our driver know," said Whittaker. "What time do we need to leave here?"

"Nine thirty should give us more than enough time," replied Cutler.

"Good enough," said Whittaker. "And then after that, what do we do next?"

"Next, I think we should take a look round Donovan's place," suggested Chambers. "It might be useful, you never know. Maybe we'll find our motive."

"Agreed," said Whittaker.

"Then we should start interviewing everyone," Chambers continued. "The entire cast. And the backstage people."

Constable Cutler raised his hand. "What about the audience?" he asked.

Whittaker looked at Cutler. "What about them?" he replied.

"I was wondering, sir," Cutler continued. "Maybe someone watching the play might have seen something. Something odd, something unusual. I don't know. Something suspicious. I just thought that maybe we should check it out."

Whittaker rubbed his chin. *It was a possibility, a slim one, but a possibility nonetheless.* "Harry, you do realise that although Miss. Cooper would have liked a much larger audience, there were one hundred and something people sitting in that audience, that night. More than enough I would say. In fact probably far too many for our purpose."

"Yes sir," Constable Cutler replied. "And it was one hundred and twenty-three."

"And Harry you should also remember that none of them actually realised that a murder had been committed," Chambers added.

"I know that, sir," Cutler replied. "Even so someone might have seen something, something important. It's worth a chance I think."

Chambers sighed, and looked at Whittaker. "They were just sitting there watching a play, sir," he said. "I doubt if they would have noticed anything if it got up and hit them."

57

Probably perfectly true, thought Whittaker. But true or not, Whittaker knew that you could never tell with people. They were predictably unpredictable. Some would be exactly as Detective Chambers had described them. Not notice a thing unless it was pointed out to them, and even then they might not fully understand its importance. Others, however, would notice something in almost everything, no matter how trivial.

"Well, you have to admit that it is possible, Derek," Whittaker said. "But there's no way we can interview all one hundred and twenty-three people. I can just imagine the number of different stories we would get." He looked at Cutler. "I'll tell you what we can do though. Get in touch with some of those local newspapers. Get them to print a request for information. You know the sort of thing, anyone with information regarding the, er …. The incident on such and such, at Wokingham Village Hall, should contact the police at …. Well, you know the rest."

Cutler smiled, he knew what to do. Over the years he had built up good contacts on all of the local newspapers. "Will do, sir," he replied. "Right after we finish here."

"Right," said Whittaker. "In the meantime let's just recap on what we do know."

"It isn't much I'm afraid, sir," said Chambers, sounding despondent.

Whittaker gave a sigh. True it wasn't much he had to admit. But looking on the positive side, it was early days, and there was still a lot of work to be done. "That's as maybe," he replied. He paused for a moment and opened his notebook. "We know that the group has been rehearsing all week, using the prop gun. We also know that according to Miss. Cooper the prop gun was placed in its normal position roundabout quarter past eight on the night of the murder."

"And by nine twenty Donovan was dead," added Chambers. "Whoever did this crime left the switch to the very last minute."

"When there would have been less risk of being detected you mean," said Whittaker.

"Precisely," said Chambers. "And with the play in progress people would have been too busy to actually notice a switch."

"Makes sense," Whittaker replied. "We need to find that fake gun, and soon." He turned to face Cutler. "By the way, did you find anything?" he asked.

"No, sir. Not a thing I'm afraid," Cutler replied. "The prop gun was not in Miss. Cooper's bag."

Chambers smiled. "Never thought it would be," he said.

"No more than I expected, Constable," said Whittaker. "But we must find it, keep looking."

"Will do, Inspector," Cutler replied. "I've already got some officers checking back stage, but I'm guessing that it's probably long gone by now."

"You could be right, Harry," agreed Whittaker. "But keep trying."

"Certainly, sir," said Cutler.

"Incidentally, do we actually know what the fake gun looked like?" Whittaker continued.

"Oh yes sir, we do," replied Chambers. "It's just a standard pistol, a bit like a starting pistol. Not a bit like the weapon that was actually used to kill Donovan. It's completely different. I just can't understand why Tim never noticed the switch."

"Perhaps he did notice," suggested Whittaker. "But point one he was in the middle of a performance. He couldn't very well start asking questions then could he?"

"Guess not, sir," agreed Chambers.

"And point two," Whittaker continued. "Perhaps he just thought that the gun was more realistic for the actual performance rather than a rehearsal."

"Good point sir," agreed Chambers. "And I guess that even though it appeared to be a real gun, you would never expect it to be loaded, and ready to fire would you?"

"That makes sense," agreed Cutler. "But you know there's a lot that puzzles me sir."

"You and me both," said Whittaker. "Go on."

"Whoever did this had all week when they could have done it, agreed," said Cutler.

"Yes agreed," said Whittaker.

"But they waited until opening night, when there was an audience present," Cutler continued. "Why?"

"Maybe they wanted someone in that audience to see James Donovan killed," suggested Chambers.

"Or perhaps they wanted the whole audience to see," suggested Whittaker.

"The question then is why?" said Chambers. "Why would they want somebody to see the killing?"

"Could be several reasons, I suppose," said Whittaker. "Maybe they wanted somebody to see it as a kind of a warning, you know, this could happen to you if you don't whatever ...."

"As a threat you mean," said Cutler.

"Could be," agreed Whittaker.

"Or maybe to show an accomplice that the crime had been committed," suggested Cutler.

"More likely just to make the whole thing even more complex I would say," said Whittaker shaking his head. "A murder right in front of so many witnesses is hardly normal is it? I mean it doesn't happen every day of the week."

"Well, it certainly succeeded in that, sir," said Chambers. "It's complex alright."

"And as we've just said, if someone had noticed the switch in an actual performance, they couldn't start asking questions could they?" said Whittaker.

Chambers agreed. "And of course, if it happened during a rehearsal, then it would just be stopped, and then the questions would start."

"Precisely," replied Whittaker. "You know, I thought this was supposed to be an open and shut case."

"It was, sir," replied Chambers. "Remember what I said about the Commissioner?"

"Oh yes, the Commissioner, bless her cotton socks," said Whittaker. "About us going down, and just make sure everything was being done by the book. Oh yes I remember. I must talk to her about that, when we get back."

"Well yes, that as well, sir," replied Chambers. "But I was thinking more of the fact that she thought it would all be wrapped up in a day or two."

"That's right, Derek, she did think that, didn't she?" agreed Whittaker.

"Well, we must be doing something wrong then, I guess," said Chambers.

"Derek, how long have you been in the force?" asked Whittaker.

Chambers thought for a few moments. "Come August, it'll be twelve years, sir."

"Twelve years, eh. As long as that," said Whittaker. "I'm coming up to twenty six years, and you know in all of that time I've never once come across an open and shut case that was really that simple to solve. Far from being a simple open and shut case, whoever did this made sure that it was anything but. Committing the crime in front of so many people made sure that it was a very complex murder, and we've got our work cut out I can tell you."

"Well, we certainly have more than enough suspects," said Chambers

"You can say that again," said Whittaker. "And we need to find out the movements of every one of them on that day, the day of the murder. We need to know where they were and when."

"How will we be sure that they tell the truth," Chambers said. "They could lie sir, especially the guilty party."

"It's certainly a strong possibility," agreed Whittaker. "In fact the guilty person will definitely lie. But remember you have to be a very clever person to lie successfully. Quite often a liar would have to lie to cover up the other lie. You also have to remember the original lie that you told, to make sure you maintain your story. Furthermore someone else might innocently make a comment that immediately shows up the lie, or at least raises doubts in your mind."

"Maybe we could do with that private detective Kendall," suggested Chambers.

Whittaker smiled, and then he started to laugh as he thought of the American private detective he had first met almost eight years previously. "Maybe," he replied. "Maybe, but without him, it looks like it's just us three," Whittaker continued. "Me, you and Harry there."

"We'll just have to muddle through then, I guess," said Chambers.

"Right," said Whittaker. "And as a start what we need now is a motive, why would anyone want to kill Mr. Donovan?"

"You remember I told you that he was a Magistrate," said Cutler. "Maybe there's a reason there somewhere. Something from his past. Maybe a judgment he made."

Whittaker shook his head. "No, I can't see that," he replied. "As a Magistrate the only cases he would have dealt with would be pretty minor stuff. Speeding, drunk and disorderly, causing an affray. Things like that. Hardly anything that would lead to his murder."

"Well, all I can say is that as a Magistrate he was strict, and quite tough," Cutler started to explain. "There was nothing soft about him. No compassion, no hint of mercy. He wasn't exactly flavor of the month you know, and I guess he might have had a lot of enemies. He certainly wasn't an easy person to like."

"Well, maybe there's our motive, right there," Chambers suggested.

"Ah, but was he disliked enough," said Whittaker.

"To see him dead you mean," said Cutler. "To commit a murder. Guess that's another question."

"And that's what we need to find out," replied Whittaker.

"Well clearly someone did dislike him enough to kill him," murmured Chambers. "The problem is maybe every one of our suspects disliked him, so we're back at square one."

"Correct, Derek. Maybe you're right," agreed Whittaker. "And, of course there's always the possibility that the young guy, Timothy Saunders, also disliked him, and really did do it after all. Maybe he did switch the guns himself. I think we need to have a word with him."

* * *

Chapter Eight
Timothy Saunders

The following morning, Whittaker and Chambers were back at twenty-eight Mill Lane. It was a beautiful morning, much to the amazement of the Chief Inspector. There was a clear blue sky, and the seemingly incessant rain had, at last, been replaced by hot sunshine.

Whittaker looked at the sky. "Wouldn't you know it?" he said. "At long last the rain has stopped, and what are we going to do? A round of golf maybe; or a day relaxing in the sun. Not on your life, we are going to spend much of the day stuck inside a prison cell."

"Good morning, Inspector," Cutler said, as he met the two men at the gate. "The forecast says that it's going to remain like this for the next four or five days. That's good news."

"Umm, and then I suppose it'll be back to the monsoon again," replied Whittaker clearly unimpressed. He looked at the constable. "Forecasts have been known to be wrong, you know. Frequently."

"It'll be fine, sir," said Chambers. "You mark my words."

"We'll see," said Whittaker unconvinced. He looked at his watch. It was nine twenty-five. "When are we supposed to be there?"

"We are expected in just over thirty minutes," Cutler replied. "So, I think we best get going, sir."

"Where exactly is he Constable?" asked Chambers, as they started to walk towards the car.

"Well, he's not here, sir." replied Cutler. "I don't have the facility you see. And I never had the need before. No he was taken to Weathersfield, a small town about eight miles away. But I understand that he is due to be released without charge, later this afternoon, or early tomorrow morning."

"I didn't think you'd be able to hold him much longer," said Whittaker, as he got into the front seat of the car.

"If he raises the question, which I fully expect he will, I don't think we should say too much though," said Cutler. "Let the prison people tell him, when they are ready."

"Probably wise," agreed Whittaker. "Right, are we all in? Seat belts buckled?" He turned towards George. "Right, let's get going then, shall we? We haven't got all day."

* * *

Twenty minutes later the car pulled up outside the Weathersfield Police Station, where Saunders was being kept in a police cell.

A young police officer took Whittaker, Chambers and Cutler down to where Saunders was being kept. Saunders was sitting at a small table that was bolted to the floor. Around it were three vacant chairs, also bolted to the floor. As he entered the cell, Whittaker was shocked to see how gaunt Saunders looked.

"Mr. Saunders," Whittaker called out. Saunders looked up at the sudden noise, but said nothing. "Mr. Saunders, I'm Chief Inspector Whittaker," the Inspector said, as he walked over to the table, followed by Cutler and Chambers. The three men sat down. "I'm from Scotland Yard, and this is Detective Sergeant Chambers, and that is Police Constable Cutler."

"I know Mr. Cutler," Saunders interrupted.

"I've known Tim for a long while, haven't I?" said Cutler. "We need to speak with you Tim, we won't be too long. Is that alright?"

Saunders made no response.

Whittaker took a deep breath. "Tim, I have to remind you that you are still under oath. You don't have to speak to me if you don't want to, but anything you do say will be taken down and maybe …."

"I didn't do it, simple as that. I told Mr. Cutler that," Saunders stammered. "I didn't mean to do it. I didn't know the gun was loaded." He started breathing hard. "It shouldn't have been loaded. It was acting. It should have been acting …."

"Alright Mr. Saunders, take it easy," said Chambers, placing his hand on to Saunders' arm. "We would just like to ask a few questions."

Slowly Saunders started to relax a little. "What would you like to know?" he asked

"To start can you tell me something about yourself?" said Whittaker. "How old are you?"

Saunders didn't see the point, but answered anyway. "Twenty-six."

"And you live in Wokingham, is that right?" asked Chambers.

"Yes sir," Saunders replied. "Have been almost all my life."

"And what about your work?" Chambers continued. "What do you do, when you're not on the stage that is?"

"Oh, the stage thing is just a part time thing, you know, a hobby if you like," Saunders replied. "I work for Gledstone Containers, a shipping line down in Brighton."

"Interesting," said Whittaker. "A lot different to play acting in murder mysteries I guess. How long have you been with the group?"

Saunders was now fully relaxed. *This was easy,* he thought. *Not at all stressful.* "This is my second year," he replied.

"New boy eh," said Whittaker. What made you join the group?"

Saunders hesitated for a moment. "Well it was Susan. Susan Turner," he replied trying hard not to blush. "She does the props."

"Oh I see," said Chambers smiling. "You and her, are you …. you know? An item, I think that's the term they use."

"I wish," Saunders said. "No, afraid not, she's got a boy-friend, and she's getting married next year." He shrugged. "Oh well, not to worry. We're still good friends."

"How is it then?" Chambers continued. "The group I mean? Do you enjoy it?"

"It's good, I like it," replied Saunders. "Janet's nice. They all are."

"What about Mr. Donovan?" asked Chambers. "Did you like him?"

Saunders suddenly became nervous once again. He became agitated, and shook his head. "No, I didn't like him," he replied.

"Oh, why not?" asked Whittaker.

"He thought he was better than anyone else," replied Saunders.

"Is that just your opinion?" asked Chambers.

Tim thought for a moment. "No sir, it wasn't just me. "Many of the others agree with me, I'm sure. He is …. Was, a very hard person to like, for some it was almost impossible. He was always putting people down you know. Always complaining, or being critical."

"Did anyone dislike him enough to want to see him dead I wonder," said Whittaker. "You don't need to say anything about that Mr. Saunders, I'm just thinking aloud." He paused for a moment. "Can we talk about the gun?" he asked, as he looked over at Chambers.

"I've seen the gun that killed Mr. Donovan," Chambers started to explain. "Unfortunately, I haven't seen the fake one. But I understand that the two guns are quite different. The murder weapon is much heavier, and a totally different shape. I'm puzzled. When you picked it up didn't you think there was anything strange about it?"

Saunders said nothing for a moment. "Oh yes, I knew it was different right from the start. You couldn't miss it, but I never thought anything was wrong, or … well, I just thought that Janet wanted something different, you know something more realistic for the performance. That's all. I mean the fake gun was so poor. You could tell that it was a fake."

It was a reasonable reply, Whittaker thought. "And it was in its usual position," he asked. "I mean when you picked it up."

"No, it wasn't," Saunders replied. "It was nearer to the edge of the table, not in the middle like it should have been. Is that important?"

"Probably not," Whittaker replied. "I just like everything to be neat and tidy you know."

"Mr. Saunders, have you ever fired a gun before?" asked Chambers.

"Oh no, sir," Saunders replied. "I never have, not even one of those you get at the fair."

Chambers knew the kind of thing he had in mind. "What did you think, holding it, and squeezing the trigger?" asked Chambers. "It must have been strange."

Saunders thought for a few moments. "It was hard. Pulling the trigger, I mean. It really hurt my finger."

"Is there anything else you can tell me?" asked Whittaker.

Saunders thought for a moment. "I don't think so," he replied. He hesitated. "Except for the blood stain."

"Blood stain," repeated Whittaker. "What blood stain?"

"On the table, next to the gun," explained Saunders. "If you look at the table, there is a metal edge. One area is broken, and there is a rough edge. I guess someone, probably Susan, must have caught their hand on it, I did tell Janet about it, but it seems like nothing's been done about it. I nearly cut myself, but I noticed it in time."

Chambers made a note. *Saunders had been fortunate,* he thought. *Perhaps there were others who hadn't noticed the rough metal.* "It was about twenty past nine when you picked up the gun."

"That's right," Saunders agreed. "Just before the end of Act Two."

"What time was it when you were in position?" asked Whittaker.

Saunders thought for a few moments. "About ten minutes I suppose."

"Was anyone else there?" asked Chambers.

"Rose, she was there," Saunders replied. "The man doing the lighting, oh and the scenery man, Mr. Palmer. He was doing something with the curtains."

"Anyone else?" Whittaker continued.

"I don't think so," Saunders replied. "I can't think of anyone. Oh, no John was there, John Bishop. But it was wrong, he shouldn't been. He should have been on the other side of the stage."

"The other side of the stage," Chambers repeated. "I don't understand."

"Oh it's simple," Saunders started to explain. "He just came offstage on the wrong side. He made a silly mistake. Don't suppose Janet was pleased."

"We'll speak to Miss. Cooper about that," replied Chambers. "Can you tell us anything else?"

Saunders thought for a moment. "I can't think of anything," Saunders replied, suddenly becoming agitated once more. "Sorry I can't be more helpful."

"That's alright, Mr. Saunders," said Chambers. "It's not a problem, don't worry. You have been very helpful. It'll be okay, you'll see."

"You take it easy, Tim," said Cutler. "Are they treating you ok?"

"Guess so. I mean yes sure," Saunders replied. "But how much longer will I be in here? When can I go home?"

Whittaker sighed. "It won't be much longer, you'll see," he replied. "Not long now before you'll be back home I would guess."

"But I didn't do it," Saunders protested. "I never killed Mr. Donovan. I'm innocent."

"I hear you, Mr. Saunders, but we still have a lot of investigating to do. I'm sorry," replied Whittaker.

"Tim, it won't be long," said Cutler. "Keep your chin up. Just a little while longer, you'll see."

Saunders nodded, and tried to smile.

"Okay Constable, I'm done here," said Whittaker. "Goodbye Mr. Saunders. It won't be long I promise."

The three men stood up and walked to the cell door, as it was opened by a warden. Whittaker stopped at the door, turned and looked back at Saunders. "Remember what I said," he called out. "You'll be out of here before you know it." He then turned and went out of the cell.

* * *

"I've been thinking, sir," Chambers announced as they left the building. "What if Donovan had been blackmailing someone?"

"Go on," said Whittaker. "I'm listening."

"Well suppose that person decided that with Donovan dead, they'd be in the clear," Chambers explained. "That would be a motive wouldn't it?"

"Well it's certainly a possibility," admitted Whittaker. "One of quite a few. So where do we go next?"

"To where Donovan lived," suggested Cutler. "Right here in Weathersfield. A place called Albany Mansions.

"And then we'll tackle the cast members," added Chambers.

"Okay," Whittaker agreed. "Donovan's place it is then. Give the directions to George."

* * *

Chapter Nine
Donovan's House

Albany Mansions had probably been quite fashionable in its day, a hundred years or so, ago. But now it was anything but. Now it was looking tired and worn. Neglected and in need of some repairs and a fresh coat of paint.

The police officer on duty at the entrance to Block B saluted Chief Inspector Whittaker as he approached. "Morning sir," he said jovially. "Not a bad day, sir."

"No, not bad at all, replied Whittaker. *For a change,* he added under his breath

"It's on the fourth floor I'm afraid, sir," the officer advised, speaking of Mr. Donovan's flat, and pointing upwards. "And the lift is out of order, again."

Whittaker looked up to the top of the building and heaved a sigh. *Oh, well, there's nothing for it,* he thought. "Come on Derek, let's get some exercise shall we. You too Constable."

"Right with you, sir," replied Chambers, taking the lead.

"Coming, sir," added Cutler.

* * *

Flat 8B was a typical male domain. Donovan's wife had died some twenty years previously. It was sparsely furnished, and completely free from any ornaments, or photographs. Clearly, however, Mr. Donovan liked his books, and his records. Opera mainly, but his musical tastes were quite diverse.

Whittaker glanced around. "You know, Derek, Donovan was murdered for a reason. Somewhere in this flat I'm hoping to find that reason." He walked over to the full-length shelving.

"Dickens," he murmured. "Agatha Christie, Alistair Maclean. Quite a mixed selection." He turned away. "Nothing here," he announced. "What about you, Derek?"

Chambers looked up. "Nothing so far," he announced. *Just exactly what am I looking for anyway?* he wondered. He glanced around the room, and walked over to a sideboard and opened the top drawer. As far as he could see there was nothing significant. A few recent household bills, unpaid, a number of receipts, an address book, and a bunch of keys. He opened the cupboard doors. Inside were a number of files. He started to look through them.

"Anything yet," Whittaker called out.

Chambers wasn't sure whether he had found anything or not. "There's a whole pile of files over here," he replied. "They seem to relate to the time when Mr. Donovan used to be a Magistrate" he said. "They seem to be reports of the court cases. There's details of names, addresses, dates, offences, the lot."

Whittaker walked over to join his colleague. "Let me see that," he said, taking hold of the file. He started to thumb through the papers. "I'm pretty sure he shouldn't have these," he said. "These are official documents." He continued looking through the documents. "As far as I can tell the last entry was seven years ago."

Derek looked up from the document that he was reading. "That's when he retired, sir," he explained. "At least when he was forced to retire." Whittaker looked over. "Clearly he wasn't happy about it. In fact, he wrote a stinger of a letter complaining."

"Did it have any effect?" asked Whittaker.

"None at all, as far as I can see, sir," replied Chambers.

"I don't get it," said Whittaker. "Why would anyone keep this sort of stuff?"

"Nostalgia," suggested Cutler. "Memories of his past. Maybe he loved his work so much, he didn't want to let go."

"Well judging by the letter he sent, he never wanted to leave the job," added Chambers. "So you could be right, Harry."

"Could be," agreed Whittaker, sounding far from convinced. "Still doesn't change anything. He shouldn't have kept them, these are Court records, that's where they should remain. But I think it's more than nostalgia."

"I think you're right, sir. He kept these for a reason," said Chambers. "Think about it. Why would anyone keep information about other people? Simple, because he was hoping to make use of that information."

"Are you talking about blackmail?" asked Cutler.

"Exactly," replied Chambers. "Blackmail, that's why he kept them. Pay up or I tell everything."

Whittaker wasn't convinced. "Maybe, but who would be that worried about someone knowing about their speeding offence from seven years ago, or being drunk and disorderly ten years ago? No it's got to be something else, some other reason. I'll check the bedroom, you keep looking in here."

Keep looking, thought Chambers, but just what was he looking for? He spied a roll top bureau in the corner of the room. *As good a place as any.* He walked over, and opened it. Inside were a number of letters, and several newspaper cuttings. He started to read through the cuttings, as Whittaker returned from the bedroom.

"There's nothing in there," Whittaker announced, sounding disappointed. He looked at Chambers. "What have you got there?"

Chambers looked up from what he was reading. "I don't know. A pile of press cuttings," he replied. "There's a dozen or more in here."

"There's a few more over here," said Cutler, standing over in the corner nearby, and pointing to a number of cuttings spread out on the table.

"What are they about?" asked Whittaker.

"They seem to be about crimes, serious crimes," replied Chambers.

"Same here," added Cutler. "It looks like Donovan had been looking at them fairly recently. Some of them have been highlighted with a red marker pen."

"But why?" asked Chambers. "Why would he be interested in them, I mean some go back a long time. Doesn't make sense, Donovan would never have come across these types of crime, as a Magistrate. I mean these crimes aren't your normal case of speeding, or causing an affray. These relate to murder, or armed robbery. There's one here about some missing money, one hundred thousand pounds. Not bad eh."

Whittaker walked over, and took hold of the papers. He glanced through them. "Why on earth would he have these I wonder?"

"Perhaps he was interested in crime," suggested Cutler.

"Perhaps he was," agreed Whittaker. "But why only a few crimes. I mean look at them, there aren't really that many, and as you say, some are years old." He paused for a moment, and looked at the papers scattered on the table. "If he was interested in crime, it was certainly very selective. Why keep this stuff? What would be the point?"

Chambers walked over to Whittaker, and looked down at the papers. "It's just a thought, sir," he began. "I'm just wondering if there's any connection between these, and his other files, those from the Magistrate's Court."

Whittaker looked over at the files. "Alright, what's on your mind?"

Chambers looked at Whittaker. "I'm thinking aloud maybe," he started to explain. "I'm wondering about those petty criminals, in those files." He pointed to the Court files. "I wonder if any of them actually progressed on to something bigger, you know, something a bit more substantial." He then pointed to the press cuttings. "Maybe some of them also appear in them. I'm also wondering if any of our suspects are mentioned in there somewhere."

"I gather we're talking about your blackmail theory," suggested Whittaker.

Chambers started to tap the press cuttings. "Well blackmail has always been a nice little earner hasn't it? And there's a lot of detail here that could be very useful, and it would also be a pretty good motive for murder, you must admit."

"It always been an excellent motive," Whittaker agreed, but he was puzzled. "But I just don't get it," he continued. "There's one thing that doesn't make sense."

Chambers looked disappointed. He was so sure of his theory. It made perfect sense to him. "So where have I gone wrong, sir?"

Whittaker looked at Chambers. "Just think about it for a moment," he said. "These crimes are long gone, over and done with. I mean look at this one, it's twelve years old. The guilty persons have already served their time, and are now walking the streets again. So what is there to use for blackmail. There's no big secret any longer. It's public record. Who would be bothered? Get my point?"

"Oh yes, sir, I get your point," replied Chambers. And for many of these cases, you are perfectly correct. "But look again, sir. Some of those cuttings are about people who were only suspected of committing a crime. Some of them were actually charged and taken to court, but they weren't convicted for lack of evidence."

"Alright, I'll give you that," agreed Whittaker. "But I still can't see the possibility of blackmail. So what exactly are you suggesting, Derek?"

Chambers took a deep breath. *What exactly was he suggesting anyway*? "I admit it's all a bit unknown," he said. "A big mystery, but I'm convinced that the key to his murder is in there somewhere." He pointed to the press cuttings.

"And I agree completely," Whittaker said. "What's your point?"

"Well, as you suggest, perhaps we can disregard the cuttings where people have been found guilty, and served their time," Chambers started to explain. "Maybe the answer to our problem lies with the not guilty cases, the unproven cases, the cases thrown out because of a lack of evidence."

"Okay, I'm listening," said Whittaker.

"Well, let's just suppose that James Donovan had, somehow, acquired something, some evidence, evidence that could change the original court decision," Chambers continued. "Evidence that would prove that they were actually guilty after all."

"That would certainly be something they would want kept secret," suggested Cutler. "A case of blackmail not for something that somebody had done, but for something Donovan had found out about them, and was threating to divulge."

"That's precisely what I had in mind," said Chambers.

"If your suggestion is right, then there's our reason for his murder right there," announced Whittaker. "Where to now?" he asked.

"I'm convinced that somewhere in those files is the name of our murderer," Chambers continued "We need to check the names in there, and compare them with our list of possible suspects.

Whittaker had to admit that Chambers could be on to something. Exactly what, was still unknown, but it was at least a possibility that should be followed up. "Right, get on with checking the names, and see if we can match anything up."

"I've just thought of a problem," Chambers announced. "Maybe the names have been changed. I mean the ladies might have got married, they would more than likely change their names wouldn't they?"

"Maybe so," agreed the Chief Inspector. "And these theatrical types might have changed their names anyway, you know what they are like. They might have what they call stage names, don't ask me why."

Chambers had to admit that it was a definite possibility. "And maybe some of them would have changed their names to cover up their illegal past," he suggested.

"Get on to Records," said Whittaker. "Get them to check those details." He pointed to the files. "Names, dates, and the crimes. See what they come up with. Find out all you can. Addresses would be good, photographs even better. Be as quick as you can."

"I'll start checking on bank accounts," said Constable Cutler.

"Good idea," said Whittaker. "Let's hope the Records people come up with something. In the meantime, Miss. Cooper has supplied that list of names that I asked for. Gentlemen we've got our work cut out. I suggest a bite of lunch, and then back to Wokingham."

* * *

Chapter Ten
Best Make A Start

Once back at the hall, Whittaker picked up the sheet of paper that Janet Cooper had provided. "Well, here it is, a list of possible suspects," he said as he handed copies to Chambers, and to Cutler. "There are eight names for members of the cast, listed there." He paused for a moment. "Including James Donovan. Well we can certainly remove him from our list of suspects I think."

Chambers read through the list. "And this is the complete cast?" he asked.

"It's the full cast," said Whittaker. "And the list also includes all of the people behind the scenes."

Cutler was puzzled. "There's only three names listed," he said. "Susan Turner in charge of the props, Guy Palmer who handles the scenery, and Pete Gammons, in charge of the lighting, and that's it."

Whittaker looked down at his list. He looked at Cutler. "Correct," he replied.

"Well, I don't see Miss. Cooper's name anywhere," Cutler continued. "Shouldn't she be included? I mean she had as much chance of switching the gun, and just as easily, as anyone else."

"Yes, you are absolutely correct," agreed Whittaker. "I'll add her name." He took up a pen, and added Janet Cooper to the list, and then drew a line through Donovan's name. He started to count up. "That makes ten altogether, no eleven possible suspects."

"Far too many if you ask me," said Chambers.

"You know Derek, I would agree with you. But what's worse, too many suspects, or none at all?" Whittaker said. "Unfortunately, the truth is that these are all possible suspects." He tapped the sheet of paper. "Somewhere in there I'm convinced, is our murderer. But which one?"

"As you said, sir, we've got our work cut out," said Cutler.

"Well, we best make a start then," suggested Chambers.

"Right, let's get Miss. Cooper to come back in then, shall we?" said Whittaker. "As good a place as any." He looked at his watch. "Let me see, it's two thirty now. She will probably be at the Queens Head. Harry would you mind?"

Cutler got up. "Right sir, I'll see if I can find her." He hurried from the room.

* * *

Fifteen minutes later, there was a tap on the door, and Constable Cutler peered in. "I have Miss. Cooper with me, sir," he said.

"Right, let's get started then shall we?" said Whittaker. "Please bring her in."

Cutler opened the door fully, and allowed Miss. Cooper to pass through. He followed, closing the door behind him.

"Ah, Miss. Cooper, do come in," said Whittaker standing up to greet her. He pointed to a chair. "Please sit down. I'm really sorry to trouble you once again like this. It must be very upsetting for you I know, but there's just a few more questions I have, a few loose ends that I'd like to get straight, you know. I hope you don't mind."

"It's not a problem, Inspector," she replied as she sat down. "If I can help find James' killer then I'm happy to help. To think that his murderer is one of the cast. It doesn't bear thinking about. I mean we've been working as a group for a while now, and all that time …. It's very distressing."

"No, I can understand that," said Whittaker. "Oh, by the way thank you for the list of names you supplied. Very helpful."

"I hope that it does help," replied Janet. "Incidentally, here is a copy of the script you wanted. Though why you wanted it is more of a mystery than the actual play."

Whittaker smiled. *It was a fair point,* he thought. Just why did he want the script? "Much obliged," he said as he took hold of the document. "You said that it would never be shown again, remember. This could become a collector's item. Could be worth a lot of money in years to come. Especially with the real life crime attached to it. And it's a first edition."

Now it was Janet's turn to smile. "I like your optimism, Inspector. Perhaps you should get the cast to sign their autographs."

Whittaker shrugged. "I might just do that, you never know," he replied. "If not, I'm still sure that it will be very helpful."

"Well, at the very least it will certainly tell you who carried out the murder at Larkhall Manor, and why."

"Well that's something at least," Whittaker replied. "It's just a pity that it won't tell me about our murderer."

"I'm very sorry about that, Inspector," said Miss. Cooper, sounding sympathetic. "Wish I could help."

"Well you never know, it might actually produce a clue at least," Whittaker replied. "In the meantime maybe you can help." He started to tap the manuscript. "Could I just ask you about the play?"

"Go on," replied Miss. Cooper. "What would you like to know?"

"I imagine that a play like that takes some time to learn, doesn't it?" Whittaker began. "I mean to learn not only the words, but the actions. When to move, and where to go, things like that."

Janet Cooper wasn't sure what this had to do with James' murder. "Absolutely," she replied. "It takes a lot of hard work, and co-operation."

"I'm sure it does," said Whittaker. "You must have rehearsed, and rehearsed, over and over, to get it just right."

"Oh yes, we had several rehearsals that week," Janet explained. "In fact we had a final rehearsal, a dress rehearsal, on that Saturday. Just a few hours before the actual opening performance."

"Is that right?" said Whittaker.

"We started at about ten minutes after two, if I remember correctly," Janet continued. "And we finished just after five thirty."

"And the prop gun was used in all of those rehearsals?" asked Chambers. "Is that right?"

"Absolutely," Janet confirmed. "The prop gun was used the whole time, including that final rehearsal."

"So, what happened then?" Whittaker asked. "I mean the performance wasn't due to start until eight o'clock, correct? So what happened between half past five, and eight?"

"Well most of the cast went for a bite to eat, and to freshen up ready for curtain up," Janet replied.

"But I thought you theatrical types had supper after the performance," said Whittaker. "At least that's what I've heard."

Janet started to laugh. "If only," she replied. "You're right, that's certainly what they do in London's West End, but sadly, we don't have the luxury of late night restaurants down here. Here we either have Martha's Tea Rooms, which closes at six, or a ploughman's in the Queens Head, but they stop that at about half past. Then their kitchen only caters for the guests. So you see, you're okay if you happen to be staying there."

"I see the problem," Whittaker replied. "But I understood that the cast were all locals, why not go home for a meal."

"Yes they are locals, well most of them are," Janet agreed. "But some of them live in the next village, or even in Weathersfield. They wouldn't really have the time to go home, and get back for the performance. Besides they preferred to have a meal together as a group, and perhaps talk about the play. You know any last minute thoughts or ideas. Just reminding each other what they were supposed to be doing, or saying."

The Inspector nodded. It certainly sounded reasonable. "You say everyone went to the Queens Head. Did that include Mr. Donovan?"

"I'm not sure, but I very much doubt it. He wasn't one for socializing I'm afraid," she replied. "Besides he had to see someone I understand."

"Do you know who that was?" asked Whittaker. "Or what it was about?"

"No, I'm sorry I don't," Janet said. "James was a very private kind of person, and he never spoke about his private life. Why should he anyway. None of our business is it?"

"Normally I'd agree with you, but a murder does change things a little. Now, everything about Mr. Donovan is my business," said Whittaker. "I don't suppose you know where the meeting was to be held?"

"Sorry," Janet replied. "I'm not much help I'm afraid."

"It's okay, not to worry," said the Inspector. "I just thought that maybe there was a connection, but there again maybe not. So apart from Mr. Donovan, everyone else went, is that correct?"

"Not quite," replied Janet. "Everyone went except for me and Tim. I wasn't that hungry, I get like that on a first night. It's silly really, but that's what nerves can do. Even here in a small village, it makes no difference. I just get all worried and anxious, you know. I just went for a quiet sit down, in my room, with a cup of tea. Tim said he had sandwiches, so he stayed behind at the hall I think."

"So either of you could have switched the gun," suggested Whittaker.

Janet looked surprised. "Am I a suspect?" she asked.

"At this stage of the game, I'm afraid that everyone is a suspect," explained the Inspector. "But I'm a long way from going from suspect to definite. All I'm saying is that you could have switched the gun. Nothing more, and nothing less."

"I understand," Janet replied. "Well, yes I suppose you're right, we could have," she admitted. "But I certainly didn't, and neither did Tim."

It was exactly the response that Whittaker had expected. "You're sure of that are you? About Tim I mean?" he asked.

"Yes I'm sure," replied Janet, trying not to sound impatient, but failing. "Incidentally you are forgetting one thing aren't you?"

Chambers sighed audibly. *Bad move,* he thought. *Please Miss, don't even go there. Don't even think about telling the Inspector that he had forgotten something.*

"Did you say something, Derek?" asked Whittaker.

"No sir, not a thing," Chambers replied. He coughed to clear his throat.

Whittaker looked back at Janet Cooper. "You were saying something, before I was interrupted." He looked puzzled. "Oh, yes, you were suggesting that I had forgotten something. What did you actually have in mind?"

"What I said about Susan, Susan Turner," explained Janet. "About when she placed the gun, remember."

Whittaker started to smile, and looked across at Derek. "Do you remember that, Derek? I do, I remember it very well." He opened his notebook, and flipped the pages. "Here we are. You said, and I quote. Susan would have dealt with the props for Act Two including the prop gun, at about quarter past eight, something like that." He paused and close the book. "Your words exactly."

"Well there you are then," Janet responded. "She would certainly have noticed that the gun had been changed, wouldn't she?"

"I've already thought of that, Miss. Cooper," said Whittaker. "You are perfectly correct, she would have noticed, or she should have. But of course she might have thought that it was your idea, to introduce a bit more realism to the production."

"But she would have queried it with me," said Miss. Cooper.

That made sense, Whittaker had to admit. "Probably right, Miss. Cooper, and I'll accept that the prop gun was in place at eight fifteen. Unless, of course, Susan Turner did the switching herself."

Janet Cooper looked horrified. "No, no I don't accept that, I just can't," she protested. "Susan didn't kill Donovan."

"No, Miss Cooper I don't think she did either," replied Whittaker. "However, we should consider that Miss. Turner might have placed the gun in position, much earlier," Whittaker continued. "You weren't one hundred percent certain were you? You only thought that's when Miss. Turner had placed the gun into position. You assumed it, remember? Did you actually see her with the gun?"

Janet had to admit that the Inspector was correct. She didn't really know anything, not for sure. "No, I didn't actually see her. I merely assumed."

"That means there's plenty of room for error," Whittaker replied. "We'll have to see what Miss. Turner comes up with, won't we Derek?"

"Yes, indeed, sir," replied Chambers, as he made a note. "We will." He turned towards Miss. Cooper. "Getting back to the time up to eight o'clock, were you with Tim all of the time? I mean until curtain up?"

"Well no, not all of the time," replied Janet. "As I said I went for a quiet sit down. But I know Tim. There's no way he would deliberately kill James."

Whittaker smiled. Once again it was the response he had expected. "One day perhaps you'll tell me, in great detail, why you think that, and why I should believe you." He took a deep breath. "In the meantime though we should remember that whatever time Miss. Turner placed the prop gun on that table, by nine twenty we know that it had been switched, and a real gun used to kill James Donovan, fired by Tim Saunders, and he would have had plenty of opportunity to switch the gun."

"Did you stay in your room the whole time?" asked Chambers.

"Oh no, after a while I went for a walk," she replied.

"Where did you go?" asked Whittaker.

"I went to the park, down by the river," she replied. "A bit of peace and quiet, just to un-wind you know."

"Chance would be a fine thing, Miss," Whittaker replied. "Don't generally have that luxury, always too much to do, you see. It would be nice though. Any ways, what time was that?"

"Sorry, I never really took much notice," Janet replied. "Let me think. It was about a quarter past seven when I got back to the hall. I'd been by the river for maybe thirty minutes, so a quarter to seven, something like that."

"Any witnesses?" asked Chambers.

"I don't think so," she replied shaking her head. "I never saw anyone anyway."

"That's a pity," said Whittaker. "You know if I were the suspicious type, which I'm not, I'd be thinking that it was possible that Donovan's meeting could have been with you or Tim."

"Well, it certainly wasn't me," Janet protested. "And I'm sure it wasn't Tim."

"That is exactly the reply I was expecting Miss. Cooper. Sadly it's hardly conclusive though is it?" said Whittaker, as he tapped the list of names that she had provided. "Right, I think that'll do for now, I've a few more people to see. Thank you once again. We'll probably talk again." He paused for a moment and looked at the names. "Incidentally, do you happen to know where I might find Miss. Turner?"

"Oh yes, well that is, she was last seen about thirty minutes ago," replied Janet. "She, and most of the others were sitting in the lounge at The Queens Head. They were actually discussing the case."

"Oh really. That's very interesting," replied Whittaker. "And do you know if they have reached any conclusions? Saved me the trouble, and identified the murderer by any chance?"

"Afraid not, Inspector, sorry," she replied. "By the way, we were all wondering about the tape, the crime scene tape. It's still in place. Some of us are quite anxious to get to our belongings. I was just wondering, you know."

"I perfectly understand," said Whittaker. "I'll give it some thought, and let you know. It shouldn't be much longer though." He stood up. "In the meantime, thank you for coming, it's much appreciated. By the way, how's the hand?"

She looked at her hand. "Oh it's alright now." She looked at Chambers. "I did put a plaster on, thank you." She stood up, walked to the door, and left the room.

* * *

Chapter Eleven
Clive Masters – The Doctor

"What did you make of that then?" asked Whittaker.

"Well there's always the possibility that she's right, you know," suggested Chambers. "Maybe she didn't kill Donovan, maybe Tim didn't either."

"Maybe," said Whittaker. "Though you have to admit we are still lacking any proof." He looked at the notes that he had made, and rubbed his chin. "I don't know Derek, is she correct, or is she just bluffing."

"Well, I'm inclined to believe her, sir," said Chambers. "I don't believe that either Miss. Cooper, or Mr. Saunders, is our murderer."

Whittaker shrugged. "You know I might actually be inclined to go along with you," he replied. "But we need that old fashion thing, we need proof."

"You mean proof of innocence?" Chambers queried. "So whatever happened to innocent until proven guilty, sir?"

Whittaker smiled. "A good point, but in my book there's another little saying."

"Which is?" asked Chambers.

"You're a suspect until proven different," replied Whittaker.

"Or until we get the proof to convict someone else," suggested Chambers.

"Maybe," replied Whittaker.

"The problem is we need to know when the gun was actually switched," said Chambers. "The current time period is too big."

"Agreed." Said Whittaker, sounding despondent. "Best press on. Who's next?" he asked.

Chambers looked down at his list. "It looks like Clive Masters," he replied. "The, er, doctor."

* * *

There was a tap on the door. "That'll be the doctor now, I guess," Whittaker announced, as the door started to open.

"You wanted to see me," said a voice?"

Detective Sergeant Chambers hadn't met too many actors, amateur or professional, before. Nonetheless he had built up a mental image of how they would look. Clive Masters matched that image perfectly, with his dark wavy hair, goatee beard, and ruddy complexion. The overall appearance completed by the purple cravat, and the red velvet jacket that he was wearing.

"Ah, Mr. Masters, is that right?" said Whittaker.

"Spot on," Masters replied. "Masters by name and master by nature."

"Do come in, and have a seat," Whittaker continued. "This shouldn't take long. Just a few questions."

"Don't give it a thought old man, happy to oblige, you know," Masters replied enthusiastically. "Ask away."

Whittaker looked at Chambers, and raised his eyebrows. "Good of you, I'm sure," he said. "Much appreciated."

"Civic duty, old boy," said Masters. "Nothing more, nothing less."

"Right, I'll get on," said Whittaker. "I understand that you play the doctor in the play, is that right?"

"Right again, old boy," Masters confirmed. "That's me. I'm always the doctor, or the local dignitary. I just look the part you see. Dignified, in command, authority personified. You know the sort of thing."

"Or the Colonel, maybe," suggested Chambers.

"Usually, yes you are right, the Colonel," agreed Masters. He held his head high, and raised his right arm. "Tomorrow men, we go into battle, many won't return, but I know you will do ...."

"But not to be this time," interrupted Whittaker.

"No, not this time," Masters replied, looking down and heaving a sigh. "Not to be I'm afraid."

"How did you feel about that?" asked Chambers.

"What do you mean how did I feel?" replied Masters.

"Well, did it upset you, or annoy you?" continued Chambers.

"Well, I wouldn't exactly say it upset me. I mean I wasn't exactly delighted either. But no use crying over spilt milk, as they say," replied Masters. "I thought it was a bad decision, a very bad decision. But that's how the chips fall, so to speak. You can't win them all, can you? And I wasn't upset enough to resort to murder if that's what you were thinking."

Whittaker wasn't convinced. "I wasn't thinking any such thing, Mr. Masters."

"What did you think about Mr. Donovan?" asked Chambers. "Did you hate him like everyone else seems to have done?"

Masters shook his head. "Hate him?" he repeated. "Not at all. I never hated him. Truth is I never thought anything of him, one way or the other. That would be a waste of my valuable brain power, you see. He was just another actor that's all, and not a very good one at that. But if the director wanted him for the part, and not me, well that was her decision, and her problem. I did tell her though, but she said there was nothing she could do about it."

"What did she mean by that?" asked Whittaker.

"I'm afraid I've no idea, old boy," replied Masters. "Perhaps she had already promised him the part before she thought of me, or maybe he was a relative, a long lost uncle or something. I really don't know." Masters paused for a moment.

90

"Perhaps he offered her money. That always works, the old bribery ploy. Never fails does it?"

"Maybe," replied Whittaker. "Or maybe she just thought he was more suited for the part."

"Really? Do you think so?" replied Masters sounding surprised. "You know, I never actually thought of that possibility. Certainly a novel idea I must say, but there's no accounting for taste is there, or the lack of it I should say."

"Did you know Donovan before?" asked Chambers. "I mean before Murder at Larkhall Manor?"

"No, I don't think so," Masters replied. "But of course the world of amateur dramatics is relatively small. I imagine we could have been in the same town at the same time."

"But you never actually came across him before now?" Chambers persisted.

"Oh, I'd certainly remember him if I had," Masters replied. "Once seen never forgotten, old boy." He paused and started to laugh. "Despite my trying very hard. Know what I mean." He tapped his nose.

Whittaker sighed. "Maybe," he replied. "How long have you been acting then, in this, er, amateur dramatics world?"

"It's about ten years I guess, as an amateur," Masters replied. "But only a year or two with this particular group."

"And what do you think of them?" asked Chambers.

Masters started to laugh. "What do I think of them?" he repeated. "I think they are incredibly lucky to have me, that's what I think. For without me they are nothing. Less than nothing. Not that they appear to acknowledge that undoubted fact, but it is still, nonetheless, the truth."

"And what about Janet Cooper?" asked Chambers.

"Ah, Miss. Cooper, you say," replied Masters. "A true lady, who does her best with the poor material she has to work with. What more can I say. Sadly she is easily lead, or should I say mislead, but she's young, and lacks experience."

"I see," said Whittaker. "With such glowing praise I wonder why you stay with them."

Masters smiled. "As I say, without me they would be nothing. They would just fade away, never to be seen again," he replied. "In all good conscience I could never allow that to happen, could I? You understand surely."

"Oh certainly, very good of you, very charitable," Whittaker replied. "However, carrying on, if I understand it correctly your part leaves the stage to the right side," Whittaker continued. "Is that correct."

Absolutely right," Masters replied. "I utter those immortal words, remember if you need me, you only need call, then I give a slight wave of the hand, and then its exit stage right. And that is the dramatic end to Act One. Gets you doesn't it? Pure drama. Poetic prose. Just nine little words, but such passion such …."

"Did you notice the prop gun lying on the small table?" asked Chambers, ignoring Masters' passing comment.

"Can't say that I did, I'm afraid," Masters replied. "Wasn't taking too much notice you see. Not that interested. Thought I'd get a G and T down at the Queens Head. All I can tell you is that it was definitely there at the beginning of the Act. I saw Susan put it there."

"You weren't in Act Two were you?" said Chambers.

"No, I wasn't, somehow they managed to survive without me. Don't know how. Anyway, I wasn't due back on stage until the final scene," he replied. "You know the one, the usual bit of old nonsense, where the crime is solved, and the criminal is finally exposed. I stayed down at the Queens. A most pleasant thirty minutes or so."

"But we know who committed the murder," said Whittaker. "It happens right there in front of the audience. It was the policeman, or whatever he was."

Masters raised his hand. "Ah, but all is not what it seems, Inspector," he replied. "Such a pity it will never be seen now. Theatre's loss I'm afraid."

Whittaker was puzzled. More than that, he was intrigued. "So who was the criminal?" he asked.

Masters laughed. "Not a chance old boy," he replied. "More than my life would be worth. Sorry but you'll just have to watch the play, should it ever be seen again, which is doubtful, unless of course my adoring fans demand they see it, with me as the Colonel. Or maybe you could try to bribe old Steve, he might be willing to talk, for the right price."

"Maybe," agreed Whittaker. "Or I could just read the script."

"Indeed, you could just read the script," agreed Masters.

"Right, I might just do that, one day," replied Whittaker.

"A bit disappointing though, don't you think old boy," Masters retorted. "I mean the fact that a Scotland Yard Inspector could only solve the crime by reading the script, not cricket is it? Not playing the game. But that's up to you I suppose. As for me, on the pain of death, I shall never divulge the name of the villain."

Whittaker was tempted to say *Oh yes you will,* but decided against. He looked up from his notes. "Is there anything else you can tell me?"

"I don't think so," Masters replied. "But if anything comes to mind you'll be the first to know. Can I go now?"

"Just one more thing," said Whittaker. "Then we're done."

"Yes, what is it?" asked Masters.

"What do you do when you're not acting?" Whittaker asked.

"What do I do?" repeated Masters. "I'm not sure I understand. You mean hobbies, things like that?"

"Oh no, nothing like that," explained Whittaker. "I was merely enquiring about your employment. How you make your living."

"Oh I see, well actually, what is it that they say? Ah yes, I'm a man of means," Masters replied. "A small private pension, thanks to a generous ancestor, my great aunt. Cynthia. A nice old bird, but crazy as a coot. But to her goes my undying gratitude."

"Very nice too," said Whittaker, thinking of the pension he was due in another ten years or thereabouts.

"I'm not exactly wealthy, you understand Inspector, merely comfortable. Adequate to my needs so to speak, to put a roof over my head, clothes on my back, and food on my table. Need I ask for more?" Masters continued. "So is there anything else I can help you with?"

Whittaker thought for a few moments. "No, not for the moment," he replied. "You can go, but I may need to speak with you again."

"Not a problem old man, happy to oblige. I've no plans for any foreign travel at the moment. I'm still waiting a call from Hollywood, or perhaps Broadway. If it comes, I shall make sure that you are the first to know."

Masters stood up, gave a slight wave of the hand, and walked towards the door.

* * *

The two officers watched as the door closed. "What did you think of our thespian friend, Derek?" asked Whittaker.

Chambers thought for a few moments. "Well I don't believe a word he said," he replied. "He never stops acting does he?"

Whittaker smiled. "Go on," he coaxed. "I'm listening."

Chambers opened the buff coloured file lying in front of him. He took out a single sheet of paper, and handed it to Whittaker. "It's a flyer," he started to explain. "An advertising leaflet all about an amateur production, put on about two years ago, The Death of Lord Henry. You'll notice that both

Donovan, and our friend Mr. Masters are included in the cast. You'll also notice that Masters once again plays second fiddle to Donovan. Donovan, surprise, surprise, plays Lord Henry, and Masters plays ....

"The doctor," said Whittaker. "Interesting."

"Very interesting," agreed Chambers. "Clearly he's not as unconcerned about Donovan, as he'd like us to believe. I reckon he hated Donovan with a passion."

"I'd agree with you, but was his hatred for Donovan enough to kill him?" Whittaker asked.

"Well, he was clearly jealous of Donovan, always getting the main part like he did," Chambers replied. "And as we know jealousy has always been a pretty good motive for murder hasn't it?"

Chambers was right, jealousy had led to several murders in the past. "So why did Masters lie I wonder?" Whittaker asked. "Why didn't he mention Lord Henry?"

"Perhaps he genuinely just forgot," suggested Chambers. "It could happen."

Oh yes, it certainly could happen, thought Whittaker. *How often had he forgotten something?* "Maybe," he replied in his usual non-committal way. "But I think it was more than that. He's hiding something, I'm sure of that." He looked down at the list of names. He underlined the name Clive Masters, and placed a large question mark next to it. "It doesn't look good for our Mr. Masters does it? I mean we have a possible motive, he had the opportunity, and he can be placed at the scene of the crime." He looked at the flyer and started to tap it. "Where did this come from anyway?" he asked.

"I did a Google search," Chambers explained. "And then printed it off."

"You did a what?" replied Whittaker.

"A google search," said Chambers. "You know, on the internet. I was looking for anything about Donovan."

"Google," repeated Whittaker. "New-fangled ideas. Don't suppose it said anything about who our murderer was. Did it?"

"No sir, I'm afraid not," Chambers replied

"Right," said Whittaker, heaving a sigh. *All these suspects, and all this questioning,* he wondered if they were getting anywhere. There were still several more to see, and they still hadn't determined when the gun could have been switched.

He turned towards Chambers. "Derek would you go down to the Queens Head, and have a word with Miss. Turner. Check on her timing. You know what we need"

Derek knew what was needed, exactly. "Will do, sir."

"Oh Derek, if she's there, and when you finish with Miss. Turner, have a talk with Catherine Barr, she plays the Colonel's wife," said Whittaker. "She might have some thoughts about Mr. Donovan."

"Leave it with me, sir," said Chambers, as he started towards the door.

"One last thing," said Whittaker holding up his hand. "Perhaps you'd ask Mr. Berry to come along to see me?"

* * *

Chapter Twelve
Susan Turner

It didn't take long for Chambers to walk the short distance from the Village Hall, to The Queens Head. The theatrical group was still there, in the lounge bar, still deep in conversation.

"Ah, Detective Chambers," said Steve Ashton, looking up as Chambers walked over. "Come to join us have you? You are most welcome. We can pick your brains." He stood up. "What will you have?"

Chambers smiled. "Nothing, thank you, I'm still on duty you see."

"Ah, duty, where would we be without it," asked John Berry. "That we can sleep soundly in our beds, and walk the streets without fear." He paused. "All because of duty," he sighed. "But it means that you cannot have a little drinkie. What a pity. So sad."

"Maybe another time," suggested Chambers. "I've actually come to have a word with you, Miss. Turner, if you can spare me a few minutes."

Susan Turner looked nervous. "It's nothing to worry about," said Chambers. "Just a few questions that's all."

"Go on he won't eat you. He's quite harmless, take my word for it. I survived with not a scratch," said Clive Masters, joining in with the conversation. "Will you detective? You won't eat her, promise?"

Chambers shook his head. "No, he's right, I won't eat you. I promise."

"There you have it," Masters continued. "The good detective has made a promise. There is nought to fear my child."

Chambers looked at Miss. Turner. "Just a few questions that's all." He looked back at Berry. "Incidentally, the Chief Inspector would like a few minutes of your time, sir. So if you could make your way back to the hall, he's expecting you."

Berry stood up. "Not a problem," he pronounced. "I think we're about done here anyway. Besides it is perhaps fortuitous. It was coming up to be my round."

The group started to laugh. "We'll catch you next time," said Ian Jackson.

"Parting is such sweet sorrow," said Masters. "That's Shakespeare you know."

"But perchance we meet again on the morrow," replied Berry. "That's mine."

"And when that time has been found," Ashton called out. "It'll definitely be your round."

Berry smiled, turned and walked to the door.

Chambers watched him leave, he then turned back to face Miss. Turner. "Miss," Chambers called. "Perhaps we could go over there, and talk." He pointed to an empty table a short distance away.

* * *

"Okay, I hope this is alright for you," said Chambers as he placed two coffees on to the table. "If I can't have a drink, I can at least have a coffee."

"Its fine," Susan admitted, taking a drink.

"I'll try not to keep you too long," Chambers began. "Just a few questions that's all. Nothing too drastic, there's no need to be nervous." Chambers took a drink. "I understand that you are responsible for the props," he said. "Making sure that they are available."

Susan started to relax. "Correct," she replied. "I make sure that they are in their right place, ready for the particular scene."

"Quite a responsibility I guess," said Chambers. "I mean if the scene wanted someone to remove a picture, and the picture wasn't there in the first place, it could be a bit awkward."

"And probably embarrassing," Susan added.

"And when someone is due to shoot a gun, that gun has to be in its proper place, right?" said Chambers.

"Of course, it would look ridiculous if the gun was missing wouldn't it?" Susan replied. "And someone just held up their hand, and pointed. Especially if the sound effects were still heard. Or I suppose they could just call out Bang."

"What about this particular gun?" asked Chambers. "The one that was used by Mr. Saunders? The fake one, the prop."

"What about it?" Susan asked.

"Well, it was your job to make sure that it was in its proper place, by the proper time, correct?" said Chambers.

"That's right. It wasn't a major problem. It was easy, I just had to place it on to the small table over in the wings, stage right," Susan explained. "Sorry, that's on the right hand side of the stage."

"Is that your right, or mine?" Chambers asked.

"It's the audience's right," she replied.

"And was it in plain sight?" asked Chambers.

I guess so," Susan replied. "I mean not to the audience of course. But anyone backstage could see it easily. Mind you, I don't suppose it was being closely watched. I mean there'd be no need would there? No one would be expecting the gun to be switched would they? Besides they'd be too busy with the production."

"Well certainly there was at least one person who was watching very closely," said Chambers. "Whoever switched the gun watched very carefully, waiting for the right opportunity, when no one else would be around."

"They would have had a lot of opportunity," said Susan. "Much of the action involves coming on stage from the left, and then leaving on the left. For much of the time the right hand side would be empty."

Interesting, thought Chambers. "But that would only be true for people actually in the scene," he said. "What about the others who maybe weren't required?"

"I get your point," agreed Susan. "And I suppose they could have been anywhere backstage."

Chambers made a note in his notebook. He needed to find out where everyone was during the performance. But more to the point he needed to determine the time the switch was carried out.

"Miss. Turner, when you placed the gun in position, did you notice what time it was?" he asked.

"I'm not a hundred percent sure of the time, but I generally put the gun in position at the start of the performance, and then I can forget all about it," she replied. "I know it's done, and I don't have to worry about it. You can do that with the smaller items, you see. The problems arise with the bigger things, furniture and things like that."

"I'm surprised," said Chambers. "Miss. Cooper tells me that you probably placed the gun in the required position at about a quarter after eight, ready for the second act starting just after eight forty."

"That's the time I had originally suggested," Susan replied. "But during the week I realised that I could place it there much earlier, probably at about ten to eight. But that day, the day, you know, I was even earlier. I'm guessing that it would have been just after seven thirty, or maybe twenty to eight. Something like that."

"But the gun wasn't actually needed until sometime near the end of Act two, an hour and thirty minutes later," suggested Chambers. "Why were you so early?"

"Just circumstances I guess," Susan replied. "After the final rehearsal finished at about half past five, most of us came down here, to the Queens Head, for something to eat. I left the pub at about twenty to seven, something like that. I went back to the hall. You know there was such a lot to do before curtain up. To make sure everything was where it should be. I was nervous of missing something. I made sure that everything was in place for Act one. That was all ready by about half past seven. Then I just thought of the gun, it was easy. It was just that one item, but very important. I thought I'd get it over and done with. I just wanted it ticked off of my list. One less thing to worry about. I mean if the gun wasn't in position on time, how would we have a murder at Larkhall Manor?"

Understandable, thought Chambers. "Makes sense I guess," he replied.

"Incidentally, has the prop gun been found yet?" Susan asked.

"No not so far," Chambers replied. "It possible that we'll never see it again." He sighed and looked down at his notes. "When you got back to the hall, was anyone else there?"

"Well Mr. Berry arrived twenty or thirty minutes after me I think, and Janet arrived at about twenty past seven, or a little bit later, but I wasn't really taking too much notice," she explained.

"Was Donovan there?" asked Chambers.

Susan thought for a few moments. "No, he wasn't. Janet was getting a bit worried. It was nearly curtain time before he arrived." She paused for a moment. "And Rose, she was late as well, just a few minutes before Donovan."

"Anyone else?" asked Chambers.

"I didn't see anyone, but there was an argument going on outside the hall," Susan said. "Couldn't help hearing that."

"When was that?" asked Chambers.

"I'm not sure, about seven o'clock, I'm guessing," Susan answered. "A little later maybe. I never really noticed."

"Do you know who it was?" Chambers continued. "And what they were saying?"

"Well, there was a woman's voice," Susan began. "Sounded like she wanted to get in to the hall. She wanted to meet someone I think."

"Do you know who?" asked Chambers.

"No, I'm sorry, I've no idea, but Steve might know," she replied.

"Steve?" repeated Chambers. Do you mean Steve Ashton? Why do you think he might know?"

"I'm sure he was the other half of the argument," Susan explained. "It seemed that he was preventing the lady from coming in, and she clearly wasn't very happy. She kept on about wanting to see someone."

"Did you see him?"

"Oh no, I just thought I recognized his voice, that's all," Susan replied. "I might be wrong, it might have been someone else."

Chambers made a mental note to check with Mr. Ashton. "What did you think of Mr. Donovan?" he asked.

"Mr. Donovan?" repeated Susan, beginning to feel nervous once again. "I'm afraid I didn't really like him. He wasn't very friendly you see, at least not to me. No respect, I wasn't important enough. I was just there to serve his needs, at least in his opinion."

Chambers closed his note book. "He didn't seem to be very popular with anyone, I'm afraid," he said. "Anyway, I'm done for the time being. Thank you for your help. You can return to the group if you like."

Susan looked over. "It looks like they are breaking up anyway. I think I'll just get a bite of lunch."

"Well, thanks once again," said Chambers. "Have a nice lunch."

She smiled and gave a wave.

Chambers sat down and watched her leave. He then looked over at the other table. "Oh, Miss. Barr, could you spare me a few minutes?"

* * *

Chapter Thirteen
John Berry

Chief Inspector Whittaker laid the paper he had been reading on to the table. He put his feet up on to the table and laid back in his chair. He removed his spectacles, rubbed his eyes, and heaved a sigh. It was a report on the murder weapon. It was not a very helpful report, either. In fact, it was no more than he had expected. There were no big surprises. There were no finger-prints on the gun, except those belonging to Timothy Saunders. Furthermore there were no identification marks on the gun, so its origins were impossible to trace. The report did nothing except to confirm something that Whittaker already knew, that the gun was the murder weapon.

Next to it was a second report. The post mortem had been carried out. As expected it merely confirmed the cause of death, and did nothing to advance the investigation one inch. Although not unexpected Whittaker had hoped that the reports, especially the one concerning the murder weapon, might have been a bit more positive.

Earlier there had been a telephone call from the Commissioner, wondering how the investigation was progressing. "Anything you need, just ask," said the Commissioner. "By the way, did you know that Donovan was a local magistrate?"

A Magistrate, really! I never knew that! Murmured Whittaker. Quite a revelation. *Very helpful, don't know how I ever managed without that information. Anything I need? Let me think. A pay rise wouldn't be a bad start.* Sadly Whittaker knew that it wasn't going to happen anytime soon.

"I've every confidence in you," the Commissioner had continued. "Keep in touch." The line went dead.

Whittaker sat up, and put his glasses on. He started to smile. *Every confidence indeed. How was the case progressing anyway?* he wondered. *Oh no problem, piece of cake really, thanks for asking. Open and shut case.*

The victim was universally hated by all accounts. *They all did it,* Whittaker murmured. *It was a group effort. They all ganged up and decided that he should die. With such poor acting, the entire audience had wholeheartedly agreed.* He shook his head. This was getting him precisely nowhere.

He looked at the list of names that Janet Cooper had supplied. "One of you is the murderer," he announced. "I just know it." He picked up his pen, his hand hovering over the paper. "But which one? Was it you Ashton? Or perhaps you Mr. Masters? Or maybe it was you Catherine Barr. Or Rose Fuller, did you do it? Or maybe it was you John Berry."

Clearly the murderer was not about to leap up and say that it was me. He sighed, and placed the pen on to the table. He sat back in his chair and closed his eyes. To date the only motive he had discovered was a strong dislike of the victim. Hardly sufficient for murder.

There was a knock on the door. Then a second, and the door opened. Constable Cutler walked in. "I have Mr. Berry outside, sir," he explained.

"Right, Harry, send him in please," said Whittaker.

"Mr. Berry," Cutler called out. "Please come in." He stood back to allow their visitor to pass.

"Ah, Mr. Berry, please have a seat," said Whittaker pointing to a chair.

"I understand that you wanted to see me," Berry said, as he sat down.

"That's right," replied Whittaker. "I'll try not to keep you. This shouldn't take too long, just a few questions that's all. Hope you don't mind."

Berry shook his head. "I don't have a problem with questions, Inspector. It's just the answers that I have difficulty with."

"Right," said Whittaker, ignoring Berry's attempt at humour. "So, Mr. Berry you play the …" He looked down at the list Miss. Cooper had provided. "Ah yes, you play the Butler."

"That's right, I'm the butler," replied Berry. "But I didn't do it."

Whittaker looked up, surprised. "Pardon?"

"I said I didn't do it," Berry replied. "Sorry, it's always the butler isn't it? Bad joke," he said. "Poor taste."

"Oh I get it, the butler, yes, very funny," said Whittaker. *And yes it was a bad joke,* he thought. He looked at his notepad, then he looked back at Berry. "Shall we get on?"

"Ready and waiting, sir," replied Berry.

"How long have you been part of this merry band of players?" Whittaker continued.

Berry thought for a moment. "Let me see, now. This is my third season I believe, for my sins. Gives me something to do with my time, you see. Since I retired, you understand."

"Retired?" repeated a puzzled Whittaker. "Surely you're too young to retire. You can't be much older than fifty."

"Well, I suppose, normally, you'd be right. I'm actually fifty seven, but I was basically forced to retire," Berry explained. "You see the company I worked for was cutting back, and I was made redundant, four years ago, come April. I was fifty three. Difficult to get another job at that age, I can tell you. That, and a lack of experience in anything else. I suppose I could've got a job in one of those DIY places, stacking shelves, but that's not for me." He paused again and smiled. "Oh, it was hard at first, but I'm okay now. Can't blame them really, the company I mean, they had to do something, or go down, and then everyone would have lost their job wouldn't they."

"What did you work at, before you were let go?" asked Whittaker.

"Oh, I worked in a factory, nothing special. Just making sure the production line kept going," Berry explained. "Funny really, it seems that keeping that line going was far more important than keeping me going. Sounds about right I guess. Thirty years I'd been pressing buttons, and pulling levers, just to keep that line operating. Thirty years, it's hard to believe." He sighed. "So, if I was being completely honest I wasn't really that upset about being let go, not really. Anyway, I got a reasonable redundancy payout, and there's also a small pension. I can't complain. That'll tide me over, but money's not everything is it."

"Maybe, maybe not," replied Whittaker, wondering if his expected pension would tide him over, when the time came. "You enjoy it do you, this acting lark I mean?"

"Oh it's a bit of fun really," Berry replied. "The secret is not to take it too seriously. That was the problem with Donovan you see."

"What do you mean?" asked Cutler.

"Look, if nothing else I'm a realist," Berry started to explain. "None of us are ever going to get an Oscar are we, or a Novello or whatever they hand out these days. I mean it stands to reason. We're amateurs, nothing more. The Royal Shakespeare Company has nothing to fear from us. But Donovan, well he thought different. He took it very seriously you see. Considered himself one of the best. Up there with the greats you know. Another Laurence Olivier." He started to smile. "No sense of humour either. Me, well I'm always ready with a funny comment. What's life without a laugh eh, that's what I say."

"You didn't like Donovan, I gather," said Whittaker.

"Didn't like him?" said Berry. "Let's just say that I won't be sending any flowers. And you'll find that many of the others think the same."

"They disliked him you mean?" said Whittaker.

"Dislike did you say? Oh yes, they certainly disliked him," replied Berry. "No question about that."

"Enough to kill him do you think?" asked Whittaker.

Berry thought for a moment. "Oh, I don't know about that," he replied. "It's your job to find that out, but as I said at the beginning, I didn't kill him, so you can strike me off your list."

"You know, I expected you to say something like that," said Whittaker.

"You know, Inspector, I just knew that would be your response," said Berry. "It goes to show how perceptive we both are."

"Um, maybe," agreed Whittaker. "Or perhaps we are both good at poker."

"Poker?" repeated a puzzled Berry.

"We are both good at bluffing," replied Whittaker.

"Oh, I see," replied Berry. "Yes, I guess you could be right."

"To continue, I understand that there was a dress rehearsal on Saturday, the day of the murder," Whittaker continued.

"That's right, there was. Started about two I think it was," said Berry. "It went okay I suppose. At least we were all feeling pretty pleased with ourselves. No great mistakes, and we all remembered our lines."

"I suppose at that rehearsal Mr. Saunders used the prop gun," said Whittaker.

"Yes that's right," Berry replied. "I mean what else would he use?"

"Okay, let's get to the actual performance then, shall we?" suggested Whittaker ignoring Berry's final comment. "What can you tell me about the time leading up to Saunders shooting Donovan?" asked Whittaker.

"Not much I'm afraid," Berry replied. "I'm only in the second act for a couple of minutes, right at the start. I take the Colonel his usual nightcap you know." He paused for a moment. "Cold tea, and not malt whiskey, contrary to popular belief." He started to smile. "Then I say, Will there be anything else, sir. The Colonel grunts something unintelligible, and I walk off, exit stage left. And that's it. I wasn't needed again until the final act about thirty minutes or more later. I'm meant to find the body the next morning. But of course we never got to the final act did we?"

"Carry on Mr. Berry," Whittaker coaxed. "You've walked off stage, then what happened?"

"As I say I wasn't needed for a while, and I went for a smoke." He held up his hand. "Yes, I know it's bad for me, but what can you do. I'm trying to cut down. Patches you know, and the gum. Waste of time. I don't have too many pleasures these days, and we've all got to go one way or another haven't we?"

"Mr. Berry, I wonder if you have seen this?" asked Whittaker, holding up a sheet of paper. "I was given this by Miss Cooper. It's a list of errors that took place on the opening night, the actual performance."

Berry smiled. "Oh yes, she does that," he agreed. "She notes every little thing down, no matter how trivial. Whether you're slow with your cue, or maybe slightly in the wrong place, or a prop isn't where it should be. You move your left hand, not your right. It all goes down. It's like a report card. I keep expecting her to give out scores, you know, five out of ten, must try harder. She's a real perfectionist you know. She writes it down and then we go through it the next day. We're supposed to correct any problems or mistakes. It's a bit like being back at school, and being sent to the head mistress, for a rap over the knuckles."

"That's right, she told me all about it," said Whittaker. He looked down the list. "It's quite detailed." He started to tap the paper. "Did you know that there's two items listed that specifically concerns you?"

Berry looked surprised. "No, I didn't. I don't believe it, I was perfect, even if I do say so myself," he replied, indignant. "Well, alright no Oscars or anything like that, but it was okay."

"Not so, I'm afraid," said Whittaker. "In fact, in the space of a few short minutes, you made two major errors."

"No way, let me see that," Berry protested, as he reached for the paper.

Whittaker kept hold of the paper, and started to read. "Point number one, you said the wrong thing."

"My lines were perfect," Berry replied. "I mean you can't go wrong with a dozen words can you?"

"You said *there won't be anything else will there, sir,*" Whittaker continued. "And secondly you exited stage right, not left. Right over to where the gun was lying on the table."

Berry took a deep breath. "So I made a couple of errors. I got a few words mixed up," he admitted. "What about it? What she going to do sue me? It's only a two bit play anyway. Hardly Shakespeare is it? I doubt that the audience even noticed."

"Maybe so," said Whittaker. "But those two errors just might be enough to prove that you murdered Donovan."

"I never killed him, I told you that if you remember," Berry protested. "I also told you that I went out for a smoke didn't I? Well the right hand side of the stage was more convenient for getting out of the building. That's why I went that way. I didn't really think it mattered that much anyway. I doubt if anyone complained."

"Was anyone else there, on the right side of the stage?" asked Cutler.

"Well Rose was there, fussing with the curtain, or something. It had got caught somewhere," Berry replied. "I don't know, I never bothered to look."

"Was anyone else there?" asked Whittaker.

"Well Tim was there, naturally," Berry replied. He paused for a moment. "That electrician guy, he was there. I think Clive was there as well. Or was he? I'm not sure now. Or was it Steve?"

"Did anyone see you?" asked Cutler. "Outside I mean?"

"How am I expected to know that?" Berry replied becoming impatient. "There were certainly a few people out and about. On the way to the pub I expect, or maybe going down to the chip shop."

"Mr. Berry I have to say that I'm having some difficulty in accepting your story," said Whittaker. "You could easily have switched the gun. As a possible alibi, it leaves a lot to be desired."

"Yes, I could have switched the gun, but so could several others," Berry replied. "Tim could easily have done it himself. I'm telling you the truth, Inspector, I'm not sorry he's gone, I'd be lying if I said different, but I did not murder Donovan. I did not touch the gun."

"Possibly, we'll see, but we'll put that to one side, for the moment," Whittaker grunted. He tapped the paper a few more times, and then laid it down on the table. He looked back up at Berry. "Can we get back to the rehearsal for a moment? Miss. Cooper tells me that after the rehearsal, everyone went to the Queens Head for a quick bite to eat, before the opening performance."

"Did they?" said Berry. "Well I never went with them."

"Okay, you never went with them. Could you tell me where you were until the start of the performance?" asked Whittaker.

"I went for a walk. I went into that little shop, Martha's, or Maggie's, or Mary's, or whatever it's called. I can't remember the name. Anyway I bought some sandwiches. I took them down by the river, and ate them."

"What time was that?" asked Cutler.

"Oh, I don't know, never really noticed," replied Berry. "But let me see. By the time I left the hall, got to the shop, and then down to the river, I suppose it was about six o'clock, possibly a bit later."

"Did anyone see you?" asked Cutler.

"I've no idea," replied Berry. "But I certainly didn't see anyone. Whether someone saw me or not I really couldn't say."

"You didn't see Miss. Cooper?" asked Whittaker.

"I just told you," Berry replied. "I never saw anyone."

"What time did you leave to return to the hall?" asked Whittaker

"Sorry, but I don't know that either, I never looked at my watch you see," Berry explained. "But I guess I was back at the hall by about seven o'clock, seven fifteen, something like that."

"And the performance started at eight," said Whittaker.

"That's right," agreed Berry. "So there was plenty of time to get ready and go through any last minute changes."

"Was everyone there when you arrived?" said Cutler.

"No, not everyone," Berry replied. "Rose arrived about ten minutes later, and Donovan didn't arrive until very late. Janet was getting quite worried, in fact. Susan was there, and Tim. Then his majesty turned up about ten minutes before the start. Made quite an entrance as usual. He'd been drinking of course." He started to laugh. "What else is new?"

"But everyone else was already there?" Whittaker stressed.

Berry thought for a moment. "I'm pretty sure that they were all there."

"One last question, Mr. Berry," said Whittaker.

"Go on I can't wait," replied Berry.

"Did you happen to notice whether the fake gun was in position?"

"Sorry, I haven't the foggiest. Not very helpful of me I know, but I never even looked," Berry replied. "No interest to me you see. The gun's there for one reason, and one reason only. For Tim to pick it up, and go and shoot the old guy." He looked at Whittaker and sighed. "Sorry. Is that it?"

"For the time being," Whittaker replied. "You can go, for now, but I might need to question you further at a later date."

"I shall look forward to it, in eager anticipation." He held up his hand, waved, and left the room.

112

"Quite a character," said Cutler.

Whittaker looked at the door. "You can say that again," he said. "The problem though, is how much is the real John Berry, and how much is play acting?"

"More to the point is how much is the truth?" said Cutler.

"Well, whatever he says, or doesn't say, he certainly had the opportunity to switch the gun," said Whittaker. "And he had a possible motive."

* * *

Chapter Fourteen
Catherine Barr

Chambers stood up, as Catherine Barr walked towards him. "Thanks for coming over, please sit down," he said. "Can I get you anything? A coffee, or something stronger perhaps. I could certainly use one. I'm going to have a scotch."

She smiled. "Really are you allowed to? I mean you are on duty aren't you? That's what you said to Steve if I remember correctly."

Now, it was Chambers' turn to smile. "Yes I am, and I did say that to Mr. Ashton. But, of course, there were rather a lot of witnesses at the time. I couldn't rely on everyone remaining silent could I?"

"And now there's just me," suggested Catherine. "Is that what you are saying?"

"Let's just say if you don't tell anyone, then neither shall I. Is it a deal?" Chambers replied.

"Deal. Your secret is safe with me," she replied. "Well then, I shall have a dry white wine."

"Good enough," replied Chambers. "I won't be long."

* * *

Chambers went over to the bar, and placed his order. Five minutes later he returned with the drinks, and placed them on to the table. He sat down. "Not a bad place," he said looking around.

"No, not a bad place at all," Catherine agreed. "How's the investigation going?" she asked.

Chambers took a long drink. "Why do you think I needed something stronger?" he replied. "Two steps forward, and three back at present. To date we have about a dozen different motives, and so many suspects that they could form a football team, with a couple of substitutes."

"Oh, I see," replied Catherine. "I hope that I can help, but I'm not sure how." She paused for a moment. "By the way am I one of the football players?"

"I'm afraid so," Chambers replied. "You all are." He took another long drink. "This shouldn't take too long," he said picking up his note book. "Hope you don't mind, but I have to make notes, my memory's not that good."

"It's not a problem," Catherine replied.

"Right, I'll get on then." He opened the notepad. "I understand that you were Donovan's wife. That is you played the Colonel's wife in the play."

"That's correct, I'm Isabel his wife, but fortunately for me, it's only in the play, and not in real life," she replied. "And extremely hard work it was, I can tell you, even in pretend. How his poor departed wife managed in real life, I'll never know."

"Oh, hard work, in what way?" asked Chambers.

"He is not, or I should say, was not the easiest of people to get on with," she started to explain. "He thought that he was better than everyone else, and would insist on telling everyone how they should play their part." She paused and shook her head. "You don't do it that way, you do it this way," she continued in a deep voice. "That's what he would say. And he would constantly suggest changes to the script. You can't say that, you should say this. I really don't know how Janet put up with it for so long."

"Did you know that he used to be a magistrate?" asked Chambers.

"Oh yes I knew that. In fact we all knew," Catherine replied. "He wouldn't let you forget it. He was constantly telling everyone how important he was. Why, under the circumstances, he was absolutely right for the role of the Colonel. It was perfect casting, according to him that is. Yet another reason, if one were needed, to dislike the man."

"I see," said Chambers, scribbling notes into his book. "This dislike of him, was that purely from an acting point of view?" he asked. "Or was there more to it than that?"

Catherine remained silent for a few moments. Then she took a drink. "I'm sure you have found out by now that he wasn't a much liked person. And that's not just me saying it. Many of the others disliked him. His manner, his aggression. His temper. He could get very angry at the slightest thing, you know. You really needed to be on your guard, and not say anything to offend. No, it was far more than just the acting. He was a thoroughly nasty man." She paused for a moment, and took another drink. "You know in the play he and I have a blazing row. Well, to be honest, I do most of the shouting, calling him names, telling him how much I hate him, and, well you get the drift. At one point I actually say to him I wish you were dead. I hate to admit it, but I really enjoyed it. In fact most of the time I'm not acting, not really." She paused once again, and started to smile. "You know I've often wondered what Steve was actually thinking when he wrote that script. Did he have Donovan in mind?"

Chambers looked puzzled. "I don't understand," he said.

"You know, although I was saying the words …. The Colonel's wife was saying them, it was like Steve was actually saying them to Donovan personally. Funny that." She looked at Chambers. "I'm sorry to say this, I don't like to speak ill of the dead, but James Donovan really was odious."

"That's seems pretty definite," said Chambers, as he drained his glass. "Sounds like a pretty good motive to commit murder."

"You could be right," she agreed. "But surely to commit a murder, you need a lot more than just a motive. You would need the will to kill someone wouldn't you? And more than that, you would need the mental ability to be able to do it. After all there are many people in this world who dislike many others, but they don't all go around killing each other do they? Furthermore, it can't be that easy to actual kill a person. I couldn't even kill a fly, literally."

Chambers had to admit that what she said was correct. It took a particular type of person to kill. "I agree, but nonetheless identifying a motive is a good aid in identifying the murderer," he replied. "Anyway, can I interest you in another white wine?"

"Let me," she replied, as he went to stand up.

"Oh no, you stay put," Chambers insisted. "This is on me, or to be honest I should say, it's on my expenses account. You can thank Scotland Yard for this." He put his finger to his mouth. "And don't forget. Not a word, it'll be our little secret, okay." He stood up and walked over to the bar.

* * *

"Here we are," Chambers announced, as he returned a short time later. He placed the drinks on to the table and sat down. "Can I ask about the dress rehearsal? The one on the Saturday. How did it go?"

"Mr. Chambers as you know we are a small, amateur group," she replied. "We try our best. Some are better than others. Even so I have to say it went well, better than any of us had expected. Except of course his lordship, he wasn't satisfied, and we had to do our scene, the one where we have an argument, just before Tim comes on, three or four times. I wasn't angry enough, Tim was too casual. He didn't take enough care that he wasn't seen. All kinds of things." She paused for a moment, and started to laugh. "Oh yes, he didn't like the way Tim was holding the gun," she continued. "I mean how many ways are there for holding a gun anyway? But eventually it was, apparently, to his liking. And then, with his parting shot telling us that it was much better, the rehearsal finished at about half past five I think."

"Yes, that time has been confirmed by some others," Chambers agreed. "And then you all came here to The Queens Head, for something to eat, correct?"

"Well not all of us came along," Catherine replied. "Let me think. Janet didn't come, neither did Tim. I think that's right."

"What about Donovan?" asked Chambers. "Was he there?"

"Oh, yes he was there, but fortunately he didn't stay long," she replied. "He said that he had an appointment to see someone. He wasn't missed I can tell you. You could feel the relief after he left."

"Do you know who he was meeting, or where?" asked Chambers.

"No, I've no idea I'm afraid, I was just grateful that he wasn't there with us."

"Am I correct in saying you aren't too unhappy about his death?" asked Chambers.

She looked shocked. "Oh no, that's not right. I didn't say that," Catherine hurriedly replied. "I admit I didn't like the man, that's true, but I would never want anyone to die because they weren't liked."

"Well clearly someone thought differently," said Chambers. "And afterwards you returned to the hall, ready for the performance."

"Correct," replied Catherine.

"What time did you get back?" asked Chambers.

"Oh, I'm not really sure," she replied. "Probably about seven, a little after perhaps. A few of the others were already there. But there was no sign of Donovan. He didn't get back until much later, about twenty to eight, something like that."

"Who else was there when you arrived?" asked Chambers.

"I'm not really sure who was there, or who arrived afterwards," replied Catherine. "I get a bit confused, but I didn't really take that much notice. I mean why would I? I think John was there, but I'm not sure. I was more concerned with putting on the play."

It made sense, Chambers thought. *Why indeed would anyone be bothered?* "The gun, the prop," he continued. "Did you happen to notice it?"

She thought for a few moments. "I can't say that I did," she replied. "Sorry."

Chambers closed his notebook. He picked up his glass and drained it. "Oh, one last thing," he said. "After the argument with the Colonel, which side of the stage did you exit?"

"Exit stage left, that's the direction," she replied.

"Well I think that about covers it, for now at least," said Chambers. "Thank you very much for your help."

"Well thank you for the drinks," she said. "Or should I say thank you Scotland Yard."

Chambers smiled and raised his finger to his nose. "Remember, our little secret."

"I'll remember," she replied, as she stood up. She gave a wave and walked towards the exit.

* * *

Detective Chambers watched Catherine Barr until she had left the building. He looked at his watch. It was just after six twenty. The Inspector wouldn't be in for dinner until about seven, so he had some time to himself. Time he intended to use wisely going through his notes of the interviews.

Chapter Fifteen
The Queens Head

The Lounge bar of the Queens Head boasts one of the finest Elizabethan inglenook fireplaces in the County. Detective Sergeant Derek Chambers knew nothing about Elizabeth the First, or inglenook fireplaces. What he did know, however, was that this one, constructed in the first year of Elizabeth the first's reign, was currently providing a very welcome fire from the cold outside.

Detective Chambers had armed himself with a double scotch and water, and found himself a comfortable seat close to the fireplace. He glanced around. The Wokingham Players had now gone, and the bar was empty, apart from one or two having one for the road, before setting off for home. He settled back into his seat, opened his notebook and started to read.

"It's a bit early for the locals," Ray, the barman, had explained. "They won't be coming in until seven, seven thirty, something like that." He rubbed down the counter. "Don't get many tourists neither," he continued. "Not this time of year. The weather you see. It's hardly the Costa del Sol."

Chambers looked over at the window. The rain had started once again, and it looked set for the rest of the evening. He looked back at the fire and shivered involuntarily.

"Good evening, Mr. Chambers," said a voice.

Chambers looked up.

"Guy Palmer," the voice explained. "I deal with the scenery, for the play. Keeps me out of trouble I suppose."

Chambers was puzzled. "Yes Mr. Palmer, what can I do for you?"

Palmer hesitated for a moment. "Could you spare me a few minutes of your time?" he asked. "There's just something I need to talk about."

Chambers was intrigued. "Certainly, Mr. Palmer," he replied. "Take a seat."

Palmer sat down, and looked around, clearly nervous.

"Can I get you a drink?" asked Chambers.

Palmer looked up. "That's kind of you. A scotch, if you don't mind."

"Water, ice?"

"Oh, ginger please," Palmer replied. "The American."

"No problem." Chambers looked over and caught the barman's eye, and ordered the drinks. "They won't be long," he said, pointing over to the bar. He waited for Palmer to begin, but he remained silent. "How long have you been dealing with the scenery at the hall?" he asked.

"Not long," Palmer replied. "A couple of years I suppose." He paused as he saw the barman approaching with their drinks.

"Here we are," said Ray, as he placed the drinks on to the table.

Chambers passed a glass to Palmer. "Your good health." He took a drink, then looked back at Palmer. "So, what can I do for you?"

Palmer took a long drink. He was breathing hard. He glanced around once again, and then looked back at Chambers. "You already know this I'm sure, but well I've got a criminal record."

"Go on," coaxed Chambers.

"It were drugs," Palmer explained in a hushed voice. "I got in with a bad crowd, twenty odd years ago. You hear things like that all the time, I know, but it doesn't register, until it's you." He took another drink. "Well I got four years inside, got out after two. Oh I deserved it right enough, and I'm not saying any different. I'd certainly done wrong, and no mistake. Stupid really, but well what can you do? Two years, don't sound a lot does it, but that affects your whole life. You know you can never get away from it. It sticks with you, no matter what. I'm not proud of it, and I'm not trying to make excuses you understand. I served my time, paid for it. It happened. I wish it hadn't but it did. I can't make it un-happen can I? More's the pity. But I didn't want anyone to know." He paused, and took a drink. "Janet, I mean Miss. Cooper, well she knew. But it didn't matter to her, you see, twenty years ago she said. Over and done with. It's the here and now that counts. That's what she said. But that Mr. Donovan, it wasn't good enough for him. He found out. Don't know how, but he knew all about it. It was a big joke to him. He wanted to tell everyone. To shame me I guess."

"And did he tell anyone?" asked Chambers.

Palmer shook his head. "No he didn't. I don't know why. He kept saying that people would be very interested to know about me, but maybe he changed his mind."

"Apart from Donovan and Miss. Cooper who else knew?" asked Chambers

Palmer thought for a few moments. "I don't think anyone else knew," he replied. "Leastways no one ever said anything."

"Okay, Mr. Palmer thank you for telling me," said Chambers. "As it happens I didn't know, and I don't really think it's relevant. Unless of course you murdered Mr. Donovan."

"Me, why would I murder him," protested Palmer.

"Well you've just given a pretty good reason," said Chambers. "You could have decided to make sure that he didn't tell anyone. To keep him quiet. It's been known."

"I never killed him, no way," Palmer replied getting agitated. "I just wanted you to know, that's all."

"Alright, Mr. Palmer, calm down. I believe you," said Chambers. "Another drink?"

"My round I think," said a voice. It was the Chief Inspector. "I think we've time before dinner. "That's a scotch for you Derek, mine's a pint of best, and you …."

"This is Guy Palmer," explained Chambers. "He is in charge of the scenery."

"Ah, Mr. Palmer," said Whittaker. "Looks like a scotch and American if I'm not mistaken."

"Absolutely right, Inspector," said Palmer, beginning to relax.

"Right, I'll be with you in a couple of shakes," Whittaker said, and then walked over to the bar.

A few minutes later Whittaker returned with the drinks. He placed the tray on to the table, and proceeded to pass the drinks around. "That's a scotch and American for you, Mr. Palmer. A double scotch for Detective Chambers, and a pint of best for me." He sat down, and took a drink. He looked around. "Well it's not exactly the Red Lion in the Kings Road, but it's pleasant enough. In fact it's very pleasant indeed."

"Perhaps you should thank the Commissioner, sir," suggested Chambers.

"You know, you're absolutely right," Whittaker replied. "I'll send an email thanking her." He smiled, and took another drink. He looked at the fire and rubbed his hands. "Very nice," he said to no one in particular. "It's turned very cold out there." He pointed towards the entrance. "And it's raining again wouldn't you know."

"Mr. Palmer has just been telling me about some trouble he got into a few years back," Chambers started to explain.

"The drugs you mean," suggested Whittaker. "Almost twenty years ago wasn't it?" He then turned to face Palmer. You got four years wasn't it?"

Palmer took a deep breath. "That's right, sir, four years. Seemed like a lifetime," he said. "But how did you know?"

Whittaker looked at Chambers. "Just a press cutting we took from Donovan's flat," he explained. "Just a small entry. What Donovan planned on doing about it, if anything, I don't know." He looked back at Palmer. "Did he ever threaten you in anyway?"

"Blackmail, you mean?" suggested Palmer. "No he never did."

"Apparently, it was a big joke to Donovan," said Chambers.

"He said that people would be interested to know all about me," added Palmer. "But nothing ever happened."

"He probably decided that it wasn't worth the effort," said Whittaker. "Not enough payoff."

"You could be right," said Palmer.

"Oh, I'm right, make no mistake," said Whittaker, taking a drink. "Tell me, all this play acting, I mean I just don't get it. I mean pretending to be something you're not. What's the attraction?"

"It's just a bit of fun, Inspector," Palmer began to explain. "An escape from reality for a while at least."

"That's as maybe, but there are some that takes it too far, don't you think?" said Whittaker. "I mean take these cops and robber things on the television. That Columbus, for a start."

"Columbo," corrected Chambers. "It's Columbo."

"Right, Columbo, or whatever his name is," agreed Whittaker. "Take him. He knows the killer right from the start. How does he do that? Fantasy land that's how. It's not for real is it? Mores the pity maybe. Imagine if I could solve this murder just like that, and relax a bit more." He snapped his fingers, and looked at Chambers. "Get a round of golf, maybe. Never going to happen is it?"

"As I said, Inspector, it's just a bit of fun," replied Palmer. "Complete fantasy I agree, but no harm done."

"Suppose not," agreed the Chief Inspector, as he took another drink.

"So, Inspector, what about this case?" asked Palmer. "Are you anywhere near solving it?"

Whittaker looked back at Chambers. "Are we?" he asked. He then looked back at Palmer. "This is no play, Mr. Palmer, and I'm not acting. I don't have a script to follow. One that tells me the villain in the last act." He paused for a moment. "So far all I have is the crime, the murder weapon, a handful of motives, and several suspects."

"Do they include me?" Palmer asked nervously.

"Oh most assuredly, you are very much included," Whittaker said. "Wouldn't want you to feel neglected would we?" He took a long drink. "You were in charge of the scenery, correct?"

"That's right, sir," Palmer replied. "Though it wasn't a big problem for this play, it was basically the same all the way through. It was mainly opening or closing the curtains."

"Can you explain that?" asked Whittaker.

"Act one is during the day, the curtains are open," Palmer started to explain. "Act two it's evening, and the curtains are closed. Act three, well we never got there did we, but act three would have been daytime again. So curtains were open."

"Understood," said Whittaker. "Where would you normally stand during a performance?"

Palmer thought for a few moment. "Depends on the circumstances, and what needed doing," he replied. "But as I said, it was the curtains that were important. I was mainly over on the right hand side."

"Right where the murder weapon was located," said Whittaker. "Maybe you switched it. Maybe you are the one we are looking for."

"I didn't do it," Palmer said quite simply.

"Well let's think about it shall we," said Whittaker. He held up one finger. "You had a motive, a bit weak maybe, but a motive nonetheless. Two, you had the opportunity, and three you can be placed at the scene of the crime. A pretty fair case I'd say."

Palmer was now beginning to get quite nervous once again. "I didn't do it, Inspector," he protested. "You must believe me."

"They all say that, Mr. Palmer," said the Inspector. "Guilty people very rarely admit their guilt. Oh no, they protest their innocence right up until the moment the key turns locking them into the cell, and even then some don't stop." He took another drink. "But I admit perhaps you are telling the truth. Perhaps you didn't do it."

Palmer drained his drink, and stood up. "On that note then, I think I'll quit while I'm ahead. I'll be on my way, and your dinner should be ready soon. Thank you for the drinks. Goodnight Mr. Chambers, and you, sir." He turned and walked away.

"Something I said?" said Whittaker, as he watched Palmer walk away.

"Could be, but he is right you know," Chambers replied. "It's just gone seven, and I have to admit I'm feeling a bit peckish."

"Me too, as it happens," said Whittaker. He drained his glass and stood up. "Let's get to it then, shall we?"

* * *

It was just after seven fifteen by the time Whittaker and Chambers arrived for dinner. The dining room was still quite empty. Ray saw them as they came in, and gave a wave. They walked over to their usual table and sat down. Ray followed them. "What will it be this evening, gents?" he asked, wiping the table. "We have chicken in white wine ...."

"Steak and kidney pie," Whittaker interrupted.

"Certainly, Inspector," replied Ray. "And you, Sergeant?"

Chambers looked at Whittaker, and then he looked back at Ray. "I'll give the chicken a try."

Ray nodded, smiled, and hurried away.

Chambers looked around, then he looked back at Whittaker. "What did you think then?" he asked.

126

"Palmer you mean?" replied Whittaker.

"Did time for drugs, didn't want anyone to know. Is that yet another possible motive?" asked Chambers. "Another reason to commit murder?"

"No, I don't think so," said Whittaker. "You heard what he said. It was twenty years ago, and Palmer did time for it. Case closed, over and done with. Okay he didn't really like the idea of his secret past being spread all over the place, but it couldn't really do him that much harm could it? I mean who would really care anyway?"

Chambers wasn't convinced. "I'm not sure about that, sir," he said. "Who really knows what harm it would do? People knowing your guilty past. Admittedly, it was a long time ago, but knowing that other people knew, your colleagues, people down at the local, work mates, could have a very significant effect on some people. People talking about you behind your back. People thinking leopards don't change their spots. Was he still taking drugs? Maybe Mr. Palmer was being over sensitive, but you know some people can be real nasty."

"Okay Derek, I hear what you say," said Whittaker. "But I have to say I still don't think Mr. Palmer is our killer. But for the time being he's still a possible. Happy with that?"

Chambers smiled. "Happy is not the word I would have used, sir, but yes that's fine for now." He paused as their dinners were brought in.

The meals were placed on the table. "Enjoy your meal, gentlemen," the waiter said. "If you need anything, just call." The waiter then turned and left the room.

Chambers looked down at the plate. "Looks good, sir," he said.

"Well you know what they say about the proof of the pudding?"

"Being in the eating, you mean," suggested Chambers.

"Precisely," replied Whittaker, cutting a piece of the pie. "How did you get on with Miss. Susan Turner?" he asked.

"She was very nervous," said Chambers. "Probably never been questioned by the police before, I guess. But she did settle down after a while."

"So, did she say anything of interest?" asked Whittaker, as he cut into his pie.

Chambers finished chewing. "Oh yes, one thing Janet Cooper is definitely wrong with her suggested timings," he replied. "The prop gun was placed into position just after seven thirty, or maybe twenty to eight."

"Seems like the window of opportunity for switching the gun just got a bit larger than we originally thought," said the Inspector.

"Correct," replied Chambers. "From seven forty to nine twenty, an hour and forty minutes, or thereabouts. I'm wondering how our murderer would have known."

"I'm not sure that he would have been that bothered about timing," suggested Whittaker. "He, or she, just knew where they would be at a certain time. They would have probably left it as late as they could anyway."

"Less risk of discovery you mean," suggested Chambers. "And less opportunity for anyone else to do anything about it anyway."

"Whoever did the swop, they knew that they would be in a good position at such and such time, and that was that," said Whittaker. "A study of the script might give us an indication as to where people were at a certain time."

"Assuming people kept to the script," said Chambers.

There was a lot of truth in that, thought Whittaker. "Did you learn anything from Catherine Barr?" he asked. "By the way this is good, just the way I like it."

"Miss. Barr was okay I guess," Chambers replied. "Didn't learn much though. Donovan was pretty much universally disliked, but we were beginning to get that anyway. But one interesting thing she did say. Everyone knew that Donovan had been a magistrate. In fact he apparently went to great lengths to make sure that they did know. There's a definite connection there somewhere I think. Almost as though he was issuing a warning of some kind. Maybe our murderer appeared in front of him at one time."

"Well, we still have people to see," said the Inspector, laying down his knife and fork. "Although I'm not altogether sure what we will gain, if anything."

"No one said it would be easy did they?" said Chambers.

"But didn't the Commissioner think it was going to be easy, or am I mistaken. An open and shut case if I remember correctly. All that we had to do was make sure everything was done by the book." He paused for a moment. "But one thing, I have to say that was an excellent meal, you can't beat a good steak and kidney pie what do you think?"

"No sir," said Chambers "You are right, you can't," he agreed. "Although the chicken was pretty good I have to say."

"That's as maybe," said Whittaker. "I'll stick with the steak and kidney, thank you."

"Right you are, sir," replied Chambers. He looked around. The dining room was beginning to fill up. "What's our plan for tomorrow, sir?"

"Tomorrow, we've got Rose Fuller in the morning," Whittaker continued. "And Steve Ashton and Ian Jackson after lunch. Exciting don't you think. In the meantime, how about a drink?"

"That's kind of you, sir," replied Chambers. "I'll have a scotch and American."

"Same here," said Whittaker. "Let's make it doubles shall we? After all the department is paying." He paused for a moment, watching the meals being brought out for the other diners. "I think maybe tomorrow, the Commissioner can treat us to some apple pie as well."

"And why not?" said Chambers.

* * *

Chapter Sixteen
Rose Fuller

"Right, here we go again," announced Whittaker, heaving a sigh. "Another day, another round."

Chambers smiled. *Another round, very apt,* he thought. It certainly seemed a bit like a boxing match in some ways. "Are we getting anywhere do you think, sir?" he asked.

Whittaker said nothing for a moment. He looked over at his notice boards. There were certainly a few more coloured pins in place, with attached notes indicating a time period. *But were they getting anywhere,* he wondered. It didn't seem like it. He started tapping the table, and stared across the room. "Well, if you mean are we any closer to solving the crime, then sadly I have to say no," he replied. "But I guess it's giving us a feeling about our suspects. An impression if you like."

"I think you mean that some of them are lying," suggested Chambers.

"Oh certainly that," Whittaker agreed. "There's a couple who have definitely lied, or at the very least, not told the entire truth. Now they may have a good reason for that. They might have forgotten something, or simply not considered it relevant."

"It's easily done, I suppose," said Chambers.

"Oh yes, very easy," agreed Whittaker. "But lying about something that happened is one thing, but I don't believe you can lie about how you feel, really feel."

"What do you mean, sir," asked Chambers.

"Well, everyone has said quite definitely that they never killed Donovan," replied Whittaker. "They are innocent."

"They said that they disliked him, but not enough to kill him," said Chambers.

"That's right," said Whittaker. "But you know I truly believe that some of them did dislike Donovan enough." He paused for a moment. "Doesn't get us any nearer identifying the murderer though. So, we shall just have to wait and see." he continued. "Right, let's press on then. Who's next on the list?"

Chambers looked down at the sheet of paper on the desk. "Oh yes, I remember now," he said. "It's Rose Fuller."

"Ah, the house keeper," said Whittaker. "All right, let's have her in."

* * *

"Ah, Miss. Fuller, or is it Mrs.?" Said Whittaker.

"Miss, will do," she replied.

"Right, Miss. Fuller, please have a seat." Whittaker pointed to a chair. "This shouldn't take too long," he continued. "Just routine really. A few questions, that's all."

"Take as long as you need, Inspector. I've nothing else to do," Rose replied. "I just hope that I can help you."

"Can I start by asking about the dress rehearsal," said Whittaker. "Or to be more precise, what happened afterwards."

"Well, after the rehearsal several of us went to The Queens Head, for something to eat," Rose replied.

"What time was that?" asked Chambers.

Rose thought for a few moments. "I don't know exactly," she replied. "It was about half past five I think. We weren't due back at the hall until seven. The performance wasn't due to start until eight."

"When did you leave the public house?" asked Chambers.

"I never really took any notice. I just gave myself enough time to get back," she said. "It was maybe about twenty to seven, I think."

"Was anyone else with you when you left?" asked Whittaker.

"No, I went back alone," she replied. "A few had already left much earlier. Donovan hadn't stayed very long. I think he left before six, he said he had someone to see."

"Do you know who that was?" asked Chambers.

"No, I'm sorry," she replied. "I've no idea. I didn't ask, and he never said. None of my business really." She shrugged. "He probably wouldn't have told me even if I had asked. He'd have considered it prying. He wasn't someone you could talk to, if you know what I mean."

"Yes I think I know what you mean," Whittaker replied. "Who else can you tell me about?"

"Well, Steve, Steve Ashton he went about thirty minutes after Donovan," she continued.

"What about the others?" Whittaker continued. "Jackson and Masters?"

"Sorry, but I can't remember," she replied. "I think they were still there when I left, but I don't know for sure."

"When you got back to the hall, did you notice the gun?" said Chambers.

"No, can't say that I did," replied Rose. "I've never really noticed it I'm afraid, it's not something you would think of is it?" she replied. "I mean you just assume don't you? It was Susan's task to put the prop where it was needed." She paused for a moment. "I guess it was there, but I couldn't swear to it. It wasn't something for my attention, I wasn't that interested."

"Maybe so," said Whittaker. "What did you think about Mr. Donovan?" he asked.

Rose was taken by surprise at the sudden switch in questioning. "I have to say that I didn't like him, but he never bothered me, like he did some of the others." She paused for a moment. "You know I don't think there will be too many tears shed at his passing. He was not a likeable man. And I think you'll find, that he wasn't very popular with anyone."

"Why was that?" Whittaker persisted.

"Many reasons I would say," she replied. "Take your pick."

"Such as?" asked Whittaker.

"Where do I start? He was arrogant, thought he was better than anyone else," Rose began. "Thought he knew it all. He was extremely rude. A horrible, horrible, man. Everyone hated him."

"Hated, you say," said Whittaker. "Was he hated enough for someone to kill him?"

"That's a very good question, Chief Inspector," said Rose. "All I can say is that I didn't kill him, if that is what you're thinking."

"I never suggested anything of the kind now did I?" Whittaker replied.

"No, maybe you didn't," Rose agreed. "But you were thinking it weren't you?"

"You are very perceptive, Miss. Fuller," Whittaker replied. He sighed, and turned to face Chambers. "I really must be more careful about what I say, or indeed, what I think, in the future."

"Why would I want to kill him anyway?" she asked. "Just because I didn't like him?

"That's a great question, Miss. Fuller," admitted Whittaker. "And one I ask over and over. Why would anyone want to kill him?"

Rose made no response, which was no surprise to Whittaker. He hadn't actually expected anything more. "It has been known," Whittaker continued. "People have often killed someone else simply because they didn't like them."

"I understand that you weren't required in the second act," said Chambers.

Rose turned to face Chambers. "That's right," she replied. "I was mainly in act one, you know. What with the arrival of the weekend visitor, and then the totally unexpected arrival of the stranded motorist."

"Ah that would be …. Let me see." Whittaker looked back at his list.

"It was Steve, Steve Ashton," Miss. Fuller said helpfully. She shrugged. "I was on stage and off stage so many times, I was getting dizzy. It carried on like that right until almost the end of Act one."

"At about eight-thirty?" suggested Chambers.

"A few minutes before, I think. And that was it. Then I wasn't required until act three, for the finale where the identity of the murderer is revealed. The crime solved in the old theatrical traditional way." She started to laugh. "All fully explained, in great detail, and making absolutely no sense whatsoever."

"What did you actually think of the play?" asked Chambers.

She started to laugh. "Steve will never be a playwright that's definite," she replied. "What did I think of it? Two words, harmless nonsense." She paused for a moment. "But great fun I guess. I mean after all why do so many people go for this kind of thing? It's all over the television, with constant crime programmes. There's that one on in the West End, whatever it's called. Been on for years. Everyone in the country must have seen it by now, probably more than once. And most of them probably didn't understand it, and probably can't remember who did it, or why."

"I know the one you mean, I can't remember what it was called though," Chambers replied. "I have to admit that I've seen it. Many years ago. I quite enjoyed it."

"Well I've never seen it, nor likely to," added Whittaker.

"You say that you weren't required for Act Two," said Chambers. "What did you do?" he asked Rose.

"What do you mean what did I do?" she replied.

"During the second act," Whittaker explained.

134

"I just stayed backstage," she replied. "Over in the wings."

"All the time?" said Chambers. "Why would you do that?"

"As I'm sure you would have realised by now, we are a small group, and very, very, amateurish," she explained. "There is always a lot to do with the production. Scenery shifting, lighting, a million and one things. I like to help out where I can. In fact I spent some time with Peter, Peter Gammons. He had some adjustments to make to the lighting"

"Right, I understand," agreed Chambers. "So you remained backstage for the whole of act two."

"That's right," she agreed.

"Whereabouts were you?" asked Chambers. "I mean which side of the stage?"

"There were a lot of people waiting over on the left side," Rose started to explain. "John Berry, he plays the butler, Donovan, and Katie. That's Catherine Barr, she played Donovan's stage wife. It's a very small area backstage as you can imagine, and it was a bit congested. You can move around a bit, through the area at the back of the stage. I was over on the left side for some of the time, but most of the time I stayed over on the right side."

"Where the small table was situated," suggested Chambers. "The table where the gun was located."

"Yes, I guess that's right," Rose admitted.

"Meaning that you could easily have switched the gun then," continued Chambers.

Rose Fuller, started to smile. "You know I missed that completely, I never saw that coming at all," she replied. "Yes you're absolutely right. I suppose I could have switched the gun, but I didn't."

"You know, I thought that you'd say that, Miss. Fuller," said Whittaker.

"You're not disappointed then," she said, smiling.

"No, I'm not disappointed in the least," admitted Whittaker. "By the way did you notice anyone else on that side of the stage?"

"Well as I said, Peter was there for a while, something to do with the lights. Too technical for me," she replied. "Then there was John Berry, he came off the stage exiting on the right. He should have gone to the other side, but he said that he was making a quick getaway, and going for a cigarette."

"I hope that you told him that smoking was bad for his health," said Whittaker. "Was there anyone else?"

She said nothing for a moment or two. "The scenery man, Guy, he was fiddling around with something. I never really took much noticed."

Whittaker sighed. How many times had he heard that, or something similar? I never noticed, I never took much notice, or quite simply I never saw anything. Not really surprising though, he had to admit. "Well, I think that's about all, for now," he said. "You may go, and thank you. You have been quite helpful."

"I'm not sure how," she replied. "But I'm pleased to hear it. Such a dreadful business. I hope you find whoever did this, and soon." She shook her head, and started to walk away.

"Incidentally," Whittaker called out to her. "What happened to your hand?"

"My hand?" repeated Rose. She looked down. "Oh this, it's just a scratch. A broken piece of glass. Foolish of me. But there you are, accidents happen."

"Guess so," said Whittaker. "You need to be more careful."

Chapter Seventeen
Steve Ashton

"Odd that, don't you think?" said Whittaker, after she had left. "That question about her hand seem to come as a complete surprise to her, and yet she knew which hand to look at with no hesitation."

"Maybe your question just refreshed her memory," suggested Chambers. "I didn't think it significant."

"You know Derek, to me, in any criminal investigation, but even more so in a murder enquiry, everything is significant, until proven not to be," Whittaker replied. He looked over at the door. "She's a very clever lady methinks."

Chambers had to agree, she was a clever lady, but was she a little too clever. "Didn't Mr. Berry say something about her fussing with the curtain?

"Yes he did, what about it?" agreed Whittaker.

"Well, she never mentioned it at all did she?" Chambers continued. "But she did say that Guy Palmer was there, and that he was fiddling around with something, but she didn't take much notice."

"Could have been the curtain I suppose," suggested Whittaker. "Remember what Mr. Palmer told us."

"I remember," said Chambers. "Opening and closing the curtains was an important function."

"Correct," said Whittaker. "But why didn't she say so?"

"You know, sir, there's a few things she said, that I find puzzling," Chambers continued.

"Such as?" said Whittaker.

"What she said about the gun struck me as odd," said Chambers. "She said that the gun didn't interest her, or words to that effect."

"Yes she did," Whittaker agreed, as he looked back at his notes. "She actually said, it wasn't something for my attention, and that she wasn't interested."

"That's right," agreed Chambers. "And yet she was supposed to be so interested in the play, always ready to help out where she could."

"What's your point, Derek?"

"You have to admit that the gun was clearly a very important prop," Chambers continued. "I mean without the gun, there would be no murder at the Manor, and therefore there'd be no play."

"Ashton said that, I remember?" said Whittaker.

"That's right," agreed Chambers. "The whole point of the play is that murder, and yet she wasn't interested enough to make sure that it was there. Doesn't make sense to me."

"Nor me," agreed Whittaker. "And clearly she had ample opportunity to switch the gun."

Chambers sighed. What Whittaker had just said was right, but there were several others who also had the opportunity, and the motive. "Her and several others," he replied. He sighed once again. "You know whoever switched the gun had two problems."

"Go on," said Whittaker.

"Firstly he, or she, had to bring the real gun backstage," Chambers started to explain. "And secondly, he, or she, had to remove the fake gun out of the hall."

"Whoever did it might have come in from outside, switched guns and then simply went out again," suggested Whittaker.

"Seems that way to me, sir," said Chambers.

"Well it's certainly a possibility," Whittaker replied sounding despondent. "But we still don't know who he or she is, do we?"

"No sir, we don't," replied Chambers. "As usual, we go a few steps forward, and then a few back again. And end up with more questions to be answered."

Whittaker took a deep breath. "Who do we have next?"

"Steve Ashton," replied Chambers. He started to smile. "The playwright."

* * *

"Ah come in Mr. Ashton, have a seat," said Whittaker. "You are the .... Now let me see." He looked at the list. "Ah yes, Mr. Ashton, apart from being the author, you are the stranded motorist, correct? Stranded in the snow, and seeking refuge at the Manor, is that it?"

"Well, yes that's right," Ashton agreed. "But I'm really a police officer. Courtesy of the miracle of fantasy and fiction I'm afraid. But you don't find that out until Act Three, when the whole mystery is explained."

"Indeed, but I thought Mr. Saunders was a policeman" said Whittaker completely unimpressed.

"Ah, but this is play acting," explain Ashton. "And that's one of the twists in the play."

"Play acting, you say," replied Whittaker. "But of course I'm dealing with real life you see. Real crime, a real murder. Not this, er, this pretending."

"Oh, Inspector, you shouldn't take it so seriously," said Ashton. "It's just a bit of fun, after all. We all know that it's nonsense really, but where's the harm?"

"Possibly," replied Whittaker. "Maybe what you say is true, but somewhere along the way, someone forgot that it was just make believe didn't they, and a real murder was committed."

"Well, that is certainly true, Inspector," agreed Ashton. "I can't argue with that. How can I help?"

"Oh, just a few questions," Whittaker replied. "Nothing too onerous. Routine really. Shouldn't take too long."

"No problem, Inspector," replied Ashton. "Only too happy to help if I can."

"Pleased to hear it," replied Whittaker. "Let's make a start then, shall we? Where were you between five thirty and seven thirty, the day of the murder?"

Ashton looked surprised. "Am I a suspect then?" he asked.

"You all are, Mr. Ashton," Whittaker replied. "Every single one of you, including the backstage people."

"That's a lot of suspects. You've certainly got your work cut out," Ashton replied. "How's the investigation actually going? Any clues yet? Does anyone stand out? I mean, anyone more likely than anyone else?"

Whittaker smiled. "Maybe two or three," he replied. "But you've no need to worry, you're way down on the list."

Ashton heaved a sigh of relief. "That's good to know," he said. "Who are these front runners?"

Whittaker put his index finger up to his lips. "My lips are sealed, Mr. Ashton. Like your audience, and the play, I'm sworn to secrecy."

Ashton laughed. "What about motive?" he asked. "Do you know why anyone would want to kill old Donovan? I mean I know he wasn't liked, but it must have been more than that surely. Revenge maybe?"

"No, no we haven't found a motive, not yet," replied Whittaker. He paused for a moment, then raised his eyebrows. "Now, if you could just answer the question."

"Certainly, not a problem," Ashton said. "Five thirty until seven thirty you say," he thought for a few moments. "After the rehearsal finished, we all went somewhere for a bite to eat. The Queens Head. Well to be honest we didn't all go. A few had other ideas. Janet wasn't there, neither was young Tim. But I certainly went."

"What about Donovan?" asked Chambers. "Was he there?"

Ashton shook his head. "No, he wasn't, I don't know why. But he wasn't one for mixing, not with us commoners anyway. But didn't someone say he had an appointment, or something. I can't remember."

"And you stayed until what time?" asked Chambers.

"I think I left at about six thirty, and I went back to the hall," Ashton replied. "Probably arrived at about a quarter to seven, or thereabouts."

"Anyone with you?" Chambers continued.

"No, no one I'm afraid."

"Did anyone see you at the hall?" asked Whittaker.

"No, I don't think so," replied Ashton.

"Did you see anyone?" Chambers again.

Once again Ashton shook his head. "No one. Guess I don't have an alibi then, or whatever it's called."

"Looks that way," said Chambers. "But I wouldn't worry too much, not yet anyway."

"And you went straight back to the hall, with no detours," said Whittaker.

"No, there were no detours," Ashton confirmed. "I went straight back to the hall."

"But why so early?" asked Whittaker. "I mean the play wasn't due to start for another hour or more."

"Oh, just nervous I guess," replied Ashton. "You see I wrote the play, and I wanted to make sure that everything was ready for curtain up. I didn't want any slipups."

"Did that include checking on the gun?" asked Chambers. "The prop?"

"The gun, oh yes the most important prop of the evening," replied Ashton. "Of course I checked on the gun. As far as I can recall it was certainly on the table when I last checked. In fact I actually saw Susan place it into position."

"What time was that?" asked Chambers.

"I couldn't say," replied Ashton. "I never took note of the time. Certainly before curtain up, but that's as close as I can get. Why not ask Susan?"

"We already have, Mr. Ashton," said Whittaker.

Ashton started to laugh. "Ah, I should have guessed," he replied. "Testing me, I suppose? So how did I do?"

"But you did check that the gun was there," Chambers stressed ignoring Ashton's comment.

"I just said I did, didn't I?" said Ashton, beginning to get impatient.

"Yes you did," agreed Chambers. "But I just need to get everything straight."

"Yes, of course you do," said Ashton, beginning to calm down. "This thing, the murder, has got all of us a bit edgy you understand. A bit jumpy. Anyway I'm sorry. Please accept my apology. The thing is the gun is very important. The whole point of the play revolves around that gun. No gun, no shooting, and consequently no murder at the manor."

"And consequently, no play. Point taken," said Chambers. "So we're sure that the prop was there, at about seven thirty, perhaps a few minutes after, according to Miss. Turner. And we are equally sure that just about nine twenty it had been switched. The prop gun removed, and a real gun substituted in its place."

142

"Looks that way doesn't it. Easy enough to do as well I imagine," said Ashton. "And very clever, I mean to actually get someone else to commit the crime, innocently like that, and that person totally unaware of what was about to happen."

"Clever?" said Whittaker. "Guess you might say that. But in my time with the force, I've never yet met a clever criminal. We'll find the real murderer never fear. They are all stupid, and he or she will make a mistake somewhere along the way. He or she will get caught out in a lie maybe. Or perhaps a witness will suddenly realise that they did see something, something important. Mark my words our villain will slip up somewhere, they always do." He paused and sighed. "But I have to admit that I would like to find that prop gun."

"I'd say that the chances of finding the gun are virtually zero, wouldn't you. I'd say that it would be long gone," said Ashton. "If it had been me I'd have thrown it into the river somewhere. I think it will never be found."

"Why do you say that?" asked Chambers.

"Well it stands to reason," Ashton continued. "The killer whoever he or she is, isn't going to leave it lying around are they. I mean, especially if there are fingerprints, they're a dead giveaway." He paused for a moment. "Sorry for the pun, it was quite unintentional."

"You might be right," said Whittaker. "Incidentally, Mr. Ashton you aren't really a playwright are you? I mean Murder at Larkhall Manor, was your first effort, if I'm not mistaken."

"Not entirely correct, Inspector. And remember that even Shakespeare started with just the one play," Ashton replied with mock indignation. "There have actually been two previous attempts. Neither of them were particularly successful though, I'm afraid. In fact neither of them were actually completed. How we artists suffer for our art."

"Umm," grunted the Inspector. "Not wishing to offend, but Larkhall Manor is not really that good is it?"

Ashton started to smile. "Oh I don't know," he said.

"Come on, now," Whittaker continued. "A handful of people in the audience, the hall half full. Hardly a major success."

Ashton started to laugh. "It's not to everyone's taste, I agree, but I actually thought that it was pretty good." He paused for a moment. "At least some parts were, shall we say, promising. But I cannot believe that you are really that concerned with my play writing career. Is this line of questioning leading anywhere in particular, Inspector?" he asked.

"Oh no, no place really. Idle interest maybe," the Inspector replied. "I just wondered why you wrote the play that's all. What influenced you?"

"What influenced me?" Ashton repeated. "An interesting question."

Chambers suddenly remembered what Catherine Barr had said about Ashton and the script. "What were you thinking when you wrote the script?"

"What was I thinking? Why did I write it?" said Ashton. "Simple really. No great mystery. I've spent some time acting. I've done a lot of plays. Some have been okay I guess, but most of them have been really bad. I just thought I'd try writing a play, that's all. I thought I could do better, or at least no worse."

"I thought that might be the reason," replied Whittaker. "Do you think you'll write another one, or are your playwriting days over?"

"Well let's say I thought I had succeeded with Larkhall Manor. Others, of course, may feel differently. That's their right, their privilege. You can't please everyone," Ashton replied. "I don't actually expect any major awards any time soon. Whether or not there'll be a follow up, who knows. Sadly of course circumstances robbed us of the complete work. You never saw the best part, the crime solved. The piece de la resistance. It may never be seen now." He paused and sighed. "We shall have to wait and see shan't we. My fans might demand it, who knows?"

"Guess so," agreed Whittaker. "Incidentally what was your opinion of Mr. Donovan?"

"My opinion, what do you mean?" asked Ashton.

"Well, what did you think of him?" Whittaker explained. "I'm getting the impression that he wasn't very popular."

"Oh I see," replied Ashton. "You know I never really gave him a thought to be honest."

"I'm surprised. You clearly did give him some thought," said Whittaker. "I understand that it was you who actually recommended Donovan for the part of the Colonel," Whittaker continued.

"That's right, I did. I just thought he looked the part, that's all," Ashton started to explain. "But I can't say that I liked him particularly. He wasn't easy to like. He wouldn't win any popularity contests, but you could say that about a lot of them here."

"Oh, didn't you get on with the others in the group?" asked Chambers.

"We're here to do a job of work, to act in a bit of silly fantasy. That's all. Nothing more, and nothing less," he replied. "It's not a social event. They aren't my long lost relatives. We're not great buddies, you know. I'm not bothered about any of them, really, and I'm willing to guess they probably think the same about me. And I wouldn't blame them if they did. In fact, you could just say that it's all one big act."

"Interesting viewpoint, Mr. Ashton," said Chambers. "Very interesting."

"Is that it?" asked Ashton. "Are we all done?"

"Not quite, Mr. Ashton," replied Whittaker. "There is one other thing you might be able to help me with. I understand that you were involved in an argument, round about seven o'clock, the day of the murder."

Ashton looked puzzled. "Argument?" he repeated, shaking his head. "No, not me. Someone else maybe."

"I don't think so," said Whittaker. "You were overhead talking to an unknown lady. You were outside the hall, and apparently she wanted to get inside, to see someone, and you apparently stopped her."

"Sorry, Inspector, but someone is in error I'm afraid," Ashton protested. "Someone has made a big mistake. It certainly wasn't me. And you said something about an unknown woman. Another little mystery, just like our play. Seems a bit too vague to me though. A bit too fanciful, even for these play actors. Who was it, this person who was supposed to have overheard this conversation?"

"I'm not prepared to say at this stage," replied Whittaker.

"Did whoever it was say that they actually saw me?" Ashton asked.

"No, no they didn't see you," admitted Whittaker. "But they said that they recognized your voice."

"Seven o'clock you said?" replied Ashton. He shook his head. "No, not me."

"They were quite definite, I'm afraid," said Whittaker.

"Well, they simply made a mistake, that's all there is to that," Ashton insisted. "It's easily done. I'm made similar mistakes myself, many times."

"Yes, as you say, easily done," replied Whittaker. "Well I think that's all for the time being. I may need to speak with you again though, don't stray too far will you."

"I'll be right here, Inspector," said Ashton. "No need to worry."

The Inspector suddenly held up his hand. "There is one last thing," he said. "About the second act. You weren't in it were you?"

"Absolutely correct," said Ashton. "And you want to know where I was, am I right?

"It would help," said Whittaker.

"Simple. I went out," Ashton replied. "No point hanging around, besides it's pretty congested back stage you know."

"You went out," repeated Whittaker. "Where?"

"Oh, nowhere in particular," Ashton replied. "It's a small village, there aren't too many places to go."

"Did anyone see you?" asked Chambers.

"Not that I know off," Ashton replied. "Anything else?"

"No, nothing else, for the moment," replied Whittaker. "Thank you. You can go now."

* * *

Chapter Eighteen
Ian Jackson

Chambers watched Ashton leave the room. He then turned towards Whittaker. "Two or three?" he said. "Two or three suspects that stand out. What was that all about?"

"He was fishing wasn't he?" Whittaker said. "I just went along with him, to see how far he was going. Gave him a bit more bait if you will. I never gave any names did I? He's none the wiser is he?"

"Okay I get it, but do you actually have any front runners?" asked Chambers.

Whittaker thought for a few moments. "Well nothing definite yet, but you have to admit that both Miss. Turner, and Miss. Fuller, had the opportunity to switch the gun."

"So did John Berry," added Chambers.

"Correct, and so that makes three," said Whittaker. He looked at the door. "I wonder why the fishing trip though, and I also wonder if he actually learnt anything." He looked back at Chambers. "Maybe our Mr. Ashton could join the list, as a possible fourth candidate. He just went out, nowhere particular, and no one saw him. A bit flimsy I would say."

"Well, I for one didn't believe anything he actually said," said Chambers.

"Oh I don't know about that," said Whittaker. "What was it that he said about the others?"

Chambers opened his pad, and started to read. "Here it is. We're not great buddies, you know. I'm not bothered about any of them, really, and I'm willing to guess they probably think the same about me. Wouldn't blame them if they did. You could just say that it's all one big act." Chambers closed his pad.

"Well, I certainly believe every word of that. Don't you?" said Whittaker. "It's about the only thing I do believe, so far. Our friend Ashton doesn't care about anything, or anyone, except Steve Ashton." He looked at his watch. "It's almost twelve," he announced. "Think we've time for one more before lunch?"

"Well, I think we could squeeze one more in," Chambers replied. "Ian Jackson is waiting patiently outside. What do you think?"

"Ian Jackson?" repeated a puzzled Whittaker.

"The weekend guest, I believe," Chambers explained.

"Go on then," said Whittaker. "Bring him in, then we'll have lunch.

* * *

"Come in, Mr. Jackson," said Whittaker. "Have a seat."

Jackson looked nervous, and was breathing hard, as he sat down.

"There's no need to be nervous, Mr. Jackson," Whittaker said. "It's just a few questions, I'll try not to keep you too long." He looked down on his list. You play the weekend guest, correct?" he continued.

"That's right," confirmed Jackson. "I'm the weekend guest, a longtime friend of the Colonel."

"How did you get on with your friend, the Colonel?" asked Whittaker.

"Umm, I think you mean did I get on with Donovan?" replied Jackson. "You've been asking that of everyone haven't you? One way or another. We do compare notes you know. Well, at least some of us do. I doubt if you found anyone who said that they actually liked him. Correct?" He waited for a response, but none came. "Well. I didn't like him, simple as that. Couldn't stand him. But no, I didn't kill him."

Whittaker took a deep breath. "Never entered my head, Mr. Jackson," he replied. "The thing is, if you had said the opposite, that you liked him, and that he was the next best thing to sliced bread, I might well have thought that you were lying, and you would have gone straight to the top of the list of suspects."

"Does that mean I'm in the clear, and can go," replied Jackson, smiling.

"Not quite," said Whittaker. "It simply means that you didn't like Donovan, the same as most of the group, and that you are merely one of several suspects."

"Oh, that is disappointing," said Jackson. "What else can I tell you?"

"Tell me about the dress rehearsal," said Whittaker. "Or more to the point, what happened after the rehearsal."

Jackson smiled. "Inspector, I'm one hundred percent sure that you already know exactly what happened."

"Maybe I do," agreed Whittaker. "But I'd still like to hear your version."

Jackson started to laugh. "What you mean is that you want to see if I'm lying or not, don't you?"

"Yes, that's correct. I want to see if you are lying or not," admitted Whittaker. "If you could just answer the question it would be greatly appreciated."

"No problem, Inspector," replied Jackson. "Well, just like most of them once the rehearsal was completed, we went down to the Queens Head.

"Was everyone there?" asked Chambers.

"No, Janet wasn't there, neither was Tim," Jackson replied. "Oh, and Donovan I don't think he was there either. I can't actually remember. Besides I recall that someone, can't think who, said that Donovan had an appointment or something."

"What time did you leave the public house?" asked Chambers.

"Oh, I never really took much notice, about a quarter to seven, something like that," Jackson replied. "I got back to the hall about seven I guess."

"Was anyone else there, when you arrived?" asked Chambers

"Well, Susan was there," Jackson replied. "And Steve was there, Steve Ashton. I think he had left the pub just before me, perhaps about half past six."

"And he was at the hall when you arrived," asked Whittaker. "You saw him?"

"No, I never actually saw him," admitted Jackson. "I just heard him. At least I think it was him."

"You heard him?" asked Chambers.

"I'm sure that it was him," said Jackson. "His voice was coming from the side of the hall. I could hear him talking with someone. Well arguing really I should say."

"Arguing," repeated Whittaker. "Do you know what the argument was about?"

"No, I'm sorry, I couldn't make much out," said Jackson. "But Steve was trying to stop someone from doing something. That much was obvious."

"Do you know who it was?" asked Chambers.

"I've no idea," replied Jackson. "All I can say was that it was a woman."

"And you're sure that it was Ashton?" said Chambers.

"Ninety nine percent sure," replied Jackson. "If it wasn't Steve, it was a pretty good impersonation."

Whittaker looked at Chambers. "That makes it two to one," he said.

Ian Jackson looked at the two men, puzzled.

"Don't worry, Mr. Jackson," said Chambers. "Just a private comment between the two of us. Nothing to concern you."

"Detective Chambers is correct, it's nothing for you to worry about," Whittaker said. "Now, can we talk about another time period? The period between seven thirty, when Miss. Turner placed the prop gun into position, and nine twenty, by which time it had been switched, and James Donovan shot."

"Well as I said I got back at about seven, or just after," Jackson started to explain. "I actually saw Susan with the gun, as she put it on to the table. I'm not sure what time that was, but about fifteen minutes later the curtain went up."

"Where were you between the time Miss. Turner placed the gun into position, and the curtain going up?" asked Whittaker.

"I went over to the other side of the stage," Jackson replied.

"Stage left?" said Chambers. "Is that correct?"

"You've got it, detective," said Jackson. "There were a few of us. John was there, Catherine, and of course, Donovan. All waiting to walk on to the stage."

"When did you make your first appearance, Mr. Jackson?" asked Chambers.

"Donovan was the first to go on, with Catherine," Jackson started to explain. He was already the worse for wear. He was very late getting back. Janet was getting very worried. Anyway he arrived about five minutes before curtain up, just in time to go on. Don't know what would have happened if he had been any later." He paused for a moment, thinking about the possible consequences. "We'll never know will we? Anyway, about ten minutes after curtain up, I go on. Then I was on stage until the end of the Act, at about eight thirty. The Colonel and I have a blazing row. He had discovered that I was having an affair with his wife, you see. His stage wife I hasten to mention."

"Go on," said Whittaker.

"Remember Inspector, it's only play acting," Jackson continued. "Anyway the thing is he threatens divorce, and cutting her off without a penny."

"Is that why she arranges to have him murdered?" asked Whittaker.

"Precisely," replied Jackson. "Ah, Inspector that is not fair. We aren't supposed to tell. I could get shot for such a transgression."

"Don't worry, Mr. Jackson, your secret is safe with me," replied the Inspector. "I won't tell anyone."

"Incidentally, how did you know?" Jackson asked.

"Old fashioned detective work," Whittaker replied. "Quite simple really."

"Don't know how you do it, sir," Chambers said.

"It's nothing really, all down to experience," replied Whittaker. He cleared his throat and looked back at Jackson. "What happened next? After the argument?"

"Well I stormed off, leaving him and his wife," said Jackson. "Not very gallant I admit, but that what the script said, so that's what I did."

"You stormed off, where to?" asked Chambers.

"There was about ten minutes of the Act still to go," Jackson started to explain. "I left the stage on the left, as per stage instructions. I just stayed there waiting for the Act to finish. I couldn't very well go anywhere else. There's not much room backstage with these village hall stages. It's not Broadway you know. Anyway I thought a little drink, or three, would go down well. I wasn't due on again until the third act, which was starting at nine thirty. As soon as the Act finished, I went down to the Wokingham Arms. A quick half, or three, you know."

"How did you leave the hall," asked Chambers.

"Simple," replied Jackson. "Once the curtain was down, I just walked over to the right side of the stage, and out the side door."

"Okay, you went off for a drink," said Whittaker. "As you left, you would have gone past the small table."

"The table with the gun, you mean," suggested Jackson. "Oh yes, I saw it, nearly knocked it over. Clumsy of me I suppose. Rushing, too anxious to get to the Arms. Anyway the gun was still there, the fake gun."

"What time did you get back?" asked Chambers.

Jackson took a deep breath. "I don't know what time it was," he replied. "It was just as Catherine came off, after her argument with Donovan, and he was left sitting in the dark. Rose was still there getting ready for the changes for the last act. I could see Tim as he picked the gun up." He paused. "I could see a look of surprise on his face. I didn't know why. The clock started to chime, and he slowly walked to the centre of the stage." He stopped and took another deep breath. "Tim stopped next to the sleeping Colonel. He raised the gun, took aim, and …. I couldn't believe what I was seeing." He stammered, and tears began to fall down his face. "Tim had just shot Donovan. Right there, right in front of everyone. It was unreal. It wasn't supposed to happen. It was a play, nothing but fantasy. I never liked the guy, but Donovan had been shot, really shot I mean, not pretend."

"You knew he had really been shot?" said Whittaker.

"Oh yes I knew, as soon as I heard the gun fire, there was no mistake," Jackson explained. "I knew that it was a real gun, with real bullets. I had five years in the army. Spent time in Iraq. Once you've heard gunfire, there's no mistaking it." He paused once again. "I knew that Donovan was dead. But I couldn't believe that Tim had pulled the trigger, but he had, I saw it."

"Okay, Mr. Jackson, I think we'll leave it right there," said Whittaker. "You have been very helpful."

Jackson looked at Whittaker. "Why would Tim do that?" he asked as he stood up, and slowly walked to the door.

* * *

Chapter Nineteen
Peter Gammons

"Well I don't know about you, Derek, but as far as I'm concerned Mr. Jackson is not our murderer," Whittaker announced. "I'm convinced of that. One down, and ten more to go."

"I agree with you, sir," said Chambers. "Mr. Jackson is definitely innocent, but who the guilty person is, still remains a mystery."

"Oh don't worry about that, Derek. He, or she, will slip up one day, never fear," said Whittaker. Although he said it, he was far more hopeful than convinced. "Right, do we have anyone else to interview?" he asked.

"Yes sir, I'm afraid so," replied Chambers. "There's one more to come. Peter Gammons, he's a stage technician, in charge of the lighting."

One more, murmured Whittaker. *Just one!* He looked at his watch. "It's now almost one o'clock," he said. "Let's have some lunch, and we'll see Mr. Gammons afterwards. Tell Harry to have him here at …. Two thirty. No need to rush our lunch is there."

* * *

The Queens Head was quite busy by the time Whittaker and Chambers arrived. Ray, the barman saw them as they entered, and glanced around looking for some empty seats. He noticed some people, in the far corner, gathering their belongings. Clearly they were preparing to leave.

"Over there, Inspector," he called out, and pointed to a table just being vacated.

Whittaker waved an acknowledgement, and instructed Chambers to grab the table. "And I'll get the order," he said.

"Right, sir," replied Chambers, who then hurried over to the indicated table.

"Good afternoon, Inspector," said Ray, as Whittaker approached the bar.

"Hello Ray," said Whittaker looking around. "Busy today, I see."

"It's the weather," Ray replied. "Not raining you see. A couple of coaches came through, probably on their way to Brighton, but fortunately for us, they stopped here." He paused and started to wipe down the counter. "Now what can I get for you?"

"I've been told that you do an excellent Ploughman's," said Whittaker. "If that is correct, I shall need to take two of them into custody for further investigation. I shall also require a scotch and American, make it a double, for Detective Chambers, and a pint of best for me."

"I'll bring it right over to you, Inspector," replied Ray.

Whittaker thanked him, and made his way over to where Chambers was waiting.

"What did you think about Jackson's comment about Ashton?" Whittaker asked, as he sat down.

Chambers wasn't sure what he thought. "Well I don't really know," he replied. "So he was having an argument with someone about something. It's all a bit too vague for my liking."

"Well, don't forget, we now have two people saying the same thing," said Whittaker. "They both say that they heard Ashton arguing with a woman. So there must be some truth in it."

"Agreed, but it's still vague," said Chambers. "We still don't know who the argument was with, or what it was about. It could mean nothing at all."

156

"Yes, you're right, it might be of no importance," agreed Whittaker. "But why deny it happened. Why not just say, oh yes I had an argument with XYZ about whatever it was. It was nothing, of no importance. End of story."

That was a good point, thought Chambers. Or was it? "Would it really have been the end of the story?" he asked. "I mean we are in the middle of a murder investigation. Everything, and anything, might be significant. You said so yourself. Even this alleged argument. We wouldn't just accept his word that it was nothing, would we? There would be no end of questions. Who was the woman? What was the argument about? Maybe he just didn't think it was important enough. Maybe he just didn't want to face a whole string of questions for no real reason."

"Maybe so," replied Whittaker. "You might have a valid point. Let's say that I agree with you for the sake of further discussion. Even so our Mr. Ashton is fully aware that we have a murder to solve, and in order to assist us I still say that he should have owned up. He should have admitted there was an argument and put up with the questioning. Get it over and done with. If he had nothing to hide why be secretive? Why did he deny that it happened? We have two witnesses that say different."

Chambers was about to respond when Ray arrived with their order.

"Here we are," announced Ray, placing a tray on to the table. "Enjoy your meal."

"Thank you, Ray," said Chambers. "It looks good."

"Oh Ray," Whittaker called out. "Can you spare a couple of minutes?"

Ray heaved a sigh, and looked around at the crowded bar. "Well, I ...."

"Just a couple of questions," said Whittaker. "Five minutes."

Ray sighed once again. "Alright, go on then," he replied as he sat down.

"Thank you, Ray," said Whittaker. "I want to ask about the day of the murder. The theatre group came down here, for a bite to eat."

"That's correct," replied Ray. "About twenty to six, I remember. Before they arrived the bar was dead, I was more than happy to see them I can tell you. What about it."

"How were they?" asked Whittaker. "I mean did anyone act oddly, or say anything out of the ordinary?"

Ray started to laugh. "Inspector, what can I tell you? They were actors. Everything they did looked odd. Everything they said was odd."

Whittaker smiled. "I understand. A silly question."

"There was one thing though," Ray continued. "You know they are a very talkative lot. Always got something to say, and not shy about saying it. Laughing and having a great time, But one of them, Ashton I think his name is. Well he didn't seem to have much to say, not like the others."

"Interesting," replied Whittaker. "Anything else?"

"Not that I can think of," Ray replied. "They spent a fair amount, and I was quite happy I can tell you. Normally at that time of day it would be a bit quiet." He stood up, and looked around. "I better get back, Inspector, but if you need anything else, well you know where I am."

"Thank you, Ray," said Whittaker. "You've been very helpful." He watched as Ray walked back to the bar. Then he turned to Chambers. "Well now, what did you think of that?" he asked.

Chambers was still not convinced that it meant anything significant. "Perhaps he was just feeling nervous," he suggested.

"Derek, let's say you're right, he's just feeling nervous. Okay, but how do you think you would feel in a similar situation?" Whittaker continued. "Think about it. Just imagine, you are sitting there surrounded by six or seven of your colleagues. They are all laughing and joking, and having a good time. But you aren't having a good time. Why not?"

"Perhaps he was worried about something," Chambers suggested. "After all it was his play they were performing. He didn't want anything to go wrong."

"Right let's say I agree, he's worried about his play," Whittaker agreed. "But he just sits there, just thinking. Not saying a word. Wouldn't you discuss the problem with your colleagues?"

"Maybe I would," agreed Chambers. "But maybe he was just too worried, he didn't like to talk about it. Maybe he was too nervous."

"Oh, Derek, I'm willing to bet that Ashton was certainly nervous," replied Whittaker. "No question about it. But I'm willing to bet that it had nothing to do with his play."

Chambers was puzzled. "Well what then?"

"Let's just say I have a hunch about our Mr. Ashton. I just have to prove it. He has certainly lied to us, hasn't he? Does he have something to hide I wonder?"

"I agree he lied," said Chambers. "But that doesn't necessarily mean anything, does it? And don't forget that there's at least two others that haven't been entirely honest and straight forward with us."

"Well that's certainly true. You know you could be right, and I could be totally wrong," Whittaker admitted, taking a bite of the French bread. "But Ashton interests me. There's a lot of things beginning to build up, and I'll keep on digging for information, and who knows what we'll find." He paused and took another bite of the French bread. "Derek, get on to Records, see if they've come up with anything yet. Who knows, perhaps Ashton might be mentioned in there somewhere."

"It's early days, sir," said Chambers.

"I know it is," agreed Whittaker. "But it won't do any harm to chase them up will it? Keep them on their toes. Can't have them idle can we?"

Chambers wasn't entirely sure about the possible harm or otherwise. "Right sir, when we get back I'll give them a call."

"This is good," said Whittaker, taking another bite of French bread. "I must tell her ladyship about this."

Chambers smiled. "You mean the Commissioner, sir?"

"Yes, of course I mean the Commissioner," replied Whittaker. "Who else would I call her ladyship?"

"Mrs. Whittaker, perhaps," suggested Chambers.

Whittaker started to laugh. "Good point Derek, good point."

* * *

The two men arrived back at the hall a few minutes before two thirty. Constable Cutler and Peter Gammons were already waiting.

"Do go in, gentlemen," said Whittaker, opening the office door, and allowing the visitors to enter. "Derek, you go and make that call will you?"

Chambers nodded and walked away.

Whittaker turned his attention to his visitor. "Please sit down." He said pointing to the chair. "It's Mr. Gammons, right? And I understand that you deal with the stage lighting. Is that correct?"

"That's right," said Gammons. "I also deal with all of the electrical problem here at the hall."

"So, let me be clear you work for the Village Hall, not the theatrical group?" Whittaker continued.

"Right again," replied Gammons. "Worked for them for six, no seven years now."

160

"Does that mean that you never had much to do with the actors, then?" said Whittaker.

"Not too much," Gammons replied. "Except for that Miss. Cooper. She gave me a list of what was needed, and we worked together."

"Tell me what you did that night?" asked Whittaker. "The opening."

Gammons took a deep breath. "It wasn't too difficult, you know. Pretty easy in fact. The first act is all during the day right, and the lighting had to give the appearance of daylight," he started to explain. "But that all changes for act two. Then it gets a bit more complicated."

"In what way?" Whittaker asked, wondering whether there was anything to be gained.

"Act two is set during the evening," Gammons continued. "And the lighting changes as the act continues. Consequently, for most of the act I'm over on the left hand side where the lighting panel is located."

"Understood," replied Whittaker. "I don't suppose you would have noticed the gun, the prop, over on the right hand side."

"The gun," Gammons repeated. "Oh yes I saw it. Just before act two started I went over to the right hand side to make a change to the lighting. You see in Act one, we have sunlight coming through the windows, but in the second act it's the evening, and the curtains are closed, and no lighting was needed." He paused for a moment, pleased with his explanation. "The gun was there alright."

"You're sure of that," said Chambers. "The gun was in position just before act two started?"

"Yes I'm sure," Gammons confirmed.

"That means that the prop gun was in position at eight thirty, or a few minutes afterwards," said Whittaker.

"That's right," agreed Gammons. "Nearer twenty to nine I'd say."

"That's very helpful Mr. Gammons," said Chambers.

"Yes indeed," said Whittaker. "So was that your total involvement with the group?"

"That's right," agreed Gammons. "Well, except for that Mr. Donovan."

"Oh, what about Mr. Donovan?" asked Whittaker.

"A right busy body he was," Gammons started to explain. "Always interfering, and changing things. He didn't like the way Miss. Cooper had it set up. The lighting was all wrong, according to him. A right know it all." He paused and shook his head. "You know I can't believe he's actually dead. Murdered like that, in front of everyone. I don't like talking bad about the dead, but he was so, well just there. You know what I mean. In your face. He had a loud voice, good for acting I guess, but he could sound quite threatening sometimes."

"You obviously didn't like him," suggested Constable Cutler.

Gammons sighed. "I never gave him much thought one way or the other. Clearly he wasn't the easiest of people to like though. You couldn't get too close to him, if you know what I mean. He considered himself pretty superior, better than everyone else."

"I don't suppose he actually had many friends," suggested Whittaker.

"I don't know if he had friends or not," Gammons replied. "But I definitely get the impression that the rest of the group weren't too fond of him." He paused for a moment, hesitant. "Probably shouldn't be saying this, and it probably doesn't mean anything anyway. But a couple of days ago, there was quite an argument going on between Mr. Donovan, and one of the actors, Mr. Ashton. I think that's his name."

"Where was this?" asked Whittaker, sitting forward.

"I live down Church Lane, number four, one of them old workmen's cottages you know," Gammons started to explain. "Artisan cottages they calls them. Anyway, I was making my way back from the village, and I'm going past The Queens Head, when I heard loud voices coming from the car park. I looked round the corner, and there's that Donovan, and the other gentlemen, and they're really having a go at each other."

"Do you know what the argument was about?" asked Whittaker.

"I couldn't make everything out, I'm afraid," Gammons replied. "It was too loud and too fast you see. Something about a letter I think. The other man, Ashton, wanted it back I think, or maybe it was a letter that he had received. I'm not sure."

Why would he and Donovan argue about a letter? Whittaker wondered. "Do you know what the letter was about?" he asked.

"I'm sorry, but I've no idea," replied Gammons. "But the discussion got quite heated I can tell you. Then Mr. Donovan suddenly appeared. He looked quite angry, and he just brushed past me. Almost knocked me to the ground."

"Interesting," murmured Whittaker. He looked at Gammons. "And what about Mr. Ashton? Did he see you?"

"Oh no, I don't think so," Gammons replied. "I last saw him walking towards the hall."

"Thank you Mr. Gammons, you have been very helpful," Whittaker said. "I don't need to delay you any longer, you're free to go."

Gammons looked at Cutler, and then back at Whittaker. He stood up, and then walked towards the door.

* * *

Chapter Twenty
Time For A Review

Chambers returned just as Mr. Gammons was leaving.

"Did you get anything from Records yet?" asked Whittaker, trying not to sound too impatient.

"Yes sir, but it's still vague, and not very helpful, I'm afraid," replied Chambers, as he sat down.

"Go on," coaxed a weary sounding Whittaker. "Let's have what you've got."

"Well, firstly we have a complete list of names. Every name mentioned in Donovan's files, and every name mentioned in the press cuttings," Chambers began. He paused and started to read his notes. "There are twenty four mentioned in Donovan's files. Six of them went on to bigger and better crimes, and they also appear in the newspaper cuttings." He paused once again, and scanned his notes. "Three of them were actually convicted and have done time for their offences. Regarding the other three the cases were dismissed through lack of evidence."

"Are any of our suspects included?" asked Whittaker, hopefully.

Chambers shook his head. "Afraid not, sir," he replied. "The three names don't match at all, sorry."

Whittaker was disappointed, but at the same time he didn't really expect it to be that easy. "So there's no mention of Steve Ashton then. Pity, I had high hopes."

"No one said that it would be easy," said Chambers.

"No, they didn't, you are absolutely right there, and no mistake," Whittaker replied. "Though, I had hoped that it wouldn't be quite so difficult."

"Remember what we said about maybe names had been changed," Chambers continued. "Anyway, I've asked Records to send on photographs if possible."

"Good. The sooner the better," said Whittaker, brightening up a little. "Hopefully that might show some result. We shall see."

"Should have them soon, I hope," said Chambers.

"Right, that's that then," said Whittaker. "Well we've seen all of the people on Miss. Cooper's list. All eleven possible suspects. I think now is as good a time as any for a review." He looked at the two other men. "Let's see what we have shall we?"

"Well, it seems to me that the only definite fact we do have, is that Donovan was not flavor of the month," suggested Chambers. "It seems that the majority hated him, some more than others."

"But the question is why?" asked Cutler. "Yes, I know what they said. He was a bully. He thought a lot of himself, and considered himself better than the lot of them. He was rude, aggressive. I know all of that, but really is that enough reason for such dislike."

"Dislike, did you say?" said Chambers. "This wasn't simple dislike, in some case this was pure hatred."

"Well, whatever it was, whatever you call it, the point surely is whether it was enough to justify killing him," said Whittaker. He didn't think it was. *No way,* he thought. *There must have been another reason, something else. But what?* "Derek, why do people kill other people?" he asked.

Chambers thought for a moment, wondering if this was a trick question. "Well, there's no end of reasons, sir," he replied. "Money. That's always an excellent reason for murder." He paused. "Then there's revenge, and jealousy." He paused once again. "Then, of course there's always the possibility that it was an accident, or even self-defense. And it should also be remembered that some people are naturally evil, they kill for the sake of it."

"True enough," said Whittaker. "You know our suspects aren't the greatest of people, but I don't really think any of them are especially evil, do you? I mean evil enough to kill for no reason." He didn't wait for an answer. "No there's something else. Something we've missed."

"Then, of course, there's always Blackmail," suggested Chambers. "That's what I thought all along."

"Yes you did," said Whittaker. "And I have to say that blackmail has always been an excellent reason for bumping someone off."

"Well it's certainly a possibility," agreed Cutler.

"I'm convinced that Donovan was blackmailing someone," Chambers continued. "But that still raises the questions of who was being blackmailed, and why?"

"What about John Berry?" suggested Cutler. "Maybe he was the one Donovan had the appointment with. Remember he never went to the Queens Head with the others. He went to get a sandwich at Martha's, and then he went down to the river. He said that he saw no one, I have to say that I think his alibi is pretty feeble."

It was a possibility, Whittaker had to admit. Another one of many possibilities, but nothing to prove it one way or the other.

"He would have had a great opportunity to switch the gun, as well," Chambers suggested. "Don't forget he walked off the stage the wrong way, right over to where the gun was waiting. He could easily have switched the gun, and then taken the fake pistol with him down to the river, and disposed of it."

"Well it's certainly a possibility," Whittaker agreed. "The timing would have been perfect as well, just about ten minutes or so before Tim picked it up, and shot Donovan."

"Too late for anyone to query the switch," said Cutler. "Makes sense to me."

"We just need some proof," said Chambers, sounding despondent. "As usual two steps forward, and three back."

"I think the answer to our problem lies within those files, and press cuttings we found in Donovan's flat," said Whittaker. "I'm convinced of that. If only we can find some link back to Bishop, or Ashton."

"I agree, and I hope that Records comes up with something, soon," said Chambers. He heaved a sigh, and stifled a yawn. He looked at Whittaker. "How was Mr. Gammons?"

"Well, I have to say that he was very interesting, to say the least," Whittaker replied.

* * *

Ten minutes later Whittaker had told Chambers everything that Gammons had said. "Well, what do you think?" he asked. "Changed your opinion about Ashton, maybe?"

Chambers thought for a few moments. "Maybe," he replied. "I'll go so far to say that if, and I did say if, if Mr. Gammons is telling the truth, then there's a possibility that Ashton is our murderer."

"You do, do you? You think it could be a possibility, then?" said Whittaker trying not to sound too smug, but not succeeding.

"Well, arguing with Donovan does sound like a possible motive, I grant you," Chambers replied. "Are at least it might be connected to a possible motive."

"Good enough," said Whittaker. "But, I suppose that there is always the remote possibility that Gammons could be lying, or maybe mistaken."

Chambers smiled. "But I don't believe you go along with that possibility, do you sir?" he said.

"No, you're correct. I don't," replied Whittaker. "The question of course is why didn't Ashton mention it?" He paused and flipped through his notes. He found the entry he was searching for, and quickly scanned the item. "He never said a word."

"And what about the letter?" asked Cutler. "Where is it now?"

"Good question," said Whittaker. "As far as I'm aware there's been no sign of a letter. No sign in Donovan's flat at any rate."

"Perhaps Steve Ashton already has it," suggested Chambers.

"Perhaps so," agreed Whittaker, sounding unconvinced. "Or perhaps it has already been destroyed."

"Or maybe it's locked away in a safety deposit box somewhere," suggested Chambers.

"Maybe," said Whittaker. "But we still don't know what the letter was about, or whether it was to Ashton, or was it from Ashton to Donovan?"

"Or maybe it was a letter to, or from, a third party," suggested Chambers.

"I think we need another word with him," said Cutler.

"We definitely need to speak with him," agreed Whittaker. "But I'm becoming more and more convinced that he is our man."

"We still lack the proof, though," Chambers said.

"Agreed," said Whittaker.

"What about John Berry?" asked Chambers.

Whittaker sighed. "Well, in theory he could have been the person we're looking for. His story certainly lacked proof of any kind, and his alibi was weak," he said. "But remember it was confirmed by Rose Fuller. She was actually standing on the right side of the stage, when he came off. Okay it wasn't the correct exit for him, but she did confirm his story about going for a cigarette." He paused. "I'm inclined to believe him. You know it's strange. Smoking is supposed to be bad for you, but in this case, I think it might just have saved Berry from a charge of murder."

"I had thought we were on to something," said Cutler. "But he could be telling the truth. I'm guessing I know, but I'm willing to bet that if we did a bit of checking around, we might actually find some eye witnesses going to the local chippie, who would have seen him."

"Alright, I'll go along with that. He's in the clear," Whittaker agreed. "What about Clive Masters?"

"Well he was certainly being secretive, there's no doubt about that," said Chambers. "The question is did he deliberately lie, or had he genuinely forgotten. When I get a chance I'll have another word with him."

Whittaker. "Okay, keep me informed," he replied. "But either way I don't really think it's significant. Donovan was universally hated, end of story. But I really don't believe that was the motive for murder."

"Neither do I," Cutler agreed.

"Nor me," said Chambers, making it unanimous.

"So that's possibly two more suspects off the hook," Whittaker announced. "Making a total of three, but we still have eight possibles." He sighed. "Still a long way to go."

Despite what he had just said, Chambers was not entirely convinced about Clive Masters being in the clear. There was still a nagging doubt. A need to clarify something once and for all. "For the time being I think we still have eight suspects," he announced. "I still want to check on Mr. Masters."

* * *

Chapter Twenty-One
The Death of Lord Henry

To say that Whittaker was pleased with the progress made, would be something of an overstatement, but it was, at least, encouraging. If their conclusions had been correct, there were now eight suspects remaining. They were heading in the right direction. There was still a long way to go, and as Chambers had said they needed to speak with Clive Masters once again.

Whittaker looked at his two colleagues. He then looked at his watch. "Just gone three o'clock," he announced. "A nice cuppa would go down a treat I think, and a slice of Dundee cake to round it off. What say you gentlemen?"

"Sounds like a good idea to me, sir," said Chambers.

"I'm with you, sir," said Cutler. "And I know the very place where we can get some. Martha's Tea Rooms. Best tea for miles around, and a selection of cakes to satisfy anyone's taste. How about it? It's time for a break."

"Can't wait," said Chambers.

"Well then," said Whittaker. "Let's go."

* * *

Located in a sixteenth century building, close to the Parish Church, Martha's Tea Rooms had been established almost forty years ago. With its old world charm, and excellent service, it had soon become a firm favourite with the local population, and visitors alike. Sadly Martha herself had passed away some years ago. The business was now owned by her grand-daughter, Emma.

It was Emma who saw the three men as they entered. She looked up, smiled and walked over. After introductions, she escorted them to a table in the far corner. "I hope that you'll be comfortable here," she said. "I'll send Anne over to take your order."

A few minutes later the order had been taken, and Anne, the waitress, had just brought over a pot of tea, and three thick slices of Dundee cake.

"I could get used to this," said Whittaker, taking a bite of the cake. He looked around. "Yes I could certainly get used to this. You know we could do with one of these in the Fulham High Street."

"I shouldn't mention it to the Commissioner, though," suggested Chambers. "Wouldn't want to make her jealous would we?"

"Perhaps not," said Whittaker brushing some crumbs into his hand, and placing them into his mouth. "Waste not, want not, that's what I always say," he murmured. "This is great tasting …."

"Good afternoon gentlemen," a voice suddenly called out.

Chambers looked up. It was Clive Masters

"Mind if I join you?" Masters continued. "Or are you busy? I was just passing, when I saw you through the window." He pointed over to the entrance. "Thought I'd stop by and say hello. See how the old investigation was going."

Whittaker looked up. "I'm very pleased to see you Mr. Masters, anytime," he said. "In fact, this is quite a co-incidence. We were just talking about you, a short while ago."

"Something nice I hope," said Masters.

"Well it wasn't too bad, shall we say," Chambers replied. "Please sit down. Strangely enough we wanted a word with you."

Masters sat down. "Always happy to help where I can," he said. "If I can help somebody as I pass along, then my living shall not …. Well you know the rest."

"Be in vain," Chambers completed the saying. "How about a coffee?"

"Very nice of you," replied Masters. "A coffee would be very welcome, black, no sugar."

"You should try the cake," advised Whittaker, taking another bite.

Masters shook his head. "Coffee's just fine, thank you. I'm watching the old waist line you see. At least that's the general idea, although the odd Gin and Tonic doesn't help."

Chambers looked over at the waitress. Upon catching her eye, he repeated the order. "And some more of the excellent Dundee cake, if you please."

"So, gentlemen, what can I do for you?" asked Masters.

Whittaker reached for his notepad. He opened it, and flicked through until he reached the page he wanted. "Just a bit of clarification you might say," he started to explain. "It was just something you said at our previous meeting."

"Oh what was that?" asked Masters looking puzzled.

"You said that you hadn't known Donovan before now," said Chambers.

"That's right," agreed Masters. "I first ran into him in Larkhall Manor. That's when I had the privilege of meeting the great man."

"So you said," agreed Chambers. "The only thing is I have information that says different."

Masters was about to answer when Anne arrived with his coffee, and the extra cake. She placed the drink on to the table, turned and walked away. Masters took a drink. "Now what was it? Oh yes I remember." He took another drink. "I really can't think of anything." Then he suddenly struck his forehead with the palm of his hand. "Oh no, you're not thinking of that dreadful play, that Lord something or other snuffs it thingy, are you?"

"Death of Lord Henry," said Chambers. "That's the one."

Masters smiled. "That's right, Death of Lord Henry. Well it was certainly the death of something I can tell you. I certainly lost the will to live." He took a drink of coffee. "Best forgotten old man. A complete disaster of the very worst kind. I can't bear to think about it, even now. No wonder I forgot about it." He took another drink. "By comparison Murder at Larkhall Manor was a triumph, a masterpiece."

"That bad, eh," said Whittaker.

"Where was that now?" Masters wondered. "Just let me think, for a moment. Ah, I remember now, it was a small hall in West somewhere or other. West …. West. No it wasn't, it was Skye Green, that's the one. What a place. Capacity audience, if I remember correctly. A sell-out, all twenty-five or twenty-six paying guests. They loved it, at least the ones who stayed awake loved it."

"I understand that it was a slightly bigger venue that you seem to suggest," said Chambers. "It was more like a hundred seats or even more."

"Yes, you're right," said Masters. "A hundred and fifty-six altogether. It just seemed like twenty-five, judging by their response, or lack of it. Mind you I can't blame them. I would have walked out myself, if I hadn't actually been in the play. It was hardly the pinnacle of my success you understand. Not exactly something to be proud of."

"Possibly, but you did meet up with Donovan didn't you?" asked Whittaker.

"Yes, you are absolutely correct," Masters replied. "I must have done something really bad in my youth, but I did have the misfortune to meet up with Donovan." He paused and took another drink. "What was it? Three years ago I think."

"It was two," Chambers corrected.

"Two," repeated Masters. "How time flies. Two years ago, and completely of no interest, or significance. Sorry about the mistake, but I assure you that it's easily done, and quite unintentional."

"Maybe," said Whittaker. "Oddly enough, once again Donovan had a major part, Lord Henry himself, and you had a smaller role, just like in Larkhall Manor."

"Yes, that's absolutely true. And once again he winds up dead," said Masters. "Perhaps dead drunk would be more appropriate. He did like his drop of drink, did our Mr. Donovan. His little tipple, as he would say."

"Even so, it must have annoyed you," said Chambers. "I mean once again playing a lesser role to him like that."

Masters shrugged. "The doctor you mean?" He paused for a moment. "Oh yes, that's right. Once again I was the doctor. What was it I said? Oh yes. He's dead I'm afraid, poisoned. About the middle of Act two if I remember." He started to laugh. "Many people said it was the finest part of the play, although they considered that it should have happened much earlier." He paused for a moment, smiling. "Like the beginning of Act one. That way we could have all been put out of our misery much sooner. They don't write things like that anymore, not these days. Thank goodness. Mind you, Larkhall comes a close second." He shook his head. "Of course it annoyed me, alright, but not in the way you think. I didn't mind playing a lesser part, but what did annoy me is that he was so bad at acting. Why did he always get these parts I wondered? Perhaps he had actually paid the director?"

"Perhaps," Whittaker replied. He took a drink of tea. "Were there any other meetings?" he asked.

"No I really believe that I can safely say that there were no other meetings, thankfully," Masters replied. He finished his coffee and stood up. "So if there's nothing else, I must be away. There's a G and T awaiting me at the Queens you understand. I can't keep my public waiting." He waved, turned and walked to the door.

Whittaker smiled as he watched him leave. "He's not our murderer," he said looking at Chambers and Cutler.

"Agreed," said Chambers. "Three down and eight to go. Still a long way to go, though."

Whittaker continued to look towards the exit. "There goes another fisherman," he murmured.

"Did you say something, sir?" asked Chambers.

"He wanted to see how the investigation was going, but he never actually enquired, did he?" he replied. "I wonder why?"

"I guess he just got excited remembering all about his first meeting with James Donovan," suggested Cutler.

"Perfectly understandable, I would say," said Whittaker, taking another bite of the cake.

* * *

Chapter Twenty-Two
18 Block C, Devonport Close

Christine Stanton turned the key in the lock of her front door. She then slid a separate bolt into position, and finally she slid the security chain into place. Then she tried the door six times to make sure that it was secure. Living alone as she did, this was her nightly routine. Satisfied that the door was securely locked, she walked over to the lounge window. She casually glanced down to the street. It had started to rain. A few people hurried past looking for shelter. *Not a night to be out in,* she thought, thankful that she was safe and warm. She pulled the curtains together, and walked back into her kitchen.

* * *

Miss. Stanton never noticed the nine year old navy coloured Ford Mondeo as it slowly drove past. She never saw it as it pulled into a side street, and stopped at the corner opposite. She never saw the driver as he applied the handbrake, and switched off the engine. He lit a cigarette and checked his watch, it was ten minutes to eight o'clock. *Time to go,* he murmured, and got out of the car. He took a small piece of paper out of his pocket, and looked at it. *18 Block C,* he read. He looked across at Devonport Close. Up at the third floor, he saw the curtains being closed over. Clearly the occupant was settling in for the evening. He looked up at the sky. The rain was getting heavier, and showed no signs of stopping. He turned up his coat collar. He took a deep breath, dropped his cigarette to the ground, and crossed the street. He then walked to the entrance door of Block C.

The entrance lobby was small, and dimly lit. There was no one around. He noticed the sign indicating that the lift was out of order. He shrugged. He wasn't planning on using the lift anyway. Lifts had a habit of breaking down when you least expected it, and he had no desire to get stuck inside one. He had business to attend to, and did not want anything to delay him. He made his way over to the staircase, and started the walk up to the third floor.

* * *

Miss. Stanton picked up the little silver tray containing her cup of tea, and three digestive biscuits. She carried it back into the lounge, and carefully placed it on to the small table by the settee. She looked at the clock. It was just eight minutes to eight. She walked over to the television set and switched it on, then she sat down. There was a programme coming on at eight o'clock that she wanted to see. A documentary about West End theatres. It was the sixth part of a series that she had been following.

For many years she had been passionate about the theatre. On every wall there were framed posters. Over in the corner there was a small bureau. Inside there were stacks of theatre programmes. Her book case was full of books about the theatre, or about the stars themselves. And barring accident, or illness, she usually went to a West End production at least once every month.

"You can keep your old films," she would say. They were nothing compared with the theatre. No comparison at all. Theatre was real acting, and it didn't rely heavily on special effects, or computer generated images. Stage actors were real actors, not like those that performed in the films. Stage actors had to get it right first time, and they didn't need stunt doubles. There was no possibility of extra takes; and no chance of editing out mistakes. They had to speak correctly, and distinctly, so that the people at the back of the auditorium could hear just as well as those in the front row. There was none of the mumbling that seemed to be prominent in every film these days. And none of that ceaseless background music.

Mind you she was the first to admit that not everything on at the theatre was to her liking. She didn't like plays with a message, or with some dark undertones. She just liked to be entertained, plain and simple. Something just to be enjoyed without it needing to be analysed this way and that. A good story was paramount to her. Murder mysteries were her favourite. She thought of the play she had gone to a few days ago, an Amateur production, Murder at Larkhall Manor. She had to admit that it was not the greatest production she had ever been to. In fact it was quite poor but at least it was entertaining, and there was none of that bad language, which was all too common in the modern day cinema. That is to say that it had been entertaining, at least for the first two acts. But then the production had been brought to a sudden and abrupt end.

She shook her head, as she thought about it. Then she started to smile. Her friend was actually part of it. She couldn't believe it. She hadn't seen her friend for many years, and then there she was, up on that stage. *She wasn't that bad either*, Christine thought, as she remembered that back at school Angela used to hate the school plays. She used to call them stupid, a waste of time. But it was such a dramatic ending to the evening. It was all there, in the local newspaper, all of the incredible details. A murder had taken place, somebody had been shot dead, right there on the stage. It didn't bear thinking about. She could still see the young man holding the gun, and pulling the trigger. He was so young, no more than twenty five, or twenty-six, she guessed. Why would he do such a thing?

She shook her head once again, dismissing it from her mind. She looked at the clock once again. Another few minutes, she murmured. She stirred her tea, and settled back into her chair. The progamme was about to start.

There was a knock on her door. She looked up. She hadn't been expecting any visitors. There was a second knock, louder this time. She heaved a sigh, and stood up. The last thing she wanted was a visitor, not now. She just wanted to settle down, and see her programme. There was a third knock. Whoever it was, wasn't going to go away.

She walked to the door. She slid the bolt back, and unlocked the door, but she kept the security chain attached. Living alone like she did, she had been advised to be aware and take precautions especially late at night. She considered that to be good advice.

She opened the door as far as the chain would allow. Peering through the gap she could just make out the figure of a man. "Yes," she said, trying not to sound nervous. "What is it?"

"Miss Christine Stanton?" a voice asked. "We spoke the other day, do you remember?"

Christine looked at the man. She did not recognize him, although his voice was vaguely familiar. As usual the lighting on the landing was poor. She looked again, straining to see. "I'm Christine Stanton," she replied, instantly regretting that she had given her name to a complete stranger. "Who are you, and what do you want?"

"I've some good news for you," the voice continued. "Can I come in for a moment?"

Christine had heard disturbing stories of visitors late at night. "No I'm sorry, it's very late," she protested.

"Yes it is late, I know. I'm very sorry. I shan't keep you long," the voice continued. "I'm sure you will like what I have to say."

She looked back at the television screen. Her programme had just started. She heaved a sigh. She just wanted the man to go away. "Can you come back tomorrow?" she asked.

The man sighed. "I'll try, but it might not be possible," he replied. "But I'm here now, why not let me in. I'll be as quick as I can. By the way Angela sent me, and she said hello."

"Angela?" Christine repeated.

The man confirmed the name. "That's right, Angela Hull, your old school friend, and she's dying to see you. You know, to talk over old times," he continued. "She was disappointed that she couldn't see you the other night, but well, after what

179

happened, it wasn't really possible, was it. I'm sure you understand? Such a dreadful business. She was so upset."

Christine's eyes lit up. She couldn't believe it. He had been sent by her old friend, Angela Hull, and she wanted to meet with her, after all these years. She began to feel quite excited at the prospect. She quickly unhooked the security chain, and opened the door. "Please, come in," she said as she stood back and allowed the man to enter.

He walked into the room, and looked around. He turned to face Miss. Stanton. "This is nice," he said, smiling. "Very nice indeed, and you keep it looking good, so neat and tidy."

She looked down. "I try, she said. "It's not always easy."

He looked down at the wet footprints he had left on the carpet. "I'm sorry about that," he said, pointing. "It's raining quite hard out there."

She looked at the marks. She hoped that they would be easy to clean. "Oh don't worry about that," she replied. "They'll dry I expect."

"You know, your husband is a very lucky man," the man said. "I hope he realises just how fortunate he is." He walked over to the side board leaving more wet footprints on the carpet. He stopped and picked up a silver frame. "Is this him?" he asked.

Christine suddenly began to feel strangely uneasy at the mention of her husband. She took the frame from his hand. "No, he's dead. That's my brother, Gary," she replied abruptly, taking the photograph from him, and returning it to its place on the sideboard.

"Oh, I am sorry to hear that about your husband," the man said. "Angela will be upset when I tell her." He shook his head. "So you live here all alone then."

"It's been ten years, now," she replied. "I'm well used to it."

"Even so, you can't be too careful, that's what I say," the man continued. "You know I was pleased to see that you were very cautious just now."

She looked puzzled. "About letting me in I mean," he continued. "You hear of such dreadful things happening. People living alone are very vulnerable you know." He walked further into the room.

"I knew that it would be alright, the minute you mentioned Angela's name," Miss. Stanton replied. "I can't wait to see her again."

"You know Angela was so sure that it was you," the man continued. "She saw you from the stage you know. She recognized you straight away." He started to laugh. "She almost forgot her lines because of you. The surprise at seeing you, you know."

Miss. Stanton smiled. "It's been a long time since we've seen each other, I'm surprised she actually recognised me."

"It was your eyes, Angela said. You couldn't mistake them," the man replied. "How about you? Did you recognise her?"

Miss. Stanton was hesitant. "You know I thought it was her when I saw her photograph on that leaflet, you know the one about the play," she replied. "But I couldn't be sure, because I didn't recognise the name."

"I know the leaflet you mean," the man replied. "But you know what these actresses are like. Many take a stage name."

Miss. Stanton agreed. "But from the moment I saw her, up there on the stage, I knew her straight away" she replied proudly. "She hasn't changed a bit."

"Really," the man replied.

"Same hair, same smile," Miss Stanton replied. "Oh a bit older, but aren't we all?"

"It must have been exciting for you," the man continued. "When you actually saw her, on the stage. I suppose you mentioned it to all of your friends. What was their reaction?

"I never told anyone," Miss. Stanton replied. "I wanted to wait until I had actually met her again after so long. To speak with her, you know, about old times.

"You never mentioned it to anyone," the man replied, surprised. "I can't believe it. If it had been me, I would have been too excited. I would have told everyone."

"Oh no, I wasn't going to spoil it," Miss. Stanton explained. "I wanted to meet with her, and then tell everyone."

"What about the play?" the man asked. "You must have told people about the play."

"No I never did," Miss. Stanton replied. "And then to hear that there had been a murder, that night, on the stage. I couldn't believe it."

"I guess not," said the man. "Dreadful, simply dreadful."

"Tell me how is Angela?" Miss. Stanton asked. "Did she ever become a teacher? She always wanted to be a teacher."

"Oh yes, she became a teacher," the man replied. "But she gave it up, and got a job with a bank. Didn't you know about that?"

"No, I never knew," Miss. Stanton admitted. "I'm surprised though, she hated arithmetic. She just wasn't good at figures."

"You just don't know what's going to happen do you?" the man replied. He looked at the television screen. "Ah, I see that you are watching that series about the theatre. It's an excellent series."

"Yes it is," she agreed.

He turned away from the television, and started to walk around the room. He suddenly stopped and looked back at Miss. Stanton. "Do you have any photographs of Angela?" he asked.

"Only two or three when we were at school," she replied. "Nothing since."

"Oh, that's a shame," he said. "I was hoping you might have had some of her as a teenager, or maybe in her twenties. Or maybe you have some letters."

"Sorry, I don't have anything like that," Christine replied. "I never knew her then."

"So you have nothing to remember her by," the man said. "No little keepsake, nothing?"

"No, nothing," she repeated. "We said that we'd keep in touch, but well we just drifted apart, you see. She moved away, I don't know where, London I think."

Then she remembered the flyer. She went over to the sideboard, and opened the top drawer. She took out a single sheet of paper. "All I've got is this." She was about to show it to the man but he had turned away and had resumed walking around the room picking up a photograph, or a figurine, and dropping them on to the floor.

"That happens. People move on," said the man, as he dropped another frame on to the floor, the glass breaking into several pieces. "You're sure that there's nothing to show that you ever knew her?"

Christine was becoming more and more nervous. "You said Angela would like to meet with me," she said. "I'd love to see her again. So when did she say?"

"Your tea is going cold," the man said, ignoring her comment. "You should drink it, seems a pity to waste it."

"When will I see Angela?" she asked.

The man looked at her. "Drink your tea," he said.

"But when will I see her?" she asked once again.

"Your tea," the man replied. "Drink it."

Christine was beginning to get quite frightened. The man was now sounding quite menacing. She wanted him to leave. She wanted to get away from him. She walked towards the door. The man followed. He raised his hand. He was holding a small metal bar. He raised his arm high, then brought it swiftly down, striking her on the back of the head. A deep gash opened up, and blood began to seep from the wound. She fell to the floor. She was dead before she hit the floor. She was still clutching the flyer.

The man looked at the lifeless body for a few moments. Then he bent down to check for any sign of life. There wasn't any.

He looked around, and went over to the sideboard. He opened the sideboard drawer, took it out and threw the contents on to the floor. He then opened the side board, and pulled the contents out, allowing them to fall. Then he went over to the book shelf and knocked the books to the floor.

He looked around once more. Scattered around were the contents of drawers, shattered china ornaments strewn around, books, and papers of every description. There was one last thing to do. He went into the bedroom, and started to search her wardrobe. It didn't take long to find what he was looking for. A small black and gold box holding her meagre collection of jewelry. He took out a couple of reasonable pieces, and put them into his pocket. He threw the remainder on to the floor. He was satisfied. It would be assumed that there had been a break in, some jewelry had been taken. She had put up a struggle, and died in the attempt.

He started to smile, as he walked to the door. He let himself out, closing the door behind him. He walked along the corridor until he reached the staircase. As he started to go down the stairs he heard the sound of a door closing. He stopped for a moment, listening. There was no further sound, and after a few minutes he continued down the stairs. Coming out of the building he turned to the right. A short distance further on, he crossed the street, and made his way to the far corner, where his car was parked.

He switched on the engine. He looked over at the building he had just left. There was a light on up at the third floor. Could he see someone looking out from the window? Looking in his direction? Looking at him?

* * *

Chapter Twenty-Three
Another Murder

"We can definitely rule out Clive Masters," said Chambers. "He's not our murderer."

"Told you so, didn't I?" said a smug Whittaker.

"Yes sir, you did," agreed Chambers. "But there was still a little uncertainty in my mind. No harm in doing a bit of checking was there? It just needed a little ….

He was interrupted by his mobile phone ringing. "Hello, Chambers speaking …."

* * *

Chambers continued to stare at his phone a few seconds after the call had finished.

"Well Derek, what was all that?" asked Whittaker.

"That was the Commissioner, sir," Chambers announced, returning his phone to his pocket.

Whittaker raised his eyes upwards. "Notice she never rang me."

Chambers shook his head, and smiled. "I suppose your phone is ready to use, sir," he asked. "I mean it is fully charged is it?"

"Probably is, I expect," the Inspector replied, sounding far from convinced. "What does she want I wonder? Crime solved, villain apprehended. Something like that I suppose. When will I be returning to deal with my other work which, no doubt is continuing to pile up."

"No sir, nothing like that," replied Chambers. "This is much worse."

"I'm listening," replied a weary Inspector. "What now?"

"There's been another murder, sir," said Chambers. "In Shadwell, a small town about twenty miles from here."

"And why should that interest me? Don't they have police in wherever you said?" asked a disgruntled Whittaker. "I suppose she wants me to investigate that one as well, does she? In my spare time maybe, or maybe I should be working at night as well as the day." He paused for a moment and took a deep breath. "Well, at least it's convenient. You tell her …."

"Well, yes she does, sir," Chambers interrupted. "The thing is there could be a connection."

Whittaker was intrigued. "Go on, let's hear it."

"Right sir," Chambers replied. "The victim is female, aged forty-five. Lived alone in a small flat. They found a flyer. A leaflet all about 'Murder At Larkhall Manor'. She was holding it when she was killed. A blow to the head according to the police doctor."

"Do we have a name?" asked Cutler

"Christine Stanton," said Chambers.

"Right," said Whittaker. "The name doesn't ring any bells. Your thoughts, gentlemen. What connection might there be between her death and the murder of James Donovan?"

Chambers thought for a moment. "Well, the obvious one is the play, Murder at Larkhall Manor," he replied. "The flyer."

Whittaker took a deep breath, and started to rub his chin. *So she had a flyer. So did dozens of other people. But dozens of other people hadn't been murdered.* "What do you think? About the flyer I mean?"

"Well it's possible that she was there, at the village hall, the night of the murder," Chambers suggested. "She might have seen something, or recognized someone."

"And that someone murdered her. Is that what you're saying?" said Whittaker.

"It's a possibility, sir," suggested Chambers "Apart from that perhaps it's just co-incidence."

"You never met that American did you?" Whittaker replied. "That private detective?"

"No sir, I didn't," replied Chambers. "I joined you shortly afterwards."

Whittaker sighed. "Well, you know, he had a theory all about co-incidence. Our Mr. Kendall disliked co-incidence. In his opinion co-incidence was really just a convenience. Something you could use when you didn't have an answer to some problem or other. He said that you should start by assuming that there was no co-incidence, but that there was a connection. Then, when you have the proof that there was, in fact, no connection, then, and only then, can you judge it to be a co-incidence."

"Sounds reasonable to me," said Cutler.

"And to me," added Chambers.

"Do we know when it happened?" asked Whittaker.

"According to the doctor it was between seven and eight, last night," replied Chambers.

"Do we have an address?" asked Whittaker.

"It's here, sir." Chambers handed him a piece of paper with the address written down. "18C Devonport Close, Shadwell."

"I know where that is, sir," said Cutler. "It's a block of flats, near the bus station."

"Right, I suggest we pay a visit to the ladies flat," said Whittaker, draining his cup, and taking the last piece of cake. He stood up, and looked at the empty plate. "Pity, another time perhaps." He started towards the door. The other two men followed close behind.

* * *

Devonport Close was the collective name for six identical three storey high blocks of flats. Number eighteen was located on the top floor of Block C. Two police cars were parked outside the main entrance. A young police officer was on guard duty at the double doors.

He looked up as Whittaker approached. "Can I help you, sir?" he asked politely.

"I'm Chief Inspector Whittaker, from Scotland Yard," he explained, showing his warrant card. "This is Detective Chambers, and that is Police Constable Cutler."

"Good afternoon, sir," the police officer said, saluting. "Constable Aldridge. We've been expecting you."

"Right Constable, what do we have?" Whittaker asked.

"Christine Stanton," replied the officer. "Aged forty-five. Divorced. Her ex-husband was a real bad one, by all accounts. Done time. GBH the last time, got ten years. Not a nice sort. The doctor says she died instantly. A blow to the back of the head, with a blunt instrument, a piece of metal tubing maybe. We haven't found the murder weapon yet."

"Any witnesses?" asked Chambers, already expecting what the answer would be.

"No one saw anything," the officer replied. "Except the lady next door, at number sixteen. Well she heard loud talking just after eight o'clock last night. Went on for a while, she said. Then the sound of breaking glass. All of a sudden all went quiet. Then there's a loud thud as the front door slammed shut. Then footsteps along the corridor, and down the stairs." He paused. "There's no lift you understand. Anyways she looked out and she saw the back of someone going down towards the stairs. She then looks out of her window, and saw the figure of a man walking down the street."

"Walking?" said Chambers. "He wasn't running?"

"No, apparently not, sir," said the Constable. "According to the lady at number sixteen, he seemed perfectly normal. Not panicking. In fact he stopped to cross the street."

"Any description?" asked Cutler, sounding hopeful.

"Oh yes, we have a description," said the Constable. "But it's very vague. Fortyish, medium height, dark hair. And that's it."

"It's certainly vague alright, but does it remind you of anyone?" Whittaker asked Chambers.

"Well it could apply to thousands of men I guess," Chambers replied. "But it could be our friend John Berry, it could also be Steve Ashton, or even Ian Jackson."

"Could be," agreed Whittaker. "Could even be our good friend Constable Cutler over there. Don't worry Constable, I'm just being facetious." He turned back to face Aldridge. "Not really helpful I'm afraid. We'll just have to wait and see."

"Was anything taken?" Chambers asked.

"Not that we know of, not yet at any rate," the Officer replied. "But whoever did it tried to make it look like a break in, but oddly enough there were some bits of jewelry laying on the floor. We don't think anything was taken, but it seems that he was looking for something. Whether he found it or not we don't know."

"Right, Constable, let's take a look inside shall we?" said Whittaker. "Can we go up?"

"Oh yes, forensics have finished their work. You can go up," replied Aldridge. "You'll find Constable Roberts at the flat. He's expecting you, and he'll let you in."

Whittaker thanked the officer. Then he, Chambers and Cutler, entered the building, and made their way up to the third floor, to number eighteen.

* * *

Police Constable Roberts saluted as Chief Inspector Whittaker approached. "Afternoon, sir," he said. He stepped forward to the door. He removed the remains of the crime scene tape, and unlocked it. He stepped aside to allow Whittaker to pass by. "It's all been checked, sir," he advised. "Fingerprints," he un-necessarily added.

"Did they find any?" Whittaker asked. "Fingerprints I mean."

"Oh yes, sir, but only the ladies, and the next door neighbour's," the Constable replied. "Though we did find a couple of footprints."

"What about them?" asked Whittaker, as he walked into the flat.

"They were right where we found the body," the Constable explained as he pointed to the taped outline of the body. "It had rained quite hard last evening you see. She must have fallen on them. A man's shoe, about size nine I'd say."

"Anything else?" asked Whittaker.

"Afraid not, sir," the Constable replied. "The print wasn't very clear, you can imagine."

Yes, Whittaker could well imagine. It was no more than he had expected. He nodded an acknowledgement, and walked further into the room, and stopped. He looked around. Scattered around were the contents of drawers, shattered china ornaments, books, and papers of every description. *Someone used to live here,* Whittaker thought. *Someone who liked their books, and porcelain figurines.* He picked up one of the books 'The History of the Theatre'. He began turning the pages. He abruptly closed the book and carefully placed it on to a small table, next to a saucer, and a small plate of biscuits.

"Someone was definitely looking for something," said Chambers as he walked up to Whittaker. But what it was is anyone's guess, and whether he found it is also a mystery."

"I wonder who the man was anyway," said Whittaker. He looked up. "Harry," he called out. "You better check with the local police to see if they have any leads that might be useful."

"Perhaps it was that real bad one the Constable mentioned," suggested Cutler. "Perhaps he killed her."

"I don't really think so," Whittaker said. "I mean why kill her now, he would have had many opportunities long before."

"And surely the neighbour would have recognized him," added Chambers.

Cutler had to admit that both points were valid.

Whittaker looked back at the debris lying on the floor. "But, let's not dismiss the idea completely," he said. "The ex-husband is a possible lead that should be followed up." He looked over at Cutler. "See if you can get a photograph. Maybe a name and a description at the very least. Have a word with the constable outside."

"Well, whoever it was, clearly Miss. Stanton knew the murderer," said Cutler.

"Not necessarily true," Whittaker said. "Perhaps he had a good story to tell, and she let him in. You know, saying something like I'm a friend of a friend. That would probably work."

That also made sense, Cutler thought. He glanced around, wondering what they were actually hoping to find. In the far corner he could see a number of photographs lying on the floor. He walked over, bent down and picked up several. "Sir, there's a whole bunch of photographs over here," he called out. "All torn as far as I can see."

"Do you see anyone we might know?" asked Whittaker.

There was silence for a few minutes. "Afraid not, sir," Cutler said. "I don't see any of our acting friends."

"I didn't really expect that it would be that easy," Whittaker replied. "But it was worth a try."

"Well, it could have paid off, sir," said Chambers encouragingly.

"You never know," said Whittaker. He glanced around once again. "See if there's anything there that could be the ex-husband," he continued. "Just gather up any pictures that you think might be useful. We could show them to the neighbour. Might produce a result."

"One thing's for sure," announced Chambers, standing over in the corner. "She clearly loved her theatre. Just take a look at all of this." He pointed to a stack of theatrical books, and programmes. "And look at this, the flyer she was holding. All about Murder at Larkhall Manor."

Whittaker looked at them. "Have you noticed anything?" he asked. "Those books, and programmes, they are all about West End theatres. Look, Phantom of the Opera, at Her Majesty's Theatre, Mama Mia at the Novello, and, what's this one, The Mousetrap at St. Martins."

"Is that still on, sir?" asked Chambers. "It must be sixty odd years."

"Well it seems to be," replied Whittaker. "Have you seen it?"

"Oh yes, sir, many years ago," replied Chambers. "And you, sir, have you seen it?"

Whittaker shook his head. "No, I'm not interested in these so called mysteries, they're all totally unrealistic."

"Oh, sir, it's just a bit of fun," said Chambers. "Shouldn't take things too seriously." He paused for a moment. "Who said that recently?"

"It was Steve Ashton," replied Whittaker. "Perhaps he's right, who knows." He shrugged, and continued to look through the pile of books and brochures. "You know I'm puzzled. With all of those programmes, why on earth would our Miss. Stanton be interested in this one?" He held up the flyer regarding Murder at Larkhall Manor. "What was it Miss. Cooper said? Oh yes, a second rate tin pot little group like the Wokingham Players. I don't get it. Another question is how did she know about it anyway?" Whittaker continued. "What roused her interest?"

"She probably saw something in the local paper, suggested Chambers.

"Okay let's say she saw something in the local paper," agreed Whittaker. "But why would she be interested in that particular play? Why would she be bothered about some amateur performance?"

"Well sir, it certainly wasn't because it was a great play, or great acting, that's for certain," replied Chambers.

"Absolutely right," said Whittaker. "So why?"

"Maybe she just wanted to support local for a change," suggested Cutler.

"She had seen everything that was on at the West End," suggested Chambers. "And looked elsewhere."

"Maybe," said Whittaker. "But I don't think so. Just look around. Do you see any other flyers, leaflets, or programmes, relating to local productions? Because I don't."

"She might not have kept them," said Cutler.

"Right, she might not have kept them," Whittaker repeated, unconvinced. "And yet she keeps the one for the Wokingham Players." He looked back at the flyer. "No, it's something else."

Chambers took hold of the flyer, and looked at it for a few moments. The photograph of every member of the cast was on display. "Maybe she knew someone in the production," he suggested. "She recognized someone there, one of the cast, but who?"

Whittaker started to smile. "I'd go along with that," he said. "But then why was she murdered?"

"You're sure the two murders are connected, then," said Cutler.

"Oh yes, there's a connection right enough, I'm convinced of that," replied Whittaker. "And if you want me to think differently you will have to convince me, three different ways, and even then be prepared for an argument. I'm sure that she saw someone or something on Saturday night. Or at least that's what our murderer thinks."

"You think she might have witnessed the murder," said Cutler.

"You mean did she see the gun switched?" said Whittaker, shaking his head. "I'm not sure about that, but I'm sure that she saw something. Something our murderer wanted kept quiet."

"There is one thing though," said Chambers. "We don't know that she was actually there do we? At the hall that night?"

"No that's right," agreed Whittaker. "We don't know. She might not have been, in which case my theory falls apart. But I'm willing to bet a pint of best that she was. Any takers?"

"You're on, sir, a pint it is," replied Chambers. "I'll check with Miss. Cooper, and see if Miss. Stanton was at the opening night."

Whittaker nodded, and looked around once again. "I think we're about done here," he said. "Let's have a word with that neighbour shall we?"

* * *

Chapter Twenty-Four
Mrs. Lily Johnson

"Right you are, sir," said Constable Roberts. "It's a Mrs. Lily Johnson." He walked to the door, and rang the bell. "By the way, the ex-husband's name, you wanted it."

"That's right, officer," admitted Whittaker.

"It was Michael, Michael Dunstan," the officer replied. "A bad sort by all accounts."

"Dunstan?" repeated Whittaker. "But I thought the victim's name was Stanton."

"That's correct, sir," replied the police constable. "I understand that after the divorce, she re-took her maiden name. She was so glad to be shot of him, she dumped the name as well."

"Makes sense," Whittaker replied. He thanked the police officer, and glanced at Chambers.

Constable Roberts rang the bell a second time. He put his ear to the door. "Ah, she's coming, sir," he announced, as he stepped back.

The door opened. Mrs. Lily Johnson looked at the police constable. "Oh you again, I've already told you all I can think of."

The Constable smiled. "Yes you have, and very helpful it's been," he replied. "Now, these gentlemen have come all the way from London," he started to explain. "Scotland Yard, they would like to ask you a few questions."

Mrs. Johnson was clearly not impressed. "It don't matter where they are from. Makes no difference to me, I've told you everything I can."

Whittaker stepped forward. "Mrs. Johnson, my name is Chief Inspector Whittaker, and I'm from Scotland Yard. And this is Detective Sergeant Chambers, and Police Constable Harry Cutler. I wonder if you could just spare me a few moments of your time."

Mrs. Johnson sighed. "As I just said, I've already told this officer everything I can think of."

"I'm sure that you have," agreed Whittaker. "And it is very much appreciated, and I'm sure that it has been a great help." He looked at Constable Roberts. "But I really would be very grateful if you could spare me some time. You never know I might actually ask different questions."

Mrs. Johnson knew when she was beaten. "You better come in then," she said, stepping to one side, and allowing the police officers to enter. "Excuse the mess, I haven't cleaned up yet."

Whittaker watched her as she started to tidy up. "Please, please, don't worry about that," he said holding his hand out. "All I want is to ask a few questions."

"You better sit down, then," she said pointing to the settee.

The three police officers sat down. Whittaker looked around. "This is a nice flat," he said. "Have you been here long?"

"Ten years," she replied, as she looked around. "I moved in here just after my husband Albert died. The house was too big you see, and full of memories."

"I can understand that," Whittaker replied. He stood up and started to walk around the room. He noticed a photograph on the sideboard. "May I?" he asked as he reached for it.

"That's my Albert," she replied. "That was taken a couple of years before he died."

"Had you been married long?" Whittaker asked as he replaced the photograph.

"Thirty five years," she replied.

"That's er …. Pearl isn't it?" said Whittaker.

Mrs. Johnson smiled, and shook her head. "That's thirty years," she corrected. "Thirty five is Coral."

"Right you are," said Whittaker returning to his seat. "I never get that right. Except for Ruby, of course. That's forty years, I know that one. The wife and I celebrated that just a few months ago."

"We just made the thirty five," Mrs. Johnson replied as she continued to stare at the photograph. "Six weeks later he died. His heart it was. Smoking, what can I say? I tried to stop him, and to be fair he tried to quit, but it wasn't to be."

"I'm very sorry, Mrs. Johnson," said Whittaker. He took a deep breath. "About Miss. Stanton, had you known her long?" he asked.

Mrs. Johnson turned around to face the Inspector. "Oh yes. I've known her ever since I moved in, she's a good friend." She paused, as she realised what she had said. A tear rolled down her cheek. "I should say, she was a good friend."

"What can you tell me about her?" asked Whittaker.

Mrs. Johnson looked puzzled.

"Did she work, for example?" Whittaker continued. "Did she have any hobbies?"

"Oh, well she had a little job, in a department store, Gardiners, right here in Shadwell" Mrs. Johnson replied. "On the scarves and gloves counter. It was only part time I think."

Whittaker looked around at Cutler. "It's in Market Square, sir," Cutler said. "Fairly popular shop I think."

Whittaker turned back to face Mrs. Johnson. "What about her hobbies," he prompted. "What did she like to do?"

"I don't think she had any, except the theatre that is. She loved it you know," Mrs. Johnson replied. "That was her life really I suppose, especially in the last five or six years. She was in one of those theatre clubs, and went to regular meetings. They were able to get cheaper tickets, things like that. Oh, and advanced information. I mean she always knew that some play was coming on, weeks before it happened, and she could book seats before anyone else."

"Did she go to the theatre very often?" asked Chambers.

"Often enough I suppose," replied Mrs. Johnson. "Every month, she'd go up to London on the coach on a Saturday, for the matinee performance. They'd go for something to eat afterwards, then back on the coach. And she'd be home by eight, eight thirty. She loved it."

"And it was always London?" Chambers continued. "Did she ever go to local theatres?"

Mrs. Johnson thought for a few moments. "No, I don't think so," she replied. "She used to say that if you want to go to the theatre, go to the best, or don't go at all." She paused for a moment, and started to smile. "And the best as far as she was concerned was London, the West End. There was nowhere else."

"Did you ever go with her?" asked Chambers. "To London I mean?"

"Oh yes, I did sometimes, but I much prefer the cinema," she replied. "Our local Vue Cinema has got eight screens now, you're spoilt for choice, and you don't have too far to travel."

Chambers had to admit that he also preferred the cinema. It was more exciting, and certainly there was scope for a lot more action on the big screen. "What about friends?" Chambers asked. "Did she have anyone special?"

"Well, there were two ladies at the shop," Mrs. Johnson started to explain. "I don't know if you could call them friends exactly, or special. And then of course there was the theatre club."

"Did she have any men friends I mean," Chambers explained.

Mrs. Johnson shook her head, and started to cry. "Oh no, not after Michael you know," she replied. "Men were a definite no-no. What is it they say, once bitten twice shy, and she had been badly bitten. He was nasty to her, abusive and he could be quite violent." She paused for a moment, and brushed a tear from her cheek. "She didn't have much of a life with him, and now I can't believe she's gone." She paused once again, and sighed. "She was so excited when she had seen that in the local paper, all about that murder play thingy."

"Murder at Larkhall Manor, you mean?" suggested Chambers. "But I thought that you said she wasn't interested in the local theatres."

"That's right," agreed Mrs. Johnson. "Normally she wasn't."

"So what was different about this one I wonder?" said Whittaker.

"She thought she knew someone who was in it," Mrs. Johnson continued. "An old school friend from twenty something years back."

"Do you know who it was?" asked Whittaker. "Man, or woman?"

"She never said," Mrs. Johnson replied. "I think it might have been that man, the one who was here last night."

"That's quite possible," agreed Whittaker. He looked at Chambers. "But why kill her?" Whittaker turned back to face Mrs. Johnson. "Do you know if she actually went to see the play?"

"I'm sorry, I don't know if she went to the play," Mrs. Johnson replied. "But I do know that she was hoping to see her friend." She paused for a moment, and started to cry. "Who would want to kill her? I mean why? She was such a lovely lady, never did any harm to no one."

"We don't know I'm afraid," replied Whittaker, shaking his head. "I'm actually hoping that you can help me find whoever did this dreadful thing."

"I'll help if I can," she replied, brushing away a tear, and sitting down.

"Mrs. Johnson, I understand that you heard someone talking just after eight o'clock last night," said Chambers. "Could you hear what it was about?"

"No, not really," Mrs. Johnson replied. "It was muffled, you see, and I'm afraid my hearing isn't that good these days. Getting old I suppose. I couldn't make out anything that was being said. The talking went on for a little while, then suddenly, it went quiet, the talking stopped. Then there was a lot of noise. Things falling, or being thrown to the floor, things getting broke."

"What happened then?" asked Whittaker.

"Nothing happened, it just went quiet again," she replied. "Then, a few minutes later, I heard a door slam, and someone going down the corridor. I went to the door and looked down the corridor, and saw the back of a man just going down the stairs."

"What did you do then?" asked Chambers.

"I went back inside. I went over to the window, and looked out." She pointed to the window.

"I understand that you saw someone walking down the street," said Chambers.

"That's right," she replied. "I saw him going past a light column. Then he suddenly stopped for a moment before he crossed the road."

"Could you show it to me?" asked Chambers. "The light column I mean."

"Certainly," she replied. She stood up and walked to the window. Chambers followed. "There it is," she said, pointing.

Three storeys below, and twenty yards further down the road was the light column. Chambers wondered how clearly anyone could be seen under such circumstances. He looked across the road. "I wonder if he had a car waiting" he murmured.

"Then what?" asked Chambers.

"I went over to Christine's flat to see if she was alright," Mrs. Johnson replied. "I knocked on the door, but there was no answer. I tried again, but there was response. I came back in here and called the police."

"Would you recognize the man if you saw him again?" asked Whittaker. "If I showed you a photograph, for example?"

She was hesitant. "Maybe," she replied. "But I'm not really sure. I didn't really get a good view of him, you understand."

Whittaker understood perfectly, and her response was to be expected. "You told the police officer that he was Fortyish, of medium height, and with dark hair," he continued.

"That's right," she replied. "It was very thick, and long."

"Have you anything else to add?" Whittaker asked. "For example, what about his weight? I mean was he a big man, heavy set?"

"I couldn't really tell," Mrs. Johnson replied. "But he wasn't what you might call fat. Just average."

Average, murmured Whittaker. *Whatever that meant.* "Could it have been her ex-husband?" asked Whittaker.

"You mean Michael?" replied Mrs. Johnson. "Oh no, it wasn't him."

"You're sure?" Whittaker replied. "You said that you didn't get a good look at him."

"Oh yes, I'm perfectly sure, there's no doubt about it," Mrs. Johnson replied. "It wasn't him. Old Michael has been dead four or five years now. Just after he came out of prison it was."

Whittaker looked at Chambers and Cutler. *Another suspect to be dismissed.* "Are you sure, about him being dead I mean?"

"Oh yes, I'm sure," replied Mrs. Johnson. "He died. It was lung cancer I think."

Whittaker looked at Chambers and raised his eyes.

"You know, even before he died, Michael hasn't been around here for as long as I've lived here," Mrs. Johnson continued. "She was well rid of him, by all accounts. Not that I would speak ill of the dead, you understand."

"Oh yes, I understand," Whittaker replied.

"Did she have any photographs of him?" asked Chambers. "Her husband I mean."

"You know I asked her about that some time ago," Mrs. Johnson replied. "She said there weren't any. She had destroyed them all. Any photographs with the two of them, he would be cut out. She hated him. Simple as that. You know, whoever did this dreadful thing must have been someone she knew though, wouldn't you say?"

"Why do you think that?" asked Chambers.

"Because she let him in didn't she," Mrs. Johnson explained. "She wouldn't have done that if it had been a stranger would she? We've been warned about strangers, especially late at night. Keep your security chain on, she was told, and don't open the door unless you know the person."

"That's excellent advice, Mrs. Johnson," agreed Whittaker. "And worth remembering."

"She must have known him, don't you think?"

"You might be right, Mrs. Johnson," agreed Whittaker. He stood up. "Well I think we've taken up enough of your time." He started towards the door, followed by his two colleagues. He stopped at the door, and turned. "Thank you for your assistance," he said. "We'll catch him, you can rely on that."

* * *

Whittaker shook his head. *What on earth had made him say that?* Oh he certainly meant it, alright. That is to say, he certainly hoped that the murderer would be caught, but regrettably he was still unable to guarantee success. And there was still a lot of investigation to be done. But at least they now had a description, albeit vague, and they had a witness. It was a start.

* * *

Chapter Twenty-Five
"We're Getting There"

"Well my friends, our murderer seems to have made a big mistake, just as I thought he would," said Whittaker. "He was seen. We now know that our murderer was male."

Cutler wasn't convinced. "The murderer of Miss. Stanton was male, certainly," he agreed. "But we don't know for certain about our murderer. We would only be sure if the two murders are, in some way, connected."

"Yes, that's perfectly correct," Whittaker agreed. "But I'm convinced that the two murders, this one, and the murder at Larkhall Manor, were committed by the same person."

Cutler wasn't convinced. "They could be two totally unconnected events," he suggested.

"They could be, but they aren't," Whittaker replied. "No way, not on your life," he said. "They are connected take my word for it."

"Well, you know, sir, he could be right," Chambers suggested.

"Yes, he could be right, it is possible," said Whittaker. "And I could be the next Commissioner of Police." He paused. "And that is never going to happen is it, not in a million years. Besides, didn't her ladyship believe that the two events could be connected? And you wouldn't argue with that would you?"

"Probably not, sir," Chambers agreed. "But you must admit, that's hardly conclusive is it?"

"No, you're right, it's not conclusive," Whittaker agreed. "The thing is, two murders so close together in time and place, are more than likely to be connected. In that circumstance I assume that they are connected, and will continue to think so until, and if ever, I'm proved to be wrong." He rubbed the side of face, and heaved a sigh. "So, what does this second murder tell us anyway? What have we learnt?"

"Well we know that the murderer was male, and that Miss. Stanton knew her killer," suggested Cutler.

"She might not have known him," Chambers said. "He might just have given her a good story, and she accepted what he said, opened the door, let him in, and …."

"Good point," agreed Cutler.

"But what we do know is that the man was in his forties, medium height and with dark hair," added Chambers.

"Dark hair, that was thick and long," said Cutler.

"Right," said Whittaker. "And we also know that there is a connection with Murder At Larkhall Manor, a small one admittedly."

"The flyer you mean?" suggested Chambers.

"Yes, the flyer," agreed Whittaker. "In the circumstances I think we can eliminate four more of our suspects. Janet Cooper, Susan Turner, Catherine Barr, and Rose Fuller, are all in the clear."

"Bit premature aren't you sir, with all due respect," Chambers said. "They might be eliminated, but only if the two crimes are, in fact, connected."

"Course they're connected, stands to reason," Whittaker replied. "That's seven down, and four to go. We're getting there."

"Hope you're right, sir," mumbled Chambers.

"Oh, I'm right, Derek," said Whittaker. "I just know it. All we have to do is find the proof."

"Oh, is that all, sir," replied Chambers. "For a minute there I thought it was going to be difficult."

"Well, as a start let's see if we can find a second connection," said Whittaker. "Let's see if Miss. Stanton actually went to the performance of Murder at Larkhall Manor that night." He turned to face Cutler. "See if the police constable has a photograph, and we'll get back to Wokingham, and have a word with Miss. Cooper."

* * *

Thirty minutes later, the three men were back at the village hall. Janet Cooper was there waiting for them. She was interested to hear if there had been any developments.

"I was just wondering, I mean the tape is still in place," she began. "I was hoping, that it would be gone by now."

"Ah yes, I certainly understand your concern," said Whittaker. He looked at Cutler. "I think we can remove it, now. Don't you?"

"Right away, sir," Cutler said and he hurried from the room.

Miss. Cooper smiled. At last she would be able to get to her things, and start to pack things away. "How is the investigation progressing?" she asked. "Have there been any developments?"

Whittaker heaved a sigh. "That's an excellent question, Miss. Cooper. If you mean have we solved the crime, then the answer is sadly no we haven't," he replied. "But we've made some headway. A few steps forward, and then a few back as usual. But there have been some developments, which may or may not be connected. We'll have to wait and see."

"Sounds intriguing," replied Janet Cooper. "Is it something you can talk about?"

Whittaker took a deep breath. "As I said, there have been some developments, not the kind I wanted, but, in fact, there's been another murder."

Janet Cooper was shocked. "Another murder!" she cried. "That's dreadful. Where? Who?"

"It happened last evening," Chambers started to explain. "In a small town, Shadwell, just a few miles from here."

"I know Shadwell. That's where I went to school," Janet Cooper replied. "What happened?"

"Well, a certain Miss. Christine Stanton was brutally killed, last night," Whittaker continued. "Struck from behind with a blunt instrument. The doctor advises that she died instantly."

"We found this in her flat," added Chambers as he handed the flyer to Janet. "'Murder at Larkhall Manor'. You will notice that she's underlined the times and place for the opening performance." He reached into his inside pocket. "This is her photograph. It's a couple of years old, but I'm assured that it's a good likeness."

Janet looked at the flyer, and then the photograph for a few minutes. She then handed them back to Chambers. "I still don't understand what it is that you need."

"I believe that the two murders are connected," Whittaker started to explain. "We think she may have been here, the night of Donovan's murder. It's possible that she saw something, or perhaps recognized someone, a member of the cast. Someone who perhaps didn't want to be recognized."

"We need to know whether she came here, that night, to see the play," added Chambers.

Janet took hold of the photograph again. She sighed. "Inspector, there were one hundred and twenty three people at that performance. How on earth do you expect me to recognize one person?"

"I know. It was a long shot but I had to try," Whittaker said, sounding quite negative.

Janet looked back at the photograph again. "I have to say that she doesn't look familiar, but I'm not surprised," she said. "But do you have an address?"

"Oh yes, we certainly have an address," said Whittaker, beginning to feel a little more optimistic. "Number 18C Devonport Close, Shadwell."

"In that case, I might just be able to help," Janet replied. "Or more accurately, Susan, Susan Turner, might be able to help. You should have a word with her. She looks after the props, but she's also my assistant. That night, when the performance was stopped, I asked the audience to leave their names and addresses with Susan, so that they could be refunded the price of their ticket. She might recognize her, or the address might turn up, you never know."

"Do you know where I can find her?" asked Whittaker.

"She was in Martha's, the tea rooms, twenty minutes ago," suggested Janet. "I'll see if she's still there, and send her over to see you."

* * *

Ten minutes later there was a knock on the office door. Then there was a second knock, and the door opened. It was Susan Turner. "Janet said that you wanted to see me."

"Ah yes, Miss. Turner, do come in," said Whittaker. "Please sit down."

Susan Turner sat down. "What can I do for you?" she asked.

"Miss. Cooper said that you might be able to help me," explained Whittaker.

"In what way?" Miss. Turner asked. "What can I do for you?"

"The night of Mr. Donovan's death," Whittaker replied. "I understand that you were given the task of getting all of the names and addresses of the people that had been in the audience."

"That's right, quite a job it was I can tell you," agreed Susan. "It was dreadful having to stop the play because …. Mr. Donovan getting killed like that. Janet wanted all of the names and addresses. It was all to do with refunding their ticket money." She shrugged. "How can I help?"

Whittaker explained what his problem was. He handed her the photograph. "I'll looking for one particular person," he said. "That's the lady I'm interested in."

Susan took hold of the photograph and looked at it. "I'm sorry, but we did have …."

"I know, I know. You did have one hundred and twenty three people that night," interrupted Whittaker. "Yes I appreciate the problem, but maybe an address might achieve a better result. She lived in Shadwell, just a few miles away."

"Not everyone bothered, you know," Susan continued. "To leave their name I mean." She thought for a moment. "Just over a hundred did, but it took such a long time, and some people became impatient, and just left. Still a long list though, one hundred names."

Whittaker smiled and nodded. "Yes it is, I know, but if you could just take a look," he coaxed. "I'd be grateful."

Susan opened her bag. She took out a notebook. "I carry this with me all the time," she explained. "I never know when

I'm going to need it. Janet is always giving instructions, you know. Stage directions, or something about the scenery, or about our schedule. She never stops." She heaved a sigh. It was quite a task she was facing. "Let's give it a try then, shall we?" she said. "Shadwell, you said."

She started to trawl through her list. "There's a few from Shadwell," she announced.

"How about Devonport Close, Shadwell?" said Chambers.

Susan continued to look through her list. Her fingers moving slowly down the page. "Here it is," she announced. "18C Devonport Close, Shadwell. Name of Stanton. Christine. Is that the one you're looking for?"

"That's the one," Whittaker agreed. "So she was here," he announced.

"Looks like it," said Susan.

Connection number two, Whittaker mumbled. "You don't happen to know where she was sitting do you?"

Susan looked back at her list. "She was in the fifth row, and over on the left side."

"The left side," repeated Chambers. "I wonder if she could have seen into the wings on the right."

Susan thought for a moment, then shook her head. "I doubt it," she replied. "But she'd be watching the play anyway wouldn't she. Why would she look over into the wings?"

Maybe if she saw something, Whittaker thought. *Something she wasn't supposed to see.* "Maybe," said Whittaker. "Might depend on what was happening there. Maybe it was more interesting than what was happening on stage."

Whittaker noticed the puzzled look on Susan's face. "Don't worry about it," he said. "I'm really just thinking aloud."

Chambers looked at Susan. She now looked more puzzled than ever. "Thank you for your help Miss. Turner," he said. "You have been very helpful."

"Oh yes, most helpful," added Whittaker quickly. "We shan't need to trouble you any further," He looked at Chambers. "Derek, see Miss. Turner to the door please."

* * *

Chapter Twenty-Six

Connection Number Two

Whittaker watched as Miss. Turner left, and waited for Chambers to return to his seat. He turned to face Cutler and Chambers. "There we have it then," he announced. "Connection number two."

"It's still doesn't prove that the two murders were committed by the same person," said Chambers. "Hardly conclusive is it?"

Whittaker had to admit that Chambers was correct. It wasn't conclusive. It was, however, certainly possible. "Yes, you're right," he agreed. "But ...."

Chambers looked at Cutler. "I just knew there'd be a but coming," he said.

Whittaker cleared his throat. "As I was about to say. At the present time we don't have a lot to go on, do we? We have two murders that may or may not be connected, but you have to admit that there are two possible connections. The flyer, and the fact that Miss. Stanton was there on opening night, the night of Donovan's murder." He started to make a list. "Second, we have a very vague description of a man, who we think murdered Miss. Stanton. And we have a whole crowd of possible suspects who may have killed Donovan." He looked down at the list. It wasn't much. "What else do we have?"

"We do have that description, don't we?" Cutler suggested. "A description of the man who murdered Miss. Stanton. It's a bit vague I know, but it's something."

"Vague, did you say?" Chambers repeated. "It's so vague it could apply to hundreds, if not thousands, of men, including myself, and you."

"I just wish we'd hear something useful from Records," said Whittaker. "I'm sure that's where the answer lies."

"Same here," replied Chambers. "I'll give them a call."

Whittaker turned towards Constable Cutler. "How did you get on with Mrs. Johnson?" he asked

Chambers looked puzzled.

"Harry had another word with her," Whittaker explained. "To see if she had remembered anything else about the man she saw." He looked back at Cutler. "Any joy?" he asked.

"Nothing new I'm afraid, sir," Cutler replied. "She was even revising the description she originally gave. She's now saying the guy was tall, with grey hair."

"Just as I expected," said Whittaker. For some reason most people were just not good at describing another person. Ask three eye witnesses to describe someone, and you will get three different descriptions.

Chambers started to smile. "Well sir, no one said that it would be …."

"Easy," added Whittaker. "I know, you don't have to keep on reminding me."

Any further conversation was interrupted by noises coming from inside the village hall. "What on earth is that ruckus?" said Whittaker.

Cutler stood up and went to the office door. "I'll take a look, sir," he said as he opened the door and looked out. "Oh it's young Fred Harkett, and his friends," he explained. "I'll deal with it."

He walked out of the office, into the hall. "Alright now lads, keep the noise down," he said. "You shouldn't be in here you know that. You best get off home, go on now, hop it."

"We want to see the Inspector," said Fred. "It's important."

"Yeah, we want to see the man from Scotland Yard," demanded one of the other boys.

"Now boys, you can't go bothering the Inspector," said Cutler. "He's a very busy man. He doesn't have time for you. Come on, home to your mothers."

"What is it Constable?" asked Chambers, as he walked over to join him.

Cutler looked at Chambers. "I'm sorry about this sir," he said. "Just some of the local kids. They're good kids really. They don't mean no harm. Leave it to me, sir, I'll send them packing."

Chambers moved closer to Fred. "What is it you want?" he asked.

"We want to see that Inspector man," Fred explained.

"He's a very busy man, you know. Why do you want to see him?" Chambers asked.

"We found something," said one of the other boys. "We think he might be interested."

"We also think there might be a reward," added Fred.

"Now Fred, I've just told you, not to bother …"

"What have you found?" asked Chambers.

Fred looked at his two friends. "Well, Brian, he was the first to notice it." He pointed to one of the other boys. Brian simply nodded. "It's here." Fred opened the plastic bag that he was holding. He reached inside. "He found this, sir."

It was a gun, a fake gun. "It's the missing prop gun," said Cutler.

Chambers took his handkerchief, and carefully wrapped it around the gun. "Come on guys this way." He hurried back to the office. "In you go. This is Chief Inspector Whittaker, boys."

Whittaker looked up, puzzled. He looked at the wrapped package that Chambers was holding. "Alright, what's this all about?" he asked.

"Sir, I think this will interest you," Chambers replied, as he placed the gun on to the table in front of Whittaker. "These three boys found it."

Whittaker looked at the gun, and then at the three boys. "Well now, that is very interesting," he said. "You haven't touched it have you?" he asked.

"What do you think? Course we've touched it," said Brian. "Couldn't pick it up without touching it could I? Stands to reason don't it?"

"He's got a point, sir," said Cutler. "Pity though because there probably won't be much left in the way of usable prints."

"No, I'd say that you're probably right," said Whittaker. "But there is a blood stain. Look. Might tell us something."

"Right you are, sir," said Chambers. "I'll get the lab testing it right away."

Whittaker looked back at the boys. "Where did you find it?" he asked.

"Down by the river," replied Fred. "Just near the bridge."

"By the river, you say," replied Whittaker. *Just as Ashton had suggested.*

"It was caught on some reeds," added Brian.

"I told you boys to be careful down at the river," said Cutler. He looked at Whittaker. "It's a bit deep there, at the bridge. I'm always telling them not to go there." He looked back at the boys. "What were you doing there, anyway?" he asked.

"We were going fishing, but then we saw the gun," explained Fred. "So what about the reward then? Should be worth something."

Chambers looked at Whittaker. "I think we could stretch to a fiver, don't you sir?" he said. "A fiver each. Expenses should cover that I guess."

"Go on then," replied Whittaker. "But it's coming out of your pay packet."

"All right," agreed Chambers. He opened his wallet, and took out three five pound notes. He looked at the boys. "Here you are, and thanks for your help," he said as he handed out the money. "By the way did you catch anything?"

The boys started to smile, then they laughed. "No sir, we never catch anything."

"Except maybe a cold," Cutler suggested. "Right now, off home with you, and don't let me catch you down by river again."

Chambers watched the boys as they hurried out of the room. He then sighed and turned back to face Whittaker and Cutler. "Well we've got the gun," he announced. "Not that it will do us much good."

"Fingerprints you mean," said Cutler. "No I guess they would be pretty well ruined by now."

Whittaker looked up. "There's still that bloodstain, remember," he said. "Someone must have cut themselves as they picked it up."

"On that rough edge, of the table," suggested Cutler.

Chambers wasn't convinced. "How many of our band of suspects were seen with cuts? Three or more. I can't remember, but certainly more than one."

"A good point," said Whittaker. He looked at the bloodstain. "But that stain is unique. That belongs to one person, and one person only. Hopefully the lab can tell us who that person is. Derek get it to the lab as soon as you can. They might pick something up, you never know."

Chambers still had his doubts. "Yes they might find something," he admitted. "They might even discover that the blood stain comes from Joe, or Jane Smith. But that doesn't mean that it was Joe, or Jane, that actually switched the gun."

Whittaker had to admit that Chambers was correct. "What can I say? But we have to keep trying don't we? To keep following up on the slightest lead? You never know, it might turn out to be a bit more definite than we think."

Cutler was puzzled. "But I thought we were getting somewhere."

"Oh sure, we've found the gun, with a blood stain," said Chambers, sounding disappointed. "It still doesn't prove who the murderer is, I'm afraid. Anyone could have touched that gun. Miss. Turner for example."

"Sadly, I admit that he's right," said Whittaker. "But we'll get him, mark my words. Sooner or later the criminal will generally slip up. He's slipped up once, he might slip up again. Maybe he, or she, will get caught in a lie. The thing about lying is that you have to remember the lie you told. Quite often you have to add another lie to the lie, because you couldn't remember the lie you told in the first place." He took a deep breath. "It gets very complicated. You also have to remember that even though you might deny that something happened, other people who were involved might inadvertently give the game away."

Chambers had heard this speech many times before. He knew it by heart, and was tempted to recite it along with the Inspector. He thought better of it, and decided to leave the Inspector to it.

"Maybe they'll simply make a mistake," the Inspector continued. "Something that will be the final giveaway. Sometimes they assume, wrongly, that some things, what they do, what they say, will just be accepted, and not checked. They think they will be trusted, and their action not questioned. Maybe they'll leave a fingerprint, or perhaps a bloodstain." He looked back at the gun lying on the desk.

"What about the guy in Shadwell?" asked Cutler. "What was his mistake?"

"Simple," replied Whittaker. "Firstly he committed a murder. The question is why?" He paused, but there was no response. "There's generally always a reason to commit a murder. That reason might be revenge, or maybe to stop someone from telling some dark secret."

"Blackmail you mean?" suggested Cutler.

"Yes blackmail," agreed Whittaker. "Although what you should remember is that in cases of blackmail there must be something that exists that provides the basis for that blackmail."

"Evidence you mean?" said Cutler.

"Yes, certainly evidence," said Whittaker. "And it must be written evidence, something you can show as proof. It can't simply be word of mouth. It needs to be something substantial, something that leaves no doubts. Maybe it's a letter, or a photograph."

"Or a newspaper cutting," added Chambers,

"Precisely," agreed Whittaker. "And if that evidence is still around then it would be an excellent motive for murder, and you could say it could be a dead giveaway."

"Then why did our guy murder Miss. Stanton?" asked Cutler.

A good question, thought Whittaker. "Maybe he killed her because he thought she knew something, or had seen something. Perhaps she hadn't seen anything at all. In which case he had made a really major mistake."

"I'm still not sure of what mistake he has made, though," said Cutler.

Whittaker shrugged. "He was seen, that's the mistake," he replied. "We have a description, it's vague, but when we do finally catch someone, we'll have something to compare them with."

Cutler was far from convinced. "But we are still no nearer to getting him are we?"

"Sadly, that is correct, I'm sorry to say," agreed Whittaker. "I'm hoping that Criminal Records will come up with something that will bring this case to a satisfactory conclusion."

"You are still convinced the two murders are linked," said Cutler.

"Yes I am," Whittaker replied. "Until something proves me wrong, then yes I'm one hundred percent convinced." He looked at Chambers. "Derek, give them my compliments, and tell them to get a move on. And see if they've found anything yet."

* * *

Chapter Twenty-Seven
Criminal Records Office

Chambers picked up the telephone and dialed the number. It was answered on the fifth ring. "CRO," a voice said. "Sergeant Walker speaking. Can I help you?"

"Alan, its Derek Chambers, remember me?" Chambers replied. He paused for a moment. "Chief Inspector William Whittaker, sends you his compliments, and he wonders if you could get a move on"

"Hi Derek. Yes I remember you," Walker replied. "I'm sure the Chief Inspector is sending me a lot more than just his compliments."

"Well to be honest, he did have something else to say, which we won't go into right now," said Chambers. "However, if you like I'll put it in an email and send it to you."

Alan Walker had a pretty good idea what the something else was. "That won't be necessary," he replied. He did not need a diagram. "What can I say? I'm really sorry it's taken so long, but it's been a mad house here. The Commissioner is constantly asking for this record or that one. And I have to say your little enquiry has taken a hell of a lot of time." He paused for a moment, and Chambers could hear papers being shuffled. "Those Magistrates Court Records were pretty thorough you know. In all there were eighty seven names to be checked."

"Yes, I thought there would be a lot," agreed Chambers.

"Incidentally where did you get them?" Walker asked. "They are Court Records, and they shouldn't have been removed."

"It's a long story, Alan. I'll tell you about it sometime," replied Chambers. "But in the meantime it is really important, so if you could …."

"Right, I'm getting there. As I say, they were all checked," said Walker. "And I have to say that the vast majority of them resulted in nothing. Apart from that one appearance in Magistrate's Court, that was the end to their career as a criminal for most of them."

"But not all of them," suggested Chambers, hopefully.

"Right, not all of them," agreed Walker. "Eight of them, out of the eighty-seven, went on to bigger and better things. Robbery with assault; embezzlement; grievous bodily harm. Even a murder. Four were convicted, and went to prison. Strangely enough though, the other four were never convicted. None of them. All four cases were eventually dropped through lack of evidence."

At last things were beginning to sound promising, thought Chambers. "I need names," he said. "And full details. Photographs if you have them. And I need everything pretty quick."

There was silence for a few moments. "Sorry, I was just checking on how much stuff I would need to send you. It's a lot. Let me have your email address." Chambers gave Walker the email address. "Right, I'll start sending. Hopefully you'll get everything within the next hour or two." He hung up.

Hopefully one of those four is right here, now, with the Wokingham Players, Chambers thought. He replaced the handset onto the cradle. He looked over at Whittaker. "Sounds promising," he said. "We'll have all they've got by ...." He checked his watch. "Two o'clock, I guess."

* * *

It was ten minutes to three before Chambers returned to the office, He was carrying a bundle of papers. "Sorry I've been so long, but I've been going through this lot. I think you'll be pleased though, sir," said Chambers. "Incidentally, we owe the Village Hall Committee, a lot of money for ink cartridges and for paper. I've been doing a lot of printing." He placed the papers onto the table.

"What have you got then, Derek?" asked Whittaker.

"Records have checked on all of the cases mentioned in Donovan's files, and the press cuttings," Chambers started to explain.

"And?" said Whittaker, getting impatient.

"There's not much more detail I'm afraid. The newspaper cuttings pretty much covered it," Chambers replied. "Eighty seven names appeared in the Magistrate Court Records, but only eight of those names, appeared later in more serious situations. Four were charged, were found guilty and served time. The other four were also charged, but all four cases were thrown out. These four."

He pointed to the papers on the table. The papers were actually split into four sections. "Right, here we are. Number one, Edward Townes, robbery with assault. Case dismissed through lack of evidence." He moved the pile to one side. "Next we have William Logan. Nice guy, accused of grievous bodily harm. Alleged that he beat up his girlfriend. But it wasn't proved. The girlfriend was too scared to give evidence. What can you do? So, once again, the case was dismissed, although he did get a warning." He moved the pile next to the first one. "Next, we have Daniel Marshall, charged with murder. But the police couldn't crack his air tight alibi, so he got away with it." The third pile was pushed to one side.

"What about the fourth one?" asked Whittaker, sounding disappointed.

"Ah, I saved this one till the end, the best for last," said Chambers. "I think this one will interest you." He sifted through the papers, and picked out a photograph. He handed the photograph to Whittaker. "That is Angela Hull."

"Who?" asked Whittaker.

"Angela Hull, but better known to us as Rose Fuller," Chambers continued.

Whittaker looked at Chambers, then looked at the photograph. "Well I wasn't expecting that."

"Neither was I," agreed Chambers. "But it seems that our Miss. Fuller has run foul of the law at least twice. Firstly, a simple speeding offence about fifteen years ago. She appeared in front of guess who, Magistrate James Donovan. Then five years ago she was working for a bank in London. Seems that one hundred thousand pounds went missing. She was suspected of embezzlement. She was charged, and taken to court, but the case was thrown out. Lack of evidence, apparently. The police got heavily criticized. So did the Crown Prosecution Service. Anyway, soon afterwards she changed her name, and apparently disappeared."

"Interesting," said Whittaker. "Go on."

"She moved down south," Chambers continued. "About eight months ago she met up with Donovan once again. She never recognized him, but he thought he knew her alright. He checked his files. It was her. He started to blackmail her, threatening to divulge what he knew."

"And just what did he know, anyway?" asked Whittaker

"Do you remember what she said," Chambers continued. "I didn't like him, but he never bothered me. She went to great trouble to tell us that. Why? The truth is that he did bother her."

"I'm listening," said Whittaker.

"It seems that he may have had evidence to link her with the missing hundred thousand," suggested Chambers. "Providing her with an excellent motive for killing him."

"Maybe, but we never found anything did we," said Whittaker.

"No we didn't," agreed Chambers

"And another thing, I'm puzzled," Whittaker continued.

"Carry on, sir," said Chambers. "I think I know where you are going."

"We know that the person who murdered Miss. Stanton was a man." Whittaker sighed, just when he thought they were getting somewhere. "I don't get it. I was sure our two murders were linked."

Chambers looked at Cutler. "Maybe they were two separate murders all along," he said.

Whittaker looked up. He started to smile. "Not a chance. They're connected, I'm sure of that. I'd stake my pension and gold watch on it."

"Surely not your gold watch, sir," said Chambers, smiling.

"I want to know everything about this Angela Hull, or whatever her name is," said Whittaker. "Her friends, especially men friends. Was she married? And I want to know a lot more about the bank and the missing money. Because as sure as eggs is eggs I'm betting that Donovan knew all about it." He paused and looked at the two officers. "And I want that information but quickly."

"No problem, sir. It's already here, and your gold watch is safe." Chambers pointed to the pile of paper. "And you'll be happy to note that this lot proves without a doubt that the two murders were well and truly connected." He started to sift through. "Here we are. You'll like this." He extracted a sheet of paper. "Rose Fuller, real name Angela Hull, went to Halley Street Primary School, in London."

"Okay, carry on," said Whittaker.

"Well it seems that Miss. Christine Stanton also went to that same school. In fact for a period, she, and Rose were in the same class, and by all accounts, they were great friends." Chambers placed a photograph on the table in front of Whittaker. "That's the two of them, taken about twenty-five years ago."

"Where did you get that from?" asked Whittaker.

"It was one of the photographs that we found in Miss. Stanton's flat," explained Chambers. "I had no idea of who those kids were, but it was included in the pile of photographs that I took." He looked at the photograph, and then placed it back on to the table. "Probably something that the killer was looking for, but fortunately he never found it. Or maybe he did see it but didn't realise what was on it."

"So it was Rose Fuller that Miss. Stanton thought she recognized on that flyer," suggested Cutler.

"That's right," said Chambers. "She wasn't one hundred percent sure. After all, the name was wrong, and it had been a few years since the two of them were in Miss. Taylor's class at Halley Street School. Nonetheless, she decided to go to see the play, and make sure. She actually tried to get to see her friend before the performance."

"But she was stopped by Ashton, right," suggested Whittaker. "The argument with the unknown woman."

"Precisely," said Chambers. "However, she would have been absolutely thrilled to see her old friend up on that stage. They had been very close and had vowed to keep in touch, but other things happened you know, and got in the way. Life took over, and they drifted and eventually lost touch. Watching her on the stage that night, I can imagine Miss. Stanton as she kept trying to catch Rose's eye. She wouldn't mean to distract her, but eventually Angela Hull would be looking straight at her. Rose remembered her old friend straight away. But instead of feeling pleased, she suddenly felt very vulnerable. She did not want her real identity to be known. Questions would be asked, and the old matter of the missing money would raise its ugly head once again. Only, this time she might not be so fortunate. She could not let that happen. Miss. Stanton had to be silenced."

"But we know for certain that the murderer was a man," said Whittaker.

"That's right," said Chambers. "That's where the second connection comes in. Rose could never kill someone herself. She didn't have the stomach for it. That's why it was Tim who actually had to pull the trigger to kill Donovan. But that wasn't the end of her problems was it? With Donovan out of the equation, she now had to deal with Stanton. She wasn't sure what Stanton had seen, if anything, or what she may have suspected. Would she divulge Fuller's real identity? She needed someone to kill her. That's where Steve Ashton came in."

"Ashton," said Whittaker. "Interesting."

"Let's go back a little, first," Chambers continued. "Clearly, if Donovan was going to be successful at blackmailing Angela Hull, he must have had some kind of evidence. A letter perhaps."

"What letter?" asked Whittaker.

"You remember the one that Gammons mentioned?" replied Chambers. "He said that two men were arguing over a letter. One of the men was Donovan, the other man was Steve Ashton."

"I remember the letter," Whittaker replied. "But that would suggest a connection between Rose Fuller, and Steve Ashton."

"Yes, I agree, and there is a definite connection between them," admitted Chambers. "Ashton had joined Wokingham Players four years ago. Rose had joined the following year, and met Ashton. Very soon they were married. For a while life had been good. The hundred thousand pounds had come in handy, and bought a few of life's luxuries. But then Donovan saw her on a poster somewhere. He put two and two together, and a plan started to form in his mind. It was shortly afterwards that she met up with Donovan again. And we know the rest of that story."

Cutler was clearly still puzzled. "I get all that about Donovan," he said. "And I get all of that about Christine Stanton being excited about seeing her old friend after so long. But why on earth would Stanton let Ashton in to her flat? I mean did she know him?"

"I don't think so," Chambers replied.

"She probably didn't know him, but she had seen him before, remember," suggested Whittaker. "She was the unknown lady that Ashton had been heard talking to the day of the murder."

"Arguing with more like," said Chambers. "He might have gone there all apologetic, you know. I'm sorry about the other day. It was a problem at the time, but can I make up for it now."

"Quite possible," agreed Whittaker. "Maybe he introduced himself as Rose's husband. Perhaps he mentioned about the play. He may have said that Rose herself was actually planning on visiting, in fact, she should be here soon. And then she'd let him in, no problem."

"The rest we know," said Cutler.

"Incidentally, we've checked with the neighbour, Mrs. Johnson once again," Chambers continued. "We showed her Ashton's photograph, and she has now definitely identified him as the man she saw that night."

"Well that's one murder dealt with," said Cutler. "What about the other one?"

"A bit more problematic I'm afraid," agreed Whittaker. "There were no witnesses to the actual switch, not much real evidence as to motive, and finally, too many suspects."

"But we do have evidence," Cutler insisted. "The blood stain on the gun."

"All that proves is that someone with a cut on their hand touched the gun," advised Chambers. "Susan Turner had a cut hand."

Cutler sighed. "Well, okay, what about Angela Hull's history?"

"What about it?" said Whittaker. "Still doesn't prove she was being blackmailed, and certainly doesn't prove she arranged for his murder."

"Looks like we need a confession," suggested Chambers.

"It would be helpful," Whittaker agreed. "In the meantime she and Ashton made a big mistake having Miss. Stanton killed. Up until then we weren't getting very far were we?"

Cutler was puzzled. "I don't follow you, Inspector."

"We know that Miss. Stanton's death was not an isolated event," Whittaker began. "Miss. Stanton provides a link with Rose Fuller. We've agreed that the two murders are connected. The question then is how are they connected? Had Miss. Stanton seen anything at the hall that night that could have been incriminating?" He paused for a moment. "Rose Fuller, or Hull, wasn't absolutely sure that Stanton would say anything to incriminate her. She might not have known about the missing money. Furthermore, was it absolutely certain that she had seen anything. Perhaps she had been murdered for no reason. Maybe in reality all that Miss. Stanton knew was that her friend was using a different name. Something quite common amongst actors."

"But Rose Fuller couldn't take a chance, could she?" suggested Chambers. "The risk was too great."

"True," agreed Cutler. "But if Miss. Stanton had not been murdered, Rose, or Angela, would still have been a suspect for the murder of Donovan."

"Correct. She would have been a suspect certainly, along with all of the others," agreed Whittaker. "But as I've just said I'm not sure we could actually prove that his death was because of her."

"Time for another word with Rose Fuller, I think," said Chambers. "Don't you, sir?"

* * *

Chapter Twenty-Eight
Rose Fuller Or Is It Angela Hull

Whittaker looked up at the sound of the office door opening. "I've Miss. Fuller with me, sir," said Chambers, as he opened the door wide.

Whittaker looked up. "Derek, show her in please." He then stood up as his visitor came into the room. "Oh, Miss. Fuller, thank you for coming at such short notice," he said, as he pointed to a chair. "Do sit down." He started to shuffle through some papers lying on his desk. He looked up. "I'm sorry about all of this" he indicated the papers. "I'm sorry to drag you in once again like this. It must be annoying for you, but you know needs must, the devil drives." He shook his head. "You know I've never really understood that saying. Anyway I've just a few thing to clear up. Nothing much. Shouldn't take too long."

"Inspector, I said to you some days ago, I'm happy to help if I can," Fuller said, as she sat down. "It's not a problem."

"I remember what you said. And it really is appreciated," Whittaker said, as he continued shuffling the papers around. "Oh by the way there's been a second murder." Whittaker looked up. "In Shadwell, a small town just a few miles from here. Had you heard anything about it?"

"No, Inspector, I don't think so," Rose replied. "Dreadful."

"Certainly a terrible thing," agreed Whittaker, shuffling through his papers once again. "The thing is we are sure that there's a connection with Mr. Donovan's murder."

"Really," said Rosie sounding quite disinterested. "In what way?"

"It's here somewhere," Whittaker murmured, as he continued to search through the papers. "Lose my head if it wasn't screwed on. I saw it just a moment ago. Where on earth?"

"How were the two murders connected?" Rose repeated.

Whittaker picked up a small black and white photograph. "Ah, here it is," he announced. He looked at Rose. "How were they connected? Simple really. It seems that the victim was here, on Saturday night," he started to explain. "She came to see the play." He heaved a sigh. "Name of Christine Stanton. Mean anything to you?"

"Christine Stanton," repeated Rose. "No, I'm sorry. Doesn't mean anything to me at all."

"Pity," replied Whittaker, as he started to tap the photograph. "Then I don't suppose you know these two children do you?" He handed the photograph to her.

She looked at it, puzzled, and then quickly handed it back. "I don't know what this is all about Inspector. I'm afraid I don't know who they are, sorry to disappoint you."

"Never mind," said Chambers. "It's just something we found in Miss, Stanton's flat. We were hoping that it might, oh well, never mind. Probably not that important after all."

Whittaker took a deep breath. "You know we have to check everything. No matter how trivial it seems."

"I can understand that Inspector," Fuller agreed. "But if you could just come to the point."

The Inspector turned to the back of the photograph. "Are you sure you don't know who these children are, Angela?"

Whether she noticed the reference, or choose not to, Angela said nothing.

Whittaker smiled "I have a confession to make," he said. "I already know who these children are. It says so, right here on the back." He started to read. "This photograph was taken on the 11th May 1985, at Halley Street Primary School." He paused for a moment, and looked at her. "Ring any bells?" he asked. "Sadly the building's gone now, demolished a couple of years ago apparently. There's a Lidl supermarket there now.

230

How things change. Pity really, but that's progress for you." She remained silent. "I reckon Miss. Taylor wouldn't be very happy about it." There was still no response. "You remember Miss. Taylor don't you?" Still there was no response. "Your old teacher? The headmistress in fact," he continued. "No, oh well never mind. By the way, the child on the left is actually Christine Stanton, the lady who was murdered the other evening." He looked up once again. "Mean anything to you now?"

Once again she remained silent. "Umm. The child on the right is actually you, Rose Fuller, or should I say Angela Hull," Whittaker continued. "I have to say I would never have recognized you. I mean, what are you there? About nine or ten I guess."

"I don't know what you are playing at Inspector," Rose replied dismissively. "But you would do well in a mystery play on the stage. It isn't me, and who this Angela, whatever name you said, is I couldn't say."

"Patience, all will become crystal clear, I assure you," Whittaker replied. "I have another photograph here. To be honest it's a press cutting, taken from *The West Sussex Gazette*. It's far more recent, only five years ago. It gives details of an appearance at the local Crown Court. Your appearance." He passed the document to her. "That is you isn't it? You were on trial at the time, charged with embezzlement. One hundred thousand pounds, apparently,"

She looked at the photograph. "Okay, that's me, what about it?" she replied. "If you care to read the item you'll see that there was no evidence, and the case was dismissed. So what's your point?"

"Oh yes, you're right. The case was thrown out, that's what it says right enough. The judge wasn't pleased with the police was he? Or the Crown Prosecution Service either. Should never have come to Court, that's what the Judge said," said Whittaker. "But that doesn't interest me a whole lot. At present, what does interest me, is the name, Angela Hull. You see it, right there." He pointed to the first line. "The same name as appears on the back of that old school photograph."

Angela Hull started to slow clap her hands, then abruptly stopped as she saw the look in Whittaker's eyes. "Okay, you've found out my real name. Brilliant, ten out of ten. No law against changing your name is there? Not illegal is it? I mean after that Court case I just wanted to get away, anywhere. I changed my name, and moved to a different area where no one knew me. Simple as that."

"No, there's no law against it at all," agreed Whittaker. "But clearly you knew Christine Stanton, and so far in this conversation you have denied any knowledge of her on two occasions. I wonder why? Could it be because you wanted your past kept secret? Could it be that you maybe thought Miss. Stanton might tell someone?"

Rose Fuller glared at Whittaker. "If you are suggesting what I think you …."

"Miss. Fuller, I'm not suggesting anything, yet. I am merely asking questions," replied Whittaker. "Questions that I desperately need answers to."

"Certainly I wanted my past kept secret," Rose admitted. "I didn't want it all dragged up again."

"Maybe you didn't," said Whittaker. "I can understand that, but perhaps there was someone else who had also found out your little secret?"

"What do you mean?" asked Angela, becoming more and more impatient.

"James Donovan," replied Whittaker. "He also found out about the name change didn't he?" He shifted through the papers once again. "He knew all about you from way back." He picked up another sheet of paper. "This is a report from a local Magistrate's Court. It is a few years old, fifteen to be exact, but it's all about a speeding offence you were involved in." He shook his head. "Why on earth you didn't just pay the original fine is beyond me. I mean what was it?" He looked at Derek.

Chambers smiled. "I'm guessing, but back then it would have been round about fifty pounds, and three penalty points."

"Fifty pounds, and three penalty points," Whittaker repeated. "But you choose to go to Court?" He paused and placed the paper back onto the desk. "James Donovan was the Magistrate wasn't he? But you know he wasn't just a Magistrate. He had a bit of a hobby did our Mr. Donovan. Some people collect stamps, others take up painting. Donovan studied crimes. Well, that is he studied criminals, especially those that he thought he could make use of, those he could blackmail."

"Fascinating, Inspector," replied Angela. "But I really don't see what this has got to do with me."

"I'm coming to that Miss. Hull," Whittaker replied, as he searched through the papers once again. He looked up. "He knew all about the missing one hundred thousand pounds. The embezzlement, I should say the alleged embezzlement."

"I don't know what you talking about," said Angela.

"The police didn't have sufficient evidence apparently," Whittaker continued, ignoring her protests. "The case was thrown out, but Donovan clearly thought differently. He had something, a letter perhaps, which maybe told a different story. Sadly, we haven't found anything yet, but I'm guessing it's locked away in a safety deposit box somewhere. It'll turn up I expect. Anyway whatever it was, Donovan thought he could make something of it. He started to threaten you, pay up or else. Right?"

"Where is this nonsense coming from?" Angela replied. "Sounds like it might make a good play perhaps. A mystery play, because it's certainly a mystery to me."

"Do you really think so?" asked Whittaker. "As good as Murder at Larkhall Manor? You know I've never thought of myself as a playwright. I must give it some thought. Maybe when I eventually retire. But let's leave that to one side for the moment shall we. You know, in fact I actually have a theory that maybe there was no letter, never was. I don't actually think Donovan had anything. I think it was all a bluff, a try on. You fell for it, and it worked, at least for a while, you paid up, but then ...."

"Inspector, I really have no idea what this is all about," Angela replied. "Frankly, I've had enough, more than enough, so if you've nothing else, I do have other things to do."

Whittaker held up his hand. "Just a few more points, I promise."

"Shouldn't take too much longer," added Chambers.

"I've been thinking about our Mr. Donovan you know," Whittaker continued. "He was probably blackmailing several others, all in the same situation that you found yourself in. Made quite a career out of it I wouldn't be surprised. A serial blackmailer, if you like. And certainly not someone to be admired, but to be murdered, well that's a different story. You know the strange thing is I don't actually think he had a thing on Rose Fuller. And I really don't think he could have proved anything on Angela Hull. Maybe you should have just ignored him. Called his bluff."

"But you decided that he had to be silenced," said Chambers. "I'm guessing that it was Steve Ashton who came up with the plan. He wrote the play. He actually suggested Donovan be given the part of the Colonel."

"The rest is history," said Whittaker. "And you know what, you might have actually got away it. Anyone could have switched the gun, it could have been very difficult to discover the real killer."

"Inspector, you once asked if Donovan was hated enough for someone to kill him," said Angela.

"I remember," replied Whittaker.

"And do you remember my reply," Angela continued. "All I can say is that I didn't kill him, if that is what you're thinking."

"I remember it very well," Whittaker replied. "My response was I never suggested anything of the kind now did I?"

"At the time, no you didn't," she agreed. "But I fear that now is different."

"Now is certainly quite different, Miss. Hull," suggested Chambers. "Now we have that second murder to deal with."

"What about Donovan?" asked Whittaker. "How did you feel about killing him?"

Angela started to smile. "I freely admit I wasn't unhappy when I heard that Donovan was dead, but as I've already told you, several times, I didn't kill him. And you can't prove otherwise."

"But you admit that Ashton murdered Miss. Stanton?" asked Whittaker.

"If you say he did he did, then I've no reason to doubt you," she replied. "I find it hard to believe, but I imagine you have the proof. But as I said, I didn't kill Donovan, and I had nothing to do with Christine's death."

"Come now Miss. Hull, or Mrs. Ashton might in fact be the correct term," Whittaker continued. "We can tie Ashton in with the murder of Miss. Stanton. We can tie Miss. Stanton in with you. We can tie you in with Donovan. Firstly, for a trivial speeding offence. But then later on, the missing money. The fact that you denied that you were in fact Angela Hull is another point against you."

She hesitated for a moment. "Many actresses adopt a stage name, it's nothing unusual. They all do it."

"And I perfectly understand all of that," agreed Whittaker. "So why deny it?"

"As I explained, I didn't want to drag up the past all over again. All of the same old questions once more. The same old accusations Why should I? I was put on trial, and the case was thrown out, I was innocent. But I lost my job because of it. I lost my home, my friends, my family. No, that's why I changed my name and went away."

"Is that also why you arranged for the murder of James Donovan, and why Christine Stanton had to die?" suggested Chambers.

She shook her head. "I told you, I had nothing to do with either murder, and you can't prove that I did."

"We have the prop gun, with the bloodstain," said Whittaker. "It wouldn't take much to prove that it's your blood."

"Still wouldn't prove anything," Angela insisted. "Except that I touched the gun, nothing more."

Chambers looked at Angela. "Perhaps, but then the question would be why did you touch it?" Angela made no reply. "It'll be interesting to hear Ashton's version, don't you think?"

"One thing though, that I think you would admit, is that the gun could only have been switched by someone in the cast," said Whittaker

"Probably," Rose agreed. "Or one of the backstage people."

"I agree," replied Chambers. "And we also know that the gun was actually switched during act two, so clearly that rules out a few people, Catherine Barr for one, Ian Jackson for another."

"The murder of James Donovan required opportunity certainly," said Whittaker. "But it also required a reason to kill, a motive. Why was he murdered? There were several people who had the opportunity. You told me about a few, John Berry for one, Peter Gammons, but there was only one person who had a reason. One person only who would benefit from Donovan's death. And that person was you."

Whittaker took a deep breath. "Angela Hull you had the motive and the opportunity, and you can be placed at the scene. That is sufficient for me to arrest you on suspicion of murder." He stood up, and placed his hand on Angela's shoulder. "I'm arresting you on suspicion of the murder of James Donovan, and as an accessory to the murder of Christine Stanton. You aren't obliged to say anything, but anything you do say will be taken down, and may be used against you." He paused once again. "Have you anything to say?"

She smiled, and simply shook her head.

Whittaker turned to Chambers. "Take her away," he said. "Then we'll have a word with Mr. Ashton. I have a feeling he might have a lot more to say about the affair." He looked at Angela. "He might even tell me about your involvement."

"Inspector, he's my husband don't forget," Angela responded. "He cannot testify against me."

"Correct, I haven't forgotten, but remember what I just said. Anything you do say will be taken down, and may be used against you," Whittaker replied. "And you know what you just said speaks volumes. I mean if you are innocent as you claim, what could your husband possibly have to say anyway?"

* * *

Chapter Twenty-Nine
A Pretty Good Likeness

Whittaker looked up as the office door opened. "I've got Mr. Ashton with me, sir," Chambers announced as he entered the room.

"Ah, Mr. Ashton, please come in," said Whittaker looking over at Constable Cutler. "Harry, clear those papers off of that seat, would you please." He looked back at his visitor. "Please, have a seat, I shan't keep you long."

Ashton sat down, and looked at Whittaker, who was busily reading something.

"Just a few things we need to clear up," said Chambers. "Routine really. A few loose ends, that's all."

Ashton looked back at Whittaker, who was still reading. "How's the investigation going?" he asked. "Caught your murderer yet?"

Chambers shrugged. "Oh, it's er …. Let's just say it's progressing," he replied. "It's been difficult. Puzzling is maybe a better word. Definitely a bit of a mystery."

"Just like your play," Whittaker added.

Ashton nodded knowingly. "I wish I could help, but …."

"There's been a second murder," said Whittaker, looking up from his reading. "Don't know if you've heard."

"I did hear something about it," Ashton replied. "But to be perfectly honest I never took much notice. I wasn't that interested you see. So who was it this time?"

"A middle aged woman," Whittaker started to explain. "Apparently someone who was here in the audience, the night your play was put on."

"Really," replied Ashton. "A bit of a coincidence by the sound of it."

Whittaker remained silent for a moment. "No, we don't think so," he replied. "The thing is we are sure that the two murders are connected. You know, sometimes it seems like we progress a little, and then hit a brick wall."

"It must be very difficult for you, Inspector," said Ashton. "But exactly what can I do for you. I've already told you all I know."

"I said exactly the same thing to Detective Chambers over there," said Whittaker. "I said that would be your response, didn't I, Derek?"

"That's right, sir, you did indeed," said Chambers. "Your very words, sir."

"And you didn't believe me, did you?" Whittaker continued.

"Right again, sir," admitted Chambers.

"But you know, I don't actually think you have told us all you know," Whittaker continued. "In fact I think there's a lot that you haven't told us." He paused for a moment. "Things that you have deliberately kept quiet about."

"For example?" Ashton said, almost as a challenge.

"Did you know that your wife was being blackmailed?" asked Whittaker.

Ashton looked puzzled. "My wife?"

"Yes, your wife, Angela Hull, or better known perhaps as Rose Fuller," explained Whittaker. "You married her three years ago, in South London." Whittaker paused for a moment, and opened a file. He took out a sheet of paper. "This is a copy of the marriage certificate. July the twentieth. Happiest day of your life. Remember it now?"

"I remember," replied Ashton. "But how did you ...."

Whittaker took out another sheet of paper. "This is a report of a local Crown Court hearing, from five years ago," he explained. "Maybe she didn't tell you about it. She didn't want anyone to know. You'll understand when I tell you the details. It seems that she had been charged in connection with the theft of a sum of money. A large sum of money that had gone missing from the bank she worked for. She was actually charged with stealing that money. Ring any bells?"

"Oh she told me all about that," said Ashton. "The whole story. The case was thrown out, insufficient evidence or something. The judge wasn't pleased. In fact he was quite put out by all accounts." He paused for a moment and started to smile. "Police incompetence or something. Can't say I was surprised," he continued. "No offence, but well there's no smoke without fire, that's what they say, present company excepted."

"Maybe," said Whittaker. "Seems that the police might have got it wrong. I say might. But you see apart from the police, there was someone else who thought that she was guilty. That someone started to blackmail her. And oddly enough she paid up just like that, which seems to suggest that maybe she was in fact guilty."

"No, Inspector, the Judge said that she was innocent," replied Ashton.

"Correction, the judge never gave a verdict," said Chambers. "He dismissed the case."

"Alright, lack of evidence or something. The point is the charge was dropped." said Ashton.

"Did you know that she was being blackmailed?" Whittaker continued. "Of course you did, I was forgetting."

"Forgetting what?" asked Ashton.

"The argument you had with Donovan a couple of days ago, something about a letter," replied Whittaker.

"I don't know what you are talking about," Ashton protested. "I told you that before. I wasn't arguing with anyone."

"You did indeed," said Whittaker. "But we have an eye witness. Someone who not only heard the conversation, but they actually saw you, and Donovan. In the car park behind the Queens Head. Still deny it?"

"Yes I deny it, of course I do," Ashton replied. "I wasn't arguing with anyone."

"You were seen, Ashton," said Whittaker. "You were seen with Donovan."

Ashton started to laugh. "Oh, Inspector. Alright, yes I was with Donovan, but we were just talking. There certainly was no argument."

"What were you talking about?" asked Chambers.

Ashton was hesitant. "The play," he replied. "We were discussing the play."

"Are you sure about that?" said Whittaker. "The person who saw you mentioned something about a letter."

"A letter?" repeated Ashton, shaking his head. "There was nothing about a letter. Oh wait a minute, I remember now. Yes there was mention of a letter. You see, in the play Donovan receives a letter all about his wife's affair. His wife in the play that is. Donovan thought it wasn't necessary, and I should remove it from the scene. And that's all there was to it."

"Nice try, Mr. Ashton, but my eye witness tells a different story," Whittaker continued. Their version concerns a letter that Donovan wanted payment for. I believe that your wife was being blackmailed by Donovan. And that is why she wanted him silenced, wanted him dead."

Ashton appeared to be shocked. "Inspector, forgive me," he said. "But am I to understand that you are suggesting that Angela was actually involved in Donovan's death?"

"I'm not suggesting anything, Mr. Ashton," Whittaker replied. "I'm saying quite clearly that I believe that she arranged for his murder. Not alone of course. Oh no, she had assistance. In fact she claims that the whole thing was actually your idea. And I'm inclined to believe her."

"I imagine that you can prove your theory," Ashton said. "If she had wanted Donovan dead, she never said a word about it to me."

"Can I prove it?" said Whittaker. "Sadly I have to admit that at present I don't think I can."

"Oh, that is a bitter blow, Inspector," I wish I could assist you, but as it happens I do have an appointment."

"Oh, no need to worry too much," said Whittaker. "We'll get the proof, you can count on it."

"Incidentally, Mr. Ashton, we've found the gun," said Chambers. "The prop gun, that is."

"Ah, some good news at last," said Ashton cynically. "So you found the gun, really. I have to admit that I am surprised. Where was it found?"

"Oddly enough it was right where you had suggested," said Whittaker. "By the river. Not actually in it, as you had guessed, but caught in some reeds, near the bridge. A couple of young boys found it."

"Well I have to say I never thought it would be seen again," said Ashton. "I said that didn't I?"

"You did say that," agreed Whittaker. "But it's very interesting that you pin pointed the exact spot."

"Oh Inspector, please, it was nothing more than an obvious suggestion on my part," said Ashton. "The river just seemed the most likely place to get rid of it." He paused for a moment. "And the river by the bridge is quite deep. Makes sense. I mean where else is there?"

"You may have a point," admitted Whittaker. "However, you could have been the one disposing of the gun. You said that you left the hall at the end of act one. You had ample opportunity to take the gun with you, and go down to the river yourself."

"Oh Inspector, please. Yes I could have, but I didn't, unless of course, you know differently, and you have some kind of proof," Ashton responded. "Did actually finding it help you in your investigation? I mean does it have my fingerprints for example? At last the killer identified."

Whittaker smiled. If only it was that easy. "Oh no, no fingerprints at all," he replied. "There may have been at one time, but the boys would have smudged them, so no longer of any value I'm afraid."

"Oh I'm sorry about that Inspector," said Ashton, sounding sympathetic. "Not really that helpful then. What a pity. Quite a blow I would think. Quite disappointing. To think that after everything you eventually find it, but it's of no value. Very unfortunate I would say."

"Maybe, maybe not," said the Inspector. "There are some blood stains. It should be easy enough to identify the blood type, maybe all is not completely lost."

"Let's hope so, for your sake then, Inspector," said Ashton. "Is there anything else, I really must get on my way."

Whittaker started to smile. "Well there is this," he replied as he placed a photograph on to the table. "This has proved very helpful. That is you if I'm not mistaken."

Ashton picked up the photograph. "Well it's not exactly recent. But it does show my good side," he said. "Maybe five or six years ago I would guess. But yes it is me. Where was I when that was taken?" He thought for a moment. "Ah yes, that was in Leicester Square. I'd been to see a show I think. That's when I got my interest in acting, amateur only I admit. What was it we had been to see? Clearly something quite forgettable." He placed it back on to the table. "Where did you get it?"

Whittaker picked up the photograph. "Oh, let's just say that we have our methods." He started to tap the photograph "I'd say it's a pretty good likeness, wouldn't you? You haven't changed that much you know. You've put on a bit of weight, but nothing too drastic."

"Too many cream cakes I'm afraid," admitted Ashton.

Whittaker ignored Ashton's comment. "Do you remember, when we last spoke I asked about an alleged argument between you and an unknown woman?"

"Yes I remember," agreed Ashton. "And if you remember I said I knew nothing about it and that your informant was clearly mistaken."

"That's right you did say that," admitted Whittaker. "But you know we now have two reports saying the same thing. They both state that you were heard arguing with an unknown woman, on the day of the production."

"Well, Inspector, all I can say is that both must be wrong, because I have no idea what you, or they, are talking about," replied Ashton.

"Clearly we were wrong, Inspector," suggested Chambers.

"And yet I was convinced that it was the same lady, the same lady who was later murdered," Whittaker replied. He looked at Ashton. "The second murder I mentioned."

"Mrs. Lily Johnson recognized you straightaway, when I showed her that photograph," said Chambers.

"Mrs. Johnson," repeated Ashton. "Just who is this Mrs. Johnson?"

"She was Christine Stanton's neighbour," explained Chambers.

"And who is Miss. Stanton," asked Ashton.

"Oh I'm sorry, didn't I say," said Whittaker. "Miss. Stanton was the victim in the second murder that I mentioned, remember. She was actually an old school friend of your wife, thirty five years ago."

"The lady that you murdered," added Chambers.

"What nonsense," said Ashton angrily. "I've never murdered anyone."

"No, it's certainly not nonsense, Mr. Ashton," said Whittaker. "You were seen leaving the premises. Mrs. Johnson saw you walking down the corridor, away from Miss Stanton's flat."

"Her word against mine I would say," said Ashton.

"Angela thought that her long lost friend might divulge her real name, and all the talk about the missing money would all be raised once again," said Whittaker.

"She was also worried that Christine Stanton might have seen something on opening night," added Chambers. "She couldn't take the risk. Stanton had to be silenced."

"You can't prove anything," said Ashton.

"Oh I think we can," said Whittaker. "We can certainly prove that Angela was being blackmailed. And we can certainly prove that you were at Stanton's flat."

"What size shoe do you take Mr. Ashton?" asked Whittaker. "No need to answer, I already know. It's a nine isn't it? We've already checked."

Chambers placed a photograph on to the table. "It's a photograph of a wet footprint on the carpet in Miss. Stanton's flat. I admit it's not the greatest quality, but that print does match your shoe."

"So we have motive, opportunity, and you were seen at the scene of the crime," said Chambers

Whittaker stood up, and placed his hand on Ashton's shoulder. "I'm arresting you on suspicion of the murder of Christine Stanton. I am also arresting you on suspicion of being an accessory in the murder of James Donovan. You aren't obliged to say anything, but anything you do say will be taken down, and may be used against you." He paused once again. "Have you anything to say?"

"Just one thing, Inspector," Ashton replied.

"And that is?"

"See you in Court," replied Ashton.

Chapter Thirty
Curtain Call

"Well Miss. Cooper, it looks like it's time for Curtain Call," said Whittaker. "That is the term for the end of the play isn't it?"

"Correct, Inspector," Janet Cooper agreed. "You know in the States they have an expression, its curtains, meaning the end of something."

"Or the end of someone," replied Chambers. "It's curtains for Joe if he don't come up with the money, meaning he better watch out."

Janet Cooper sighed. "Well it was certainly the end of James, wasn't it?" she said. "A very sad end."

Whittaker took a deep breath. "Certainly he didn't deserve to die, but neither did Miss. Stanton," he replied. "But one thing, or should I say one act, led to another, until the curtain came down."

"At last, you've reached the final act, Inspector," Janet said.

"It certainly seems like it, Miss. Cooper," the Inspector replied. "There were times however, several times in fact, when I thought we'd never get there. I shall certainly think a lot differently about the theatre from now on, that's for sure."

"Well it certainly been quite a performance, wouldn't you say?" she replied.

"You could say that," replied Whittaker. "Although what the critics would say about it I really can't imagine. I don't think we'll get any awards but we did our best."

"Well so much for Murder at Larkhall Manor," Janet murmured. "It wasn't much good as a play, but who would ever think that such a mediocre mystery play like that could actually be used as a murder weapon?"

Whittaker hadn't considered it in quite those terms before, but she was absolutely right, it had been a murder weapon, just like any gun, or a knife, or a piece of lead piping. He wondered if there had been any other cases involving a play as a murder weapon.

"You're right," he replied. "And Steve Ashton planned the whole thing. James Donovan had to be silenced. Ashton wrote his play, as a means of committing a murder, knowing that Donovan would demand the Colonels part. In fact he wouldn't need to demand the part, it would be offered to him. He was well suited to the role. Ashton even recommended Donovan take the part. You told me that Miss. Cooper." He paused for a moment, remembering what Clive Masters had said. "Perhaps he offered her money. That always works, the old bribery ploy, that's what Clive Masters had suggested."

Janet Cooper started to laugh. "No, no money was offered, more's the pity," she said. "No I gave him the part simply because Steve had recommended him. Simple as that."

"Donovan's fate was sealed," said Whittaker. "The shooting in Act two. It was a simple enough matter to switch guns. And the murder takes place right there in front of everyone. Clever, very clever. But just like the play, the plot was full of holes, and in the end it didn't stand up to scrutiny. And just like the fantasy, neither did the reality. One hundred and twenty odd people saw what happened, but in reality there wasn't a single witness."

"And all because he was blackmailing Rose Fuller," said Janet. "I mean Angela Hull."

"Blackmail of a kind," agreed Whittaker. "Blackmail is one of the oldest reasons for murder there is I'm afraid. The thing is I very much doubt that Donovan actually had anything on Rose Fuller."

"What do you mean?" asked Janet.

"It was all a bluff," Whittaker continued.

"And she fell for it," suggested Cutler. "She paid up."

"In reality, she probably didn't have much choice," Whittaker continued. "She never knew whether Donovan had anything on her, or not. All that she knew was that if she didn't pay, he might have had enough to put her away for at least twelve years. If she was actually guilty she wouldn't want that spread around would she? She had too much to lose. She paid up. But then Donovan got greedy, he demanded more money."

"But what if she was actually innocent?" said Cutler. "As you said Donovan was bluffing. Why didn't she just report him to the police?"

"Think about it," said Whittaker. "Let's say she had gone to the police, and Donovan really did have something on her. What then?" He paused for a moment. "The whole story would have come out again. Precisely what she had hoped to avoid. All about the bank she had worked for, the missing money, the Court case. All of the old questions would be raised once again."

"Maybe you're right, sir," said Chambers. "But all she had to do was refer to the old case, and the fact that it had been thrown out."

"Might have worked," said Whittaker. "But I'm not so sure. Someone had threatened her with blackmail. That could have suggested that maybe she wasn't innocent after all. To sow a seed of doubt, so to speak." He paused for a moment. "And just suppose for a moment that she calls his bluff. She reports him to the police, and he actually did have something to show that she wasn't innocent after all. Could prove awkward wouldn't you say? She couldn't take the risk. No, Donovan had to be silenced."

Janet heaved a sigh. "Had to be murdered you mean."

"Angela wasn't his only victim though," said Whittaker. "You might say that James Donovan was a serial blackmailer. But I have to say he didn't deserve to be murdered. He should have been brought to justice."

"He certainly paid a very high price," replied Janet. She paused for a moment. "But what about Tim? Didn't Steve care that Tim would be blamed, and possibly convicted for a crime he didn't commit?"

"There was never going to be enough evidence to convict Tim, and Ashton knew that," Whittaker started to explain. "But I guess that he also hoped that there would never be enough evidence to convict anyone else especially himself and his wife. And you know, with so many possible suspects he might have been proved right, and got away with it."

"But what about the details that you got from your Records Office?" asked Janet. "They certainly showed that Rose, I mean Angela, was being blackmailed."

"They showed that perhaps she was being blackmailed, but there was no real proof," Whittaker explained. "At least we certainly never found anything, and in fact I'm not sure that there was anything to find. And with Donovan dead it was unlikely that there would be any proof. And more importantly Angela was only one of several suspects, it might have been difficult to prove that she was actually the guilty party."

"Steve Ashton murdering Christine Stanton was a big mistake," said Chambers. "And being seen and identified proved to be the piece of the puzzle that finally revealed the big picture."

"Poor Miss. Stanton," said Janet. "But why was she murdered?

Whittaker heaved a sigh. "Poor Miss. Stanton, is right," he replied. "She was just in the wrong place at the wrong time, I'm afraid."

"What do you mean?" asked Janet.

"Her old school friendship sealed her fate," Whittaker explained. "And going to see your play. She recognized Rose Fuller. After thirty five years or more she recognized her straightaway. But she knew her by her real name, Angela Hull."

"And Angela recognized her friend," Chambers added. "She couldn't believe that there she was sitting in the audience."

"That's right," agreed Whittaker. "So once again Rose became concerned that her real identity would be exposed. The sad truth is that Miss. Stanton never actually posed a threat. She knew nothing about Angela working in a bank, or about any missing money. She hadn't seen her school friend, or anything about her, for twenty-five years. But once again Rose Fuller didn't know that and she couldn't take a chance. Miss. Stanton had to be prevented from saying anything. So murder number two."

"If that hadn't happened, I'm not sure we would have solved Donovan's murder," said the Inspector. "At least I'm not sure we could have proved anything."

"What will happen to the two of them?" asked Janet.

Whittaker thought for a moment. *What would happen to them,* he wondered. "Miss. Cooper, I really don't know," he replied. "You see I only catch them, then it's up to the barristers and the courts to decide."

"I suppose so," Janet said. "But with all the hard work necessary on your part, perhaps you would be entitled to a say."

"No, no way," Whittaker replied. "I wouldn't want the extra responsibility anyway. I'm happy to leave that to others. Catching them is hard enough. Hopefully, they'll be convicted, and sentenced, but that will depend on the judge and jury. You know, innocent until proven guilty. At least Tim Saunders is in the clear. I'm pleased about that."

"Sir," Chambers tugged at his sleeve. "It's four o'clock. We best get going. We don't want to get caught up in traffic."

"Janet, it's been good to meet you, pity it was under such dreadful circumstances," Whittaker said. He turned to face Chambers. "I'm ready, Derek?" He turned back to face Janet. "Our work is done here. Now comes the reports, and, of course, the trial. Oh, and remember what I said about the play. Give it a bit more thought, and don't give up on it. You never know."

"Alright, Inspector," Janet replied. "I'll give it some thought, but I don't think I'll change my mind."

Derek came over. "Goodbye Miss. Cooper," he said holding out his hand.

"Goodbye Sergeant, it's been nice meeting you," she replied.

It was then Whittaker's turn to say goodbye. "Let me know when your next production is on, and where," said Whittaker. "I'll arrange for a squad of coppers to attend. But for now, good bye."

The two men turned and walked towards the exit.

"Not leaving without saying good bye to me, were you, sir," said a voice. It was Constable Harry Cutler. "Let me see you to your car."

"Oh no, we wouldn't forget you," Whittaker replied. He put his arm on Harry's shoulder, as they slowly walked to the car. "You keep in touch. You've got my number."

Cutler promised to keep in touch.

"Well Harry, what did you think of your first murder case?" asked Chambers, as they reached the car.

Constable Cutler thought for a few moments. "What do I think?" he replied. "Well I think one is enough, more than enough." He held out his hand. "Goodbye Sergeant, it was a pleasure working with you."

Chambers took the offered hand and shook it. "You take care, Harry, and don't forget, give me a call. We'll go out for a drink."

"Well, Harry that's that one over, and done with," said the Inspector.

"On to the next then," Cutler replied. "Whatever it is."

The Inspector smiled. "Whatever it is," he repeated. He looked up at the clear blue sky, with not a cloud in sight. "I'll be seeing you Harry."

Whittaker turned to face Chambers. "You know, I never did get my round of golf did I?"

"No, sir, you didn't," agreed Chambers. "And you never got pneumonia either."

* * *

Chapter Thirty-One
Home Sweet Home

Room 4/24 didn't look any different. Not that Chief Inspector Whittaker had actually expected to see any changes. "Home sweet home," he said as he entered his office.

"Back in our back yard, so to speak," suggested Chambers, as he placed their bags down.

"It all looks the same as it did when we left," Whittaker continued. He walked over to the window, and looked down at the street. "Nothing has changed."

"Nothing, except that pile of files has definitely got bigger, sir," said Chambers pointing to the desk.

Whittaker turned, and looked at the array of files, and notes that littered his desk. He looked over at Chambers' desk. It was also covered with documents of all kinds. "At least our jobs are secure," he said. "They couldn't possibly manage without us could they?"

"True, sir," said Chambers. He walked over to his desk, and switched on his computer. "Apart from them files, I'm betting there will be a good few emails to answer."

The Inspector sat down. He cleared a space on his desk. He laid back in his chair, and placed his feet on to the desk. He closed his eyes. "I suppose we better get back into it," he murmured. Then he started to laugh. "But not just yet, eh."

Chambers was about to make a reply, when there was a knock on the door.

"Here we go again," said Whittaker, as he sat forward. "Come in."

The door opened, it was the Sergeant. "Welcome home, sir," he said. "And you Mr. Chambers, welcome back. Good to see you both. We've missed you."

"Thank Sergeant, that's very kind of you," said Whittaker, sitting up.

"Ah, I just thought you might like a nice cup of tea and a slice of Dundee cake," the Sergeant continued. "A sort of welcome home present."

"That is very good of you Sergeant", said Chambers, stepping forward. "The tea and cake will get a good home with us, never fear."

"Oh to be honest, sir, it was her ladyship's suggestion," the Sergeant explained. "She said that she hopes that you had a nice few days away, that you had a nice rest, and that you were now fully refreshed."

"Oh she does, does she? A nice few days away?" said Whittaker. "Well you can tell her ladyship, you can just tell her what she can do with …. No, scrap that. I'll tell her myself."

"Sir," said Chambers placing his hand on Whittaker's arm. "Remember your blood pressure. Just have your tea, sir, before it gets cold."

Whittaker nodded and smiled. "Maybe later," he murmured. He looked back at the Sergeant. "Well you can thank her ladyship, and tell her that it was anything but restful, and that I'll give her a full report, when it's ready. In the meantime you can thank her for the good wishes, the tea, and the Dundee cake."

"Will do, sir, she'll be pleased to hear it I'm sure," the Sergeant replied. "Was there anything else, sir?"

Whittaker looked at the files lying on his desk. "Okay, what's been happening with this lot while we've been gone?" He pointed to the files. "What about the Deptford job?"

"Well, we've identified the body," the sergeant replied. "It was Bob Groom."

"Thought it might be," replied Whittaker. "Any leads?"

"A few sir, there're all there in the files," replied the Sergeant. "Call me when you're ready, sir, and we'll go through it." He turned and went out.

"Now that wasn't too painful was it?" Chambers said as he passed a slice of cake to the Inspector.

"Guess not," the Inspector admitted. He looked at the files, and heaved a sigh. "Right, suppose we better get on with it."

Chambers was hesitant. "Might I suggest we finish our tea, and then have another, together with a second slice of Dundee, and then we'll make a start."

The Inspector took a bite. He looked around. "You know Derek, with all its faults, and all the pressure." He looked at the pile of files awaiting his attention. "I wouldn't swap it for anything."

"No, neither would I," agreed Chambers. "But I wouldn't want too many cases like this last one."

"I know what you mean," agreed Whittaker. "Murder at Larkhall Manor was a real shocker, wasn't it?"

"In more ways than one, sir," added Chambers.

"I hate to say it," Whittaker continued. "But there were times when I thought we might not solve it."

"But solve it, we did," said Chambers. "With some help from Records of course."

"With a lot of help," Whittaker admitted.

"So apart from catching two murderers, we have also captured an embezzler," said Chambers.

"One hundred thousand pounds," added Whittaker. "Pity we never actually recovered the money though."

"Never mind, sir," said Chambers. "You win some, you lose some. You can't win 'em all."

"No but we do try," said Whittaker. "At least we got our murderer."

"That we did, sir," replied Chambers. "By the way, sir, there were two or three other possible blackmail victims, in Donovan's files."

"Yes there were," Whittaker agreed.

"Worth looking into I would think, sir," suggested Chambers.

"Absolutely," said Whittaker. "Already on my list of things to do."

Chambers smiled. "As if we don't have enough already."

"True enough," replied Whittaker, as he looked at the pile of files that awaited him.

"Do you think Miss Cooper really meant it, about not doing the play again?" asked Chambers. "Be a pity I think."

Whittaker thought for a moment. "She does at present, but with the publicity I'm willing to bet that she'll be swamped with offers. Maybe if a producer wanting to put it on in the West End. She won't be able to resist. She loves the theatre too much."

"You may be right, sir," said Chambers. "But there will have to be some changes to the play, I would guess."

"Oh yes there'll have to be changes, no doubt about that," Whittaker agreed. He took a drink of tea, "Well now that's over, I have to confess that although you thought I was a simple policeman, I am actually a genius."

Chambers started to laugh. "Maybe you learnt something from that private detective after all."

"Maybe, but you know what they say about new tricks and old dogs," said Whittaker.

"Guess there's some truth in that," Chambers replied. "But you know they also say you're never too old to learn."

"Yes they do say that," agreed Whittaker. He took a drink of tea. "But sometimes the old ways are best."

"The good old days, you mean?" Chambers said, smiling. "Incidentally, I've worked out how that play works out. Simple really."

"What, you mean that the stranded motorist was really the policeman," said Whittaker. "Pretty obvious I would say. After all you wouldn't get a policeman going round committing murder would you?" He paused for a moment, and heaved a sigh of satisfaction. "And, of course the affair between the guest and the Colonels wife, all pretty obvious, said it all really."

Chambers shook his head. *Affair? What affair?* "Guest? What guest? Chambers asked.

"Oh Derek," Whittaker replied. "Ian Jackson, the weekend guest, remember. Long-time friend of the Colonel, and having an affair with the …."

"The Colonel's wife, I remember," replied Chambers. "But how on earth did you work it out?"

"Oh years of experience, I suppose," replied Whittaker. "Solid detective work, not a problem."

"So, how long have you known?" asked Chambers.

Whittaker smiled. "Oh, let me think, probably ever since I read the script."

* * *

THE KAMMERSEE
AFFAIR

The lake was flat and calm, with barely a ripple. Its dark waters glistening, reflecting the moonlight, as though it were a mirror. Fritz Marschall knew that neither he, nor his friend, should really have been there. They, like many others before them, had been attracted to the lake by the many rumors that had been circulating. He thought of the endless stories there had been, of treasures sunken in, or buried around the lake. He recalled the stories of the lake being used to develop torpedoes and rockets during the war. Looking out across the dark water, he wondered what secrets were hidden beneath the surface.

http://www.amazon.co.uk/The-Kammersee-Affair-
ebook/dp/B009LHE1E4/ref=sr_1_1?s=digital-
text&ie=UTF8&qid=1349541802&sr=1-1

http://www.amazon.com/The-Kammersee-Affair-
ebook/dp/B009LHE1E4/ref=sr_1_1?s=digital-
text&ie=UTF8&qid=1349541867&sr=1-
1&keywords=the+kammersee+affair

THE THACKERY JOURNAL

On the night of April 14th 1865 President Abraham Lincoln was attending a performance at The Ford Theatre, in Washington. A single shot fired by John Wilkes Booth hit the President in the back of the head. He slumped to the floor, and died a few hours later without recovering consciousness. Was Booth a lone assassin? Or was he part of a wider conspiracy? What if Booth had merely been a willing party to a plot to replace Lincoln with General Ulysses S. Grant. Let us suppose that Booth had been set up by a group of men, a group of Lincoln's own Army Generals; Generals who had wanted Ulysses S Grant for their President, and not Lincoln. And let us also suppose that the funding for the assassination had come from gold stolen by the Confederate Army.

http://www.amazon.com/The-Thackery-Journal-ebook/dp/B00EFALJCE/ref=sr_1_1?s=digital-text&ie=UTF8&qid=1376140117&sr=1-1&keywords=the+thackery+journal

http://www.amazon.co.uk/The-Thackery-Journal-ebook/dp/B00EFALJCE/ref=sr_1_1?s=digital-text&ie=UTF8&qid=1376140088&sr=1-1&keywords=the+thackery+journal

THE MACKENZIE
DOSSIER

Kendall could just see the television screen. There was a photograph of Governor Frank Reynolds. Across the bottom of the screen the ticker tape announced in large black letters 'Governor Reynolds Murdered'. The voice over was filling in whatever detail was available. Apparently his body had been discovered earlier that morning. He had been found lying in his garage. He had been shot twice. One shot to the upper chest, the other hitting his shoulder. 'Police believe that the weapon used was a 38 mm caliber pistol,' the reporter said. Kendall froze. Anthony Shaw had also been killed by a 38 mm bullet. Kendall was not quite sure of what it all meant. What connection was there between Anthony Shaw, and the State Governor, and the business mogul, Ian Duncan? And what about Senator Mackenzie? Where did he fit in? And who or what was Latimer? Only a short while ago Kendall was a small time private detective, a Private Eye, investigating an insignificant little murder with no clues, no witnesses, and no motive. In fact, no nothing. Now he had so many pieces of a puzzle he didn't know how they fitted together. He didn't even know if they all came from the same puzzle.

THE MARINSKI
AFFAIR

The Marinski Affair began as a dull mundane case involving a missing husband. Okay, so he was a rich missing husband, but he was nonetheless, still only a missing husband. The case soon developed into one involving robbery, kidnapping, blackmail and murder. But was there really a kidnapping? And exactly who is blackmailing who? Who actually carried out the robbery? Who committed the murders? Who can you trust? Who can you believe? Is anyone actually telling the truth? What have they got to hide? And what connection was there with a jewel theft that occurred four years previously? All is not as it seems. Tom Kendall, private detective, had the task of solving the mystery. He was usually pretty good at solving puzzles, but this one was different, somehow. It wasn't that he didn't have any of the pieces. Oh no, he wasn't short of clues. It was just that none of the pieces seemed to fit together.

http://www.amazon.com/The-Marinski-Affair-ebook/dp/B00AFW98D8

http://www.amazon.co.uk/The-Marinski-Affair-ebook/dp/B00AFW98D8

EPIDEMIC

Tom Kendall, a down to earth private detective, is asked to investigate the death of a young newspaper reporter. The evidence shows quite clearly that it was an accident: a simple, dreadful accident. That is the finding of the coroner and the local police. Furthermore, there were two witnesses. They saw the whole thing. But was it an accident, or was it something more sinister? Against a backdrop of a viral epidemic slowly spreading from Central America, a simple case soon places Kendall up against one of the largest drug companies in the country.

http://www.amazon.com/Epidemic-ebook/dp/B00BS9AIH2/ref=sr_1_4?s=digital-text&ie=UTF8&qid=1363206048&sr=1-4&keywords=epidemic

http://www.amazon.co.uk/Epidemic-ebook/dp/B00BS9AIH2/ref=sr_1_4?s=digital-text&ie=UTF8&qid=1363207975&sr=1-4

A KILLING IN THE CITY

'To make a killing in the City' is a phrase often used within the financial world, to indicate making a large profit on investments, or through dealings on the stock market - the bigger the profit, the bigger the killing. However, Tom Kendall, a private detective, on holiday in London, has a different kind of killing in mind when he hears about the death of one of his fellow passengers who travelled with him on the plane from Miami. It was suicide apparently, a simple overdose of prescribed tablets. Kendall immediately offers his help to Scotland Yard. He is shocked when he is told his services will not be required. They can manage perfectly well without him, thank you.

http://www.amazon.com/Killing-In-The-City-ebook/dp/B0093N363S/ref=sr_1_1?s=digital-text&ie=UTF8&qid=1346663548&sr=1-1&keywords=a+killing+in+the+city

http://www.amazon.co.uk/Killing-In-The-City-ebook/dp/B0093N363S/ref=sr_1_1?s=digital-text&ie=UTF8&qid=1346663588&sr=1-1

KENDALL

Tom Kendall had been with the 32nd Precinct, New York Police Department for just under ten years. But now he wants a change. Now he wants to start his own Private Detective Agency. He had grand ideas. He wasn't interested in just any old case. Oh no, he would handle only the big time cases, the expensive ones.

He would be able to take his pick, the ones that he wanted, where the stakes were high and so were the rewards. He knew exactly the kind of case that he wanted. Anything else would not do, and it would just be turned down flat.

http://www.amazon.co.uk/Kendall-Book-5-John-Holt-ebook/dp/B00LGZYZHW/ref=asap_bc?ie=UTF8

http://www.amazon.com/Kendall-Book-5-John-Holt-ebook/dp/B00LGZYZHW/ref=asap_bc?ie=UTF8

A CASE OF
MURDER

Whittaker passed the drinks over. "Anyway, it seems that he's got himself into a bit of bother," he continued. "A very serious bit of bother."

"Bother?" repeated Kendall.

Whittaker heaved a sigh. "Yes you know," he replied. "Trouble."

Kendall nodded. "Oh trouble, I get you," he said. "So what sort of bother are we talking about?"

Whittaker took another drink. "Well it's a case of murder I'm afraid."

"Murder," repeated Mollie.

Whittaker said nothing, but simply nodded agreement.

Another murder, thought Kendall. Just what I need. "Just stop right there, for a moment, and re-wind will you," he said. "Then let's have it from the top, slowly."

DIAGNOSIS
MURDER

"Mr. Kendall, in the past few months there have been a number of doctors who have mysteriously disappeared, or whose deaths were either alleged to be accidents, or were suicides, or they were actually murdered."

Kendall made a mental note to find out about these 'other doctors.' "A number of doctors you said. How many are we talking about?"

Mrs. Eaton thought for a few moments. "To my knowledge there have been at least eight cases in the past six months. There may be a whole lot more that I know nothing about."

THE ART OF
MURDER

When two valuable oil paintings are missing, Kendall is asked to investigate on behalf of the Insurance Company. Reluctantly he accepts the job. Then a body is discovered, and then another. "So what do you think?" asked Mollie. "What do I think?" Kendall repeated. "Well with two people dead, I think someone has been practicing the art of murder."

https://www.amazon.co.uk/gp/product/B07W8HGCL4/ref=dbs_a_def_rwt_bibl_vppi_i3

https://www.amazon.com/Art-Murder-Kendall-John-Holt/dp/1088470165

JACK DANIELS
CASEBOOK

All three novellas featuring Jack Daniels Private Detective "The Candy Man", "A Dead Certainty", and "Trouble In Mind" - all available in one volume.

The name's Daniels, Jack Daniels – just like the whiskey you know. I'm a Private Detective. And I can't help butting my nose into other people's business. It's what I do. You get used to it. It becomes a way of life almost. After a while it comes natural to you, automatic, like breathing, or eating, although not quite as enjoyable. It's a habit that I just can't break. I just can't help it.
But sometimes it can lead you into trouble .....

https://www.amazon.co.uk/Jack-Daniels-Casebook-Holt-John-ebook/dp/B00WEGS622/ref=asap_bc?ie=UTF8

https://www.amazon.com/gp/product/B00WEGS622/ref=dbs_a_def_rwt_bibl_vppi_i13

https://www.facebook.com/John-Holt-Author-553064201380567/

http://www.amazon.com/John-Holt/e/B003ERI7SI/ref=dp_byline_cont_ebooks_1